FIRE
IN THE
MIND

ARJAY LEWIS

Fire In The Mind: Doctor Wise Book 1
Copyright ©2017 Arjay Lewis

Cover Design: Marianne Nowicki, PremadeEbookCoverShop.com
Interior Layout & Design: Fusion Creative Works, fusioncw.com

ISBN-13: 978-1545504499
ISBN-10: 1545504490

Published by:
 Arjay Entertainment, Inc.
474 South Main Street
Phillipsburg NJ 08865

"The mind is not a vessel to be filled but a fire to be kindled."

— Plutarch

"I dream in fire but work in clay."

— Arthur Machen

DEDICATION:
TO MY WIFE, DEBRA,
WITH WHOM ALL THINGS
ARE POSSIBLE.

PROLOGUE

In the last ten minutes of his life, Philip Mishan stumbled down the street as he tried to run on legs that for too long had carried his bulk at nothing more than a trudging walk. Over fifty and very overweight, he panted as he gave the appearance of an out-of-shape executive who decided to jog to work in his best suit.

He pushed his way along the fashionable shops of Upper Mountainview, New Jersey, and shoved open a glass door painted with PHILIP MISHAN, FINE JEWELRY. It almost shattered from the force of his thrust.

Behind the counter, an attractive young woman, startled by noise, blurted out, "Mister Mishan! Are you all right?"

"Got to… call the police," he puffed as he loosened his tie, his voice strained. "That's what I have to do… tell them… the whole… damn story."

"You're flushed, Mr. Mishan," the woman said.

He looked at the girl, Wendy. At one time, he'd thought she was merely a frivolous young woman. But his partner informed him that he had no choice but to employ her. Soon after her arrival, he had learned to see the iron hidden under the velvet.

All in all, it wasn't too bad. She was nice to look at, like his jewelry. His last lover, Tomas, had been nice to look at as well. Pretty things were the focus of his life.

But the handsome young man had expensive tastes, and Phillip had pushed his partner to make more money. A lot more money. When his partner didn't respond fast enough, Phillip had made threats.

That had been his undoing.

"You're sweating, Mr. Mishan," Wendy said, her eyes growing wide with fear.

"It's hot in here," he said. "A phone...I have to call..."

Wendy reached behind the counter, extracted a cordless phone and held it out to him.

He stumbled toward it. He felt dizzy and decided it was from running.

"Are you having a heart attack?" Wendy asked, staring at his face as it became more and more red.

"No, no," he said as he yanked his jacket off, a beautiful Yves St. Laurent jacket in pale blue wool he'd bought years ago. "Damn it's hot," he said as he reached for the receiver in the girl's hand.

"Mister Mishan, your jacket!"

He looked at the cloth and saw wisps of smoke rising from it. He stared at it, fought to rationalize what was happening.

With a *WHOOSH,* the coat burst into flames.

Mishan dropped it with a cry and stepped back aghast.

"Oh my God!" shouted Wendy. "Stomp it out!"

"The bastard!" Mishan yelled as he watched the coat burn. All at once he knew what the only explanation could be.

He glanced about the store and realized how many flammable liquids were stored there. That's when it occurred to Mishan that his partner had planned this.

He knew the bastard had to be there. Had to see what he wrought. He turned to Wendy. "Oh God! I've got to get out of here. I've got to get under a shower or into a tub…"

Wendy looked at the burning coat and then at him as if he'd gone mad. "You can't just let that—"

"Get a fire extinguisher!" Mishan screamed. Then, all at once, he felt the presence. He looked out the plate glass window until his eyes found the one man he feared.

There he stood across the street dressed all in black, with that annoying smirk on his face.

"An extinguisher!" Philip Mishan repeated, but it was nothing more than a hollow whine. They were the last coherent words he would ever say.

With another loud *WHOOSH*, his body was engulfed in flames. His clothes, skin, and hair were on fire. The air was filled with the stench of charred flesh. He screamed pathetically as Wendy backed away, unable to hear him over her own shrieks of terror.

She turned and ran to the back exit of the store, slamming through the heavy metal door, just as the entire store became engulfed in flames.

On the street, a crowd formed on the sidewalk opposite the store, as close as the billowing smoke and flames would allow. In the distance, fire sirens sounded just as the flames burst the plate glass window and began to lick at the brick facade. The inferno stretched its orange tongues up the rest of the three-story building.

The man in black turned and wandered through the crowd, the smile still on his face. As the sirens of fire trucks approached, he strolled away in the opposite direction.

ONE

The wheels rattled and the train shook as it traversed the expansive bridge over the Delaware River. It click-clacked toward the end of three thousand miles as I crossed into New Jersey.

My home state, I thought.

Home.

Never mind that it had been years since I'd been here, or even on this coast.

I shifted my sore rear end in the uncomfortable seat and tried to squirm into a better position to no avail. My paralyzed right leg stuck out in its unbending glory, which forced me into one uncomfortable position.

Taking the train was the slowest and most difficult way to travel. A bus would have been more direct, but for a trip that spanned days, I thought a train with a sleeping berth the better choice.

My transportation had ricocheted me around the country: Los Angeles to Chicago—change trains; Chicago to Washington DC—change trains; and now the final trip north to New Jersey. If I had taken a plane, I might not have been able to find the space for my leg. And I definitely couldn't have brought my cane.

It's not much to look at, a wooden stick with the head of a cobra at the top. It fits in my hand well and gives me the balance I occasionally need with my leg.

Of course, airport security might have had a problem with the twenty-four-inch sword hidden within it.

Like almost everything I currently possessed, it was a present from my friend, mentor, and the man who probably saved my life, Doctor Fritz Kohl. I needed a cane anyway, and he decided this one might prove useful in an emergency.

Or to carve an extremely large steak.

I looked out the window at the rolling hills, lush and green with the spring. It was a beautiful time to travel; it was neither too hot nor too cold, and the country burst with new life, new growth.

My dissertation had recently been accepted at the Southern California University of Health Sciences. However, my only real interest for the last four years had been my work with Doctor Kohl as I devoured his teachings in parapsychology.

Parapsychology—the study of phenomena that investigates mental abilities, extrasensory perception, and the like.

Seven years ago, I would have laughed at the idea of studying such pseudoscience or anything that spoke of the world of the invisible.

Back then, I had just graduated summa cum laude from Johns Hopkins University Medical School, I was engaged to a beautiful woman, and both of us were about to start our residencies at the Rutgers Medical Center.

Cathy…

Her image flashed in my mind. Her short, blonde hair and lanky body with those surprising breasts.

Cathy hanging upside-down in the twisted wreckage…

I winced at that memory and then focused on my breath. I was on my own, without Doctor Kohl, and I needed to use the techniques he'd taught me to control my mind.

I returned home a doctor—the thing my parents always wanted. Not the kind my famed neurosurgeon father would prefer, but a doctor nonetheless.

I'd had my PhD for exactly one month.

I'd been sober for twelve.

Amazing that I had been able to study and even start the work on my dissertation while each evening was spent in a stupor.

I watched the hills roll by, each mile was more and more familiar. I could see why I was drawn to face the past. At the end of the line would be my oldest friend, Jon Baines.

Then, all at once, there was a *buzz*.

Something's wrong…

It was so strong, I didn't have to stop and analyze it at all. I sat up with my senses awake.

A buzz is my personal code for a quick extrasensory insight, a flash of awareness, what might be termed precognition. Sometimes, it comes as a picture, occasionally as a sound or voice. This time, it was the feeling I needed to be someplace.

With my cane, I pushed myself from my seat as if in a dream.

I don't always need the cane as I am not yet thirty and in good shape. I am strong enough from the exercises I was taught in physical therapy while recovering from the accident. But the cane does help me get up and down from a seat and, of course, on stairs.

I've cultivated the professorial look, with my tweed jacket, short trimmed beard, and my long hair tied back in a ponytail. I like to think I have a hipster meets Freud look.

I stepped out of my sleeper berth, basically a small room with a fold-down bed, seats, and a bathroom, and I went into the hall, where I was led to turn toward the dining car.

Something's wrong…

Whatever attracted my extra senses pulled me in that direction.

I have learned to trust this feeling. Not like when I first became aware of what I laughingly call my gifts, as Doctor Kohl always referred to my abilities. I'd always considered the unwanted impressions that bombard my mind as my curse.

After all, the event that opened them got Cathy killed.

Cathy hanging upside down in the wreckage…

That thought stopped me for a moment, and there was a pain in my chest. I wanted to break down, as I had so many times over the years.

Even worse, I wanted a drink. Just one little goddamn drink, that would make me forget my sore rear end, help my muscles relax, and shut off the endless flow of unwanted input.

"My name is Leonard, and I am an alcoholic," I recalled from my last Alcoholics Anonymous meeting before I started the journey.

I know the real reason I didn't take the plane. That cart with all those little bottles that would pass so close to me. So immediate, so available.

No, no, I just had a momentary lapse. They told me in AA it would be like this.

I cleared my mind and focused on the buzz to lead me, to point the way. I wanted to follow it, let it run me. Nice and simple, don't think, just allow myself to be pulled. I'd know what it was all about when I got there. I just had to remain in the present moment.

I stepped into the dining car, and everything looked perfectly normal. I paused when I couldn't see anything unusual or wrong. Then I started to walk, slowly, and tried to see if anything caught my eye.

Something about to happen…

At first, I noticed nothing, and I wondered if it was a false alarm. But no, that was the rational part of my brain, and I have spent years learning to look past it. I trust these impressions, even if I don't know their cause.

As I looked around the room, I saw a couple sitting at a table having their meal. Down at the woman's feet, right in the aisle, sat her purse. The bag appeared to glow with an inner light that pulled my eye.

Watch…

Everything moved in slow motion; the world around me and even my own motions seemed ponderous. My heartbeat boomed like a drum in my ears. I was in the midst of an event and compelled to be part of it.

The purse was not in any way extraordinary, a large black leather bag open on the floor, but I saw the wallet that lay on top, in plain view.

I slogged my way toward the purse as if I was swimming through mud.

There was a man at the next table whose napkin fluttered to the floor like a dying bird. It landed scant inches from the open purse.

Slowly, his hand went down to grab the napkin, and in one excruciatingly long movement, grasped the cloth and slipped into the purse, expertly extracting the wallet using the napkin as cover for the theft.

I was in exactly the right position. I merely shifted my weight and in one movement, smacked his fingers with the rubber tip of my cane.

The wallet fell languidly back into the purse, and all at once, the world sped up.

"Oh, I'm sorry," the woman who owned the purse said to me as she reached to pick up her bag. "Is my purse in your way?"

"Thank you," I said, not needing to share with her what happened. I heard no sound from the next table, but as I passed, I saw the man biting his lip and rubbing his sore hand. He was a fellow of average size, thin, and good-looking in a Bohemian way.

Our eyes made momentary contact.

He knows, flashed through his mind. In that meeting of our eyes, I got a glimpse, a gentle touch, of his thoughts. He was nervous, surprised that he'd been stopped. He was also angry that such a simple heist was foiled by my intervention.

I broke eye contact and paused as if unsure of my destination for a moment, then I turned and headed back in the direction of my cabin. The raven-haired would-be thief gave me a sidelong glance as I went.

I rocked back and forth to maintain my balance in the moving hallway. Once I got into the berth, I pulled the bed down from its folded position and lay down.

Is that all I was called to do? I thought, annoyed. *Stop a two-bit thief from pilfering some lady's credit cards?*

I never asked for any of this. I never wanted it. What kind of huge cosmic joke gave me these insights and appointed me some ersatz champion? I didn't want the job. These things came, and I wish they wouldn't.

Doctor Kohl had an expression for the entire phenomena of psychic ability. He referred to it as a "fire in the mind."

I burn with that fire, and I was damn tired of the heat.

TWO

At six o'clock, the train made one of its last stops before New York City, in the town of Mountainview, New Jersey.

You would think the railroad authorities wouldn't bother with such a sleepy burg since the population isn't huge.

The stop was necessitated by the advent of the prestigious Garden State University years ago. Due to its proximity, students come in from around the country and use trains as one of the major modes of transport.

The sky was overcast, and it appeared that the sun had set early. In the dark and gray, I stepped slowly down the metal steps from the train and gingerly set myself on the ground. I had a thin raincoat on and my backpack. I'd traveled with Doctor Kohl to so many places—and for many of them I needed to bring essentials: sleeping bag, towels, even food. That's because haunted houses and out-of-the-way locales were part of being an active parapsychological investigator.

"You can't do this vork in a lab," I remember Fritz told me with his thick German accent. "That's vat the mistake vas in the sixties ven they began to study ESP. They put people in a sterile environment and expected results. But I haff found that is is only out in the vorld that you can achieve actual results."

It had begun to rain. The heavy droplets fell in a steady rhythm that smacked my head and made a chill run down my spine. I wanted a drink even more. A nice cognac to warm my fingers and toes and make me forget about dead fiancées, thieves in dining cars, and old teachers.

"Len!" I heard a boisterous voice bellow.

The tall man, more leggy than my six feet four inches, galumphed up to me with all the excitement of large, friendly dog. He pulled me into a bear hug with such abandon, I was afraid I'd fall over, backpack and all, and lie helpless on the ground with my arms and legs waving uselessly like a rather large beetle.

"Jon?" I gasped, as I tried to hold onto what little breath I had.

"Who else?" he boomed in my ear. "Come on, the car is right over here."

He brought me along to a space where one of those large SUV's stood waiting like a trained elephant one would ride in India. He released me from his jovial clutches long enough to open the tailgate.

I took off my backpack and put the mass of cloth and metal into the open cargo space. I then moved to the passenger door and attempted to sit. The bucket seat was up close to the dashboard, but in a few moments, I found the controls and pushed it all the way back. Then I got my stiff right leg in, as well as the rest of me, and closed the door.

"Sorry, I didn't put that back," Jon Baines said from the driver's seat as he started the car. "Jenny rides with it all the way up."

"Jenny?" I asked.

"Yeah. I told you I got married, right?"

"Uh…no," I said. To be honest, he hadn't told me much at all. Two weeks ago, I had received a call from my old friend as I sat in my sparse California teaching assistant's dorm room.

"Hello?" I'd said.

"Is this the esteemed Doctor Leonard Wise?" the familiar voice said.

This is Len," I said to the voice, puzzled.

"Well, Mr. Big Shot *Doctor*, you might like to hear from an associate dean from a university who wants you to give a lecture."

That's how it started. I learned my old college chum was that associate dean, and he wanted me to come to my old alma mater in New Jersey to give a talk about parapsychology—for money, no less.

But married?

I looked over at my oldest friend in the light from the dashboard. His hair was short, and his hairline was further back than it was seven years ago at Cathy's funeral.

He was so young, mid-twenties, then but now—at least thirty-two and married—I guess it made sense.

I'd be married if Cathy were alive. That's what was supposed to happen.

"When did all this…?" I asked, trailing off.

Jon laughed his big laugh and gave me a carefree grin. "It took a while, actually. I met this girl about six years ago, and dated her for five before she finally said yes."

"Why did it take so long?"

"She planned to not get married. She likes to follow a plan. But after years of begging, I wore her down. You'll like her, Len—I mean, *Doctor*."

"Enough with the Doctor crap, Jon. It's no big deal."

"No big deal? You graduate first in your class in medical school—"

"That was years ago—"

"Then you go off to California to study psychiatry—"

"Neither was my path," I interrupted as I attempted to sound sage.

"Yeah, right. Then you go off to study with Kohl—one of the biggest names in the field—and finally get your PhD. It took you long enough. Len, you ought to be proud."

"I am, Jon," I said. "Just not stupid enough to think that *any* degree means anything in the real world. Your lecture was the first job offer I've had. There isn't much call for doctors of parapsychology."

"Hell, Len, for twenty bucks, I can get you a certificate that makes you a reverend who can perform weddings."

"It might come to that," I grumbled as I watched the wet pavement and how our headlights reflected on the shiny surface. Just like the night Cathy died. Roads are treacherous in the rain, especially the busy, hilly roads of my native state.

"Earth to Leonard," Jon said, and I realized he'd been speaking.

"I'm sorry," I said and tried to focus. "Long trip. What were you saying?"

"I was saying that there may be more opportunities than you think. You've received a lot of press over the last year."

I made a sound that was a cross between a grunt and a groan. "Yeah, mostly in the *National Enquirer*: Super Psychic Hunts Down Treasure in Haunted Mansion."

"Come on, Len. It was the Associated Press, and it *was* impressive. You actually found physical evidence that only the person who died in that house could know."

"I got lucky. Doctor Kohl deserves the credit, he trained me."

"But you're the one who found the stuff. And that house was famous—so many other people tried…"

And I didn't finish the job. The words jumped into my head as I watched us move along. The windshield wipers smacked to a steady beat. "So where am I staying?" I asked. "Some motel on Route Three?"

"Staying?" Jon clucked, taken aback. "Len, you're staying with us—Jenny and me. Come on, I didn't bring you here to stick you in some motel. We have a lot of catching up to do."

I smiled. "I'm sorry. It's just I haven't been here since…the funeral."

"I know, Len," he said. "That's why I think some home cooking and friends would be good for you."

"You didn't invite me out here just to offer me a handout, did you, Jon?"

"Len, you are giving a lecture, and you're a hell of a lot cheaper than most lecturers."

With his eyes on the road, Jon released his right hand, reached into the back seat, and brought up a single-page flyer. Emblazoned across a bad photo of me were the words:

PARAPSYCHOLOGY & EVIDENCE GATHERING
Is energy reading the new forensic science?
LECTURE
by Leonard Wise PhD

The flyer was designed with garish colors and it made me wonder if I would be giving a lecture or be part of a circus. Perhaps if I did magic like my brother, the Las Vegas star, it might attract a larger audience.

"I think I have pulled off a coup. I got you before you became so busy that I couldn't afford you. After all, I've got a budget to keep balanced."

"I thought associate dean was more of a figurehead position."

"No, Len. I'm the one who does the work. But Dean Walters can shake hands with the best of them—and charisma—he gets people to donate money like it was *their* idea. That's really what a dean does. I'm learning a lot from Walters."

"Good attitude," I said as he pulled the car into a driveway.

We were on one of Mountainview's slumbering streets, with houses lined up on similar plots of land. Each had a two-car garage and enough variation to not look like a "created" neighborhood, though I was sure it was.

The garage door opened with the push of a remote control, and we drove inside. The door rumbled down behind us as we got out of the car.

Jon ran back to the tailgate and with a grunt, extracted my backpack.

"What the hell you got in here, Len? Rocks?"

"Pretty much everything I own, Jon. I have a low-possession lifestyle."

He held up his two open fingers in a peace sign. "Groovy, man."

"Part of my training," I shrugged.

We walked to a nearby door that he went in first, bellowing, "He's here!"

I felt like this was an entrance into a party where hidden guests would leap out and yell, "Surprise!"

The garage door led us past a laundry room, and he steered me to a bedroom next to it. It was simple but tastefully decorated, with yellow drapes and bedspread. He dropped my heavy bag on the small bed, which it almost completely covered.

"This OK?" he asked.

I nodded. "Fine, fine."

"Come on," he said and patted my shoulder. "I'll fix you a drink."

"Got any herbal tea?" I asked, my mouth full of cotton.

"Maybe," he said with a frown as we walked into the kitchen.

"Well, there you are!" a female voice said.

I looked up and stopped. There stood a woman I knew—or was it her? For a moment, I thought my tired mind had begun to hallucinate. Before us was Cathy.

My Cathy stood in front of us.

Jon didn't even notice that I had stopped and was gawking in his hallway. He pushed past me to give this woman a kiss.

She wasn't a ghost or the creation of my brain. This woman was real, flesh and blood.

They both turned to look at me.

"Len, this is Jenn…but most people call her Jenny," he said with pride, then he hesitated for a moment.

"Are you all right?" Jenny/Cathy asked.

I shut my open mouth so fast and hard, I heard my teeth clunk together. "Yes!" I said too brightly. "I'm sorry, I'm fine." I held out my hand. "I'm Leonard, Leonard Wise."

"*Doctor* Leonard Wise," Jon added.

I shook Jenny's hand and tried hard to focus on her face, to find anything that didn't match my memory of Cathy. Her hair was a slightly different shade, perhaps her bosom a tad larger—I could see now that she was several inches shorter. But there was no doubt. She was the physical embodiment of my Cathy, from the color of her eyes to the way she held her head.

Jenny was aware I was staring.

"Is something wrong?" she asked, her tone playful. "Did I grow a second head?"

"I'm sorry," I said and glanced away. "Jon didn't mention the resemblance."

"Resemblance?" Jon frowned. "What are you talking about, Len?"

"You're kidding," I said. "You don't see it?"

"What?"

I met his eyes, and for the briefest moment, touched his mind. He didn't see it, not at all. Christ, the three of us had been great friends back in the day.

I remembered the night of the party—the last night I could bend my knee. Jon came up to me, drunk as could be. He hugged me and told me how lucky I was, how much he would've liked to find a woman just like Cathy.

Apparently, he did.

"He must be talking about my resemblance to several great starlets," Jenny said to fill the silence with good humor. "After all, I'm a dead ringer for a *young* Meryl Streep."

"If you were taller, thinner, and your hair a different color," Jon said to play along.

"Or Kathleen Turner?"

"Not even close!" Jon roared.

"Sandra Bullock?" Jenny went on.

"She's too skinny, I like you the way you are," Jon said and gave her a peck on the top of her head.

"Yes," I said, forcing a smile. "That must be it. I mistook you for all three of them."

Jenny nodded with a grin. "I think we'll get along fine, Len."

"How about that drink?" Jon suggested, steering us to the nearby kitchen where he opened a cabinet.

"I was more interested in tea," I said.

"I have chamomile," Jenny offered, opening a cabinet lower to the floor. She must have been a foot shorter that Jon. She pulled out an almost empty box and lit a fire under a steel teapot on the stove.

I fought my desire to watch her move, to find the differences I desperately sought.

I looked over to Jon, who was opening a brand-new bottle of my favorite cognac. The bouquet of the amber liquid teased my nose even from several feet away as he poured it into a brandy snifter.

I closed my eyes for a second or two and tried to create some distance. I needed to put myself into the role of the observer, the way Doctor Kohl taught me, where I perceived everything, but held no attachment. It was just pictures in my mind. Inhale and exhale.

I opened my eyes to find both Jon and Jenny staring at me.

"Sorry," I said, embarrassed. "I didn't get a lot of sleep on the train."

They both nodded and became the perfect hosts. They asked me about the trip, and we stood around the darkened kitchen drinking our tea and cognac. I kept my focus on Jon, and each time I turned to Jenny, I was again struck by the uncanny likeness to my dead fiancée. I did pretty well, though. I didn't stare or lose my train of thought again.

"So, you're giving the lecture on Tuesday, Len," Jon was saying. "Is that enough time?"

"It's already written," I assured him. "I'll run over my notes one or two more times. This is Sunday, so yes, Tuesday works."

Two days away. Two days of living with my oldest friend and a clone of my long-lost love. I considered that I could lock myself in the guest room and never come out.

"That's great!" Jon said. "And I love the title, Parapsychology and Evidence Gathering. It was an immediate sellout."

"Really?" I said. "I was hoping there *might* be some interest—"

"Interest? There are still people calling," Jon said. "I'm telling you, Len, this a great time for what you do. I mean, with the interest in higher consciousness and all."

"And you're there to take it to the bank," I said with a laugh.

Jon pretended to be wounded. "I try to give a diverse learning experience. If the university can get some favorable press and a few sold-out lectures, even better."

"Jon, I think Len is tired," Jenny said, and I became aware that she was staring at me for a change.

"Of course, of course," Jon said. "You know how I get, Len. Go to bed. Jenn will show you around tomorrow. There have been a lot of changes to this town in seven years."

"That would be, uh…nice," I said as I avoided her eyes.

We all said our good-nights, and I went to the bedroom, pulled my huge bag off the bed, and put it in the closet. There was a small bathroom with a shower, and I unpacked my toiletries, showered the smell of travel off me, and got into bed naked.

My mind wanted to keep racing, but I focused on my breath, putting myself into a light meditative state until I dropped off.

THREE

I cleared my throat. "So, in conclusion, I see the next step for forensic science to include not only the use of more sophisticated DNA technologies but the use of trained investigators who study the energy of a scene, working hand in hand with the police and scientists to pursue the truth. Which is, of course, the true desire of *any* science. I thank you."

The capacity crowd rose to their feet and applauded as a single creature while I walked off the stage. The lecture had originally been scheduled for one of the smaller halls, but due to demand, had been moved to the larger auditorium in the Shadowvale Communications Center. The name came from the original estate the college was founded upon, although no buildings still existed from that 1880s original construction.

Jon was backstage in the wings and gave me two thumbs up, then pushed me back out again to bow and thank the crowd.

I smiled at the applauding group. It went better than it had any right to. When I'd started, I experienced a moment of stage fright, which was magnified by a man in the first row. Too old to be a student, he sat with crossed arms and legs, wearing a rumpled suit and a scowl that dared me to impress him. Fortunately, I was very prepared, and my experience as a teaching assistant for Doctor Kohl kicked in. I got off of the outcome, and focused on my message.

Monday and Tuesday had passed quickly, and I had adjusted to life at the Baines's house. There was a moment of embarrassment Monday when Jenny came in to shake me awake at eleven, and I almost leaped out of the bed in my altogether. She giggled at my attempts to cover my nakedness, just as I remembered Cathy would giggle at moments of my discomfort.

I dressed and took a half-hour for my morning meditation before I came out and headed for the kitchen, where fresh coffee awaited.

"How did you sleep?" Jenny asked.

"Like the dead…what time is it?"

"Almost noon. Guess you needed to catch up. I took the day off from work to show you around."

"I feel guilty about sleeping so late."

"It gave me a chance to clean the house."

She told me about her job. She worked at Associated Insurance, a major indemnity firm, where she was the head claims adjuster. She and Jon had met while they were both going after their MBAs when Jon found out he had no talent for medicine. He'd spent their senior year proposing.

"Jon mentioned you kept saying no. How come?" I asked.

She sighed heavily. "Jonathan Baines is like a force of nature. I grew up in Salt Lake City, Utah…"

"Mormon?" I asked.

"With bells on. I was one of the middle children in a family of ten."

"Ten! Geez."

"I was in a protected environment, where each girl was supposed to grow up, have a bevy of children, and stand by her man. I *never* wanted that. And I didn't want my dear Jonathan, who is like a big puppy—"

"Always has been."

"I didn't want him to have to face my family and all those questions about his spiritual life," Jenny said as she stared at her coffee cup held tightly in her hand. "I didn't even drink coffee until I went to college. And then Jon, well, let's just say I put off intimacy for over a year."

"He's a patient man."

She sighed. "He romanced me relentlessly—and oh so sweetly—until I assented. Same thing with proposing. I said no, and he'd go off on a sulk. But he always came back with nothing but love in his heart. Eventually, I realized he wasn't going to chain me to the kitchen or turn me into a baby machine, so I finally said yes."

"What about your parents?"

"We had a small wedding and wrote them afterward. They haven't tried to rescue me, or even visit me, so I figured they just decided I was the odd child." She glanced at her watch. "If you're ready, I have a tour planned."

Jenny took me out and around Mountainview, showing me malls and stores that had sprung up over the years of my absence. She finally took us to a late lunch with Jon at the university cafeteria. I was pleased to see that the ensuing years had left it untouched since I took my premed ten years earlier.

It was a delightful afternoon, and Jenny was the perfect hostess. I forced myself not to stare at her and just tried to enjoy her for herself. She possessed a ready wit and a ringing laugh, and I did my best to be amusing, just to hear that laugh.

That night, we all went out to dinner to an Italian restaurant on the edge of town. It was a newly renovated place with a lot of woodwork, open space, decorative flowers, and drapes. The food was simple and tasty. Jon bought wine, but I stuck to the water. After dinner, we strolled the streets; the spring air was mild, so our jackets kept us warm enough.

Back at home, they had cognac, and I had the herb tea.

"Quite a dinner," I said, as Jenny puttered about, and Jon and I sat at the kitchen table.

"Yeah, I Fratelli is an out-of-the-way place, but the food is good," Jon said. "Getting acclimated?"

"Jenny is a good guide," I said. "I'm starting to recognize things."

Jenny pulled out her phone and told me and Jon to say cheese as she clicked off a photo. Then she sat down, and her eyes went from Jon's face to mine.

"What is it?" I asked. "Now is there something hanging from *my* nose?"

She giggled. "No, it's just that you are younger than Jon, but Lenny you seem much older."

I looked at my teacup. "Maybe I've seen more of life than I should."

"It's probably just your beard," Jon said.

Tuesday morning, I shaved it off.

It was something to see my bare face again. I had the beard the entire time I lived in California, and it sometimes had become sloppy and long, but I usually kept it close-cropped and well trimmed.

Jenny was right. Removed, it took years from my appearance.

Tuesday, I wandered on my own as Jenny had to go back to work. It was good for me to be alone. I needed to center myself in the new surroundings—and practice my speech.

So Tuesday night, with the lecture over and done, I came off-stage for the last time ready to relax for the rest of my visit.

"Len, that was great!" Jon said. "You received the best response of anything we've done this entire *year*."

Jenny came up alongside her husband and held my face to give me a quick peck. I rose, blushing.

"That was great, Lenny!" she said, giddy and breathless.

The light in her eyes unsettled me.

"Come on, Len," Jon said, "we have to meet and greet."

"What?" I said, unsure of what he meant.

"All the lecturers do it. We have coffee and cake in the next room, and you try to act like an intellectual."

"I don't do impressions," I said as they dragged me off.

We walked down the corridor and into a small anteroom set up with folding tables laden with food and urns of coffee. Many of the listeners were there, and I was pulled quickly away from the Baines by people who wanted to question me about points I'd made.

Lectures are hard enough when I am in control of the situation, but parties annoy me. So many minds, which all put out a constant *chatter,* like background noise. So many thoughts to surround and suffocate me.

Does he like me…?

I knew this dress made me look fat…

I wonder if my guy is for real. He can't be that nice…

All around me. Many people have a fear of groups, but mine is based on the fact that I can't completely shut out all the voices, all the feelings. I can't even be sure which mind each thought comes from.

I focused on the image of white walls to separate me from the invasive psychogenic yammering. I slapped on a fixed smile, shook hands, and tried to listen to real voices, not the ones intercepted by my brain.

One drink would stop it. Just one good sized belt of scotch or a nice snifter of brandy and the voices would stop. Then I could relax. My mouth went dry with the desire for the taste of any fermented beverage. But, I focused on my breath, made myself listen to words, and calmed down. I moved from person to person and gave the best responses I could off the top of my head.

Danger…

The buzz came unexpectedly, and I lifted my head from a conversation to look around the room.

"Uh, Doctor, are you all right?" said the matronly lady who had been telling me about her personal psychic, who had predicted she would be at the lecture tonight.

"Uh, fine," I said and turned my attention back to her. "Would you excuse me…" I walked a few steps away.

"But I didn't tell you…" she started to say, then her escort distracted her.

I gazed around the room and tried to find the source of that buzz. It had been brief but powerful. The problem was that if I opened myself up completely, I'd be drowned in the soup of the collective mental prattle.

"That was a very nice speech," a woman's voice said.

I turned to see a petite African-American woman behind me, standing next to a man six feet tall and rail thin.

"Thank you," I said, and as I looked into her kind eyes, I couldn't help but smile.

"You made everything so clear and easy to follow," she said.

"I wanted to get the ideas across, not impress people with my vocabulary."

All three of us laughed. I noted that they were both older, at least sixty, perhaps more. The woman was in a dress, neat but plain. The man wore a suit that had seen better days but had been well cared for, and he added a dashing bow tie that only made him look skinnier.

"So, what brought you? You two appear to be a little old to be students."

This drew another laugh, and the tall black man held out his hand, which I shook happily. "Not at all, Doc. I work here. I wanted to see the guest lecturer that all the fuss was about."

My eyebrows went up. "Oh, are you a professor?"

The pair exchanged a pleasant look and the woman said, "He's the custodial engineer."

I frowned as I tried to comprehend the title.

The man moved close to me and said quietly, "That's a fancy name for a janitor. I'm Jim Stevens and this is my wife, Ronnie."

I smiled. "I would think you would be tired of this place if you worked here all day."

Jim shrugged. "The kids are grown and on their own, and Ronnie and I like to go to things like this."

"Especially your speech. You are truly a gifted speaker," Ronnie added.

"Thank you. So, Mr. Stevens—"

"Just Jim, Doc."

"I guess you're looking forward to the summer, maybe some time off?"

"Nah, I like to work. In the summer, I work at a state facility."

Ronnie frowned a bit. "They call him in during the year, too. Sometimes for overnights, an' I don't like that."

Jim shrugged again. "It's hard to get folks in on the overnights. I don' mind."

"Well, nice meeting you both. I'd better keep mingling."

"Nice meetin' you too, Doc," he said with a smile as the pair of them wandered off.

Several other groups pulled me in, and all the while, I tried to locate the source of my buzz with no luck. The crowd subsided, and I drank a cup of the bad coffee.

"So, do you really believe that psychics can be an integral part of an investigation?" a deep voice behind me said.

I turned to see the speaker. It was the man from the front row. He was my height, perhaps an inch taller, still rumpled, and his clear blue eyes burned into me like a laser. Yet I received none of the brain chatter from him. He was totally focused on my answer.

"Why, yes," I responded, a bit unnerved. "I think someone sensitive to the mental energy, specially trained as an investigator, could be a remarkable help."

"You know someone who can do that?" he said almost as an accusation. "Someone who could actually do what you say?"

"Yes," I shot back, not cowed. "Me."

"You?" he frowned.

"This isn't a bunch of theory to me," I said. "I live what I spoke about. I've been involved in research—"

He held up his hand. "I know. I read up on you before I came. Haunted houses and the like. I'm talking about investigating a crime—not ancient history."

I blinked. "The techniques are the same. I don't see that a recent event would be any different. Can you tell me why you're asking?"

"Hmm. Right to the point. I like that," he said. His hand went into his jacket and extracted a leather billfold, then he flashed a gold shield with a police identification card. "Doctor, I'm Detective-Sergeant Bill McGee. I'm with the Mountainview police."

My eyebrows went up. "How can I help you, Detective?"

He glanced about, checking the room with the practiced eye of a cop. Then he spoke in a low tone. "If I were to ask you to become… involved in a case, Doctor, could I trust you to keep it confidential?"

I frowned. "Why?"

Again, he glanced about the room, just to make sure no one was close enough to hear. "Unorthodox methods—well, they wouldn't go over very well around here. If my captain found out that I was talking to a psychic…" He shrugged his massive shoulders.

"I'm technically a parapsychologist, but I get your point. It might not inspire confidence from your superiors."

He nodded. "I've only been with the force for a year. And I have—" he smiled "—a colorful background. But I'm stuck on a case, and when I read about you online, I decided to hear you speak."

"That's very kind—"

"Kindness has nothing to do with it, Doctor. Let's just say I'm willing to try anything at this point. Hell, I'd deal tarot cards or throw runes if it would help."

"Well, nice to know I'm in the same category," I smiled.

He smiled back. "No offense. But if you can…"

"I'm in town for a few more days. Tell me how I can assist."

"OK. Come by the Mountainview police station tomorrow—first thing," he said, his jaw becoming set.

"Tomorr—" I said, surprised. I thought fast. "Would you give me access to the crime scene and forensics?"

"Of course. Just so you know, I intend to tell anyone who asks that you are a forensic pathologist."

"No problem," I said, as I recalled the days I worked on cadavers in medical school. With my training, I would be able to speak the jargon with any coroner I ran into. "What kind of case is it?"

"Murder. Can you handle that?" he said, his eyes daring me.

"Well," I said, not taking the bait. "I'll do the best I can."

He took my hand in a firm handshake. "Thanks, Doctor. I'll meet you at the Mountainview Police Department at oh-nine-hundred!"

I disentangled myself from his grip and nodded as I fought the urge to salute. As he left, I noticed the room was almost cleared out, with only a few volunteers left to help Jon and Jenny.

"What was that about?" Jenny asked as I approached.

I met her eye. McGee wanted to keep my involvement with the case a secret. I trusted Jenny, but I didn't know if I was even going to be any help.

"Old friend," I lied. "I'm meeting him for breakfast tomorrow."

"Oh?" she said and watched me closely. "It's nice that you ran into him."

"Yeah, nice."

I rode home with them, and Jon offered to drop me off downtown the next day.

I lay in bed, sleepless. I was finally going to be involved in a police inquiry. I'd succeeded in cases with Doctor Kohl, but this would be the first time I worked on a criminal investigation.

And a murder, no less.

This was what all the practice to hone my abilities with Doctor Kohl had been about. Now I would find out if I could use them in ways that would work in the real world.

FOUR

As we drove downtown Wednesday morning in his SUV, Jon glanced at me and said, "Len, I'm telling you that was a great show last night."

"Show? Here I thought it was an educational experience."

"Yes, it was studious, intelligent, thought-provoking, and all the other PhD crap you want to call it. But it was a great *show*. I got calls from three newspapers about interviews with you, me, the school. I'm telling you, your entire approach to parapsychology and energetic reading is the right thing at the right time. This could do wonders for fund-raising."

"Glad I could help."

"Help? It's a godsend this time of year. By spring, everything is old hat, and the students are only interested in graduation. To get this much interest…"

"I'll do anything you need."

"That's great." He glanced over from the road and patted my shoulder. "It's also nice to see you again. And Jenny is so impressed by you."

"I'm impressed by her, Jon," I said, and wondered if I should ask my next question. "Tell me, when you started dating—did you notice the resemblance?"

"Resemblance?"

"To Cathy," I explained.

"Who...Jenn?" he said, a puzzled look on his face. "What do you mean?"

"Well the hair is different and she's shorter, but I saw it right away."

He shot me a quick glance. "I don't know what you're talking about, Len. Jenn doesn't look like Cathy at all."

• • •

I was dropped off just past Bloomdale Avenue, across from the Mountainview police station, at oh-eight-fifty-five, as McGee might put it. In the lot and adjacent streets, I could see traditional black and white police cruisers among different makes of cars.

The building itself was a large, angular structure that rested on the corner of Bloomdale Avenue and Valley Road, with a curved tower that faced the larger street. It was built with a light tan brick, granite foundation, and impressive pillars lined up along the front facade.

Carved into the stone over the main entrance was Mountainview Municipal Building, but a newer sign next to it read Mountainview Public Safety Building. This accommodated the fact that the municipal offices had moved to a new building years earlier.

It appeared that the fire department was on the second floor with the police department dedicated to the entire larger first floor.

I walked toward the front of the building which was one of the entrances to the police station. I was wearing a dark blue suit with a plain tie borrowed from Jon. It was big on me. We were the same height, but he had an extra twenty pounds or more. But I had worn my own good Harris tweed jacket the previous night, and I wanted to look more formal. My long hair was pulled back into a ponytail, and I tried to look as intelligent and forensic as possible.

Actually, it looked more like I was going to a funeral. I hoped it wasn't mine.

I was grateful there was only one step to the door, as going up steps are my biggest challenge, especially without a handrail. Going down is a lot better because I can jump steps if I'm in a hurry.

McGee stepped out as I climbed the step and gave me another of his engulfing handshakes.

"Morning, Doctor. Glad to see you made it."

"Couldn't stay away. Where to?"

"You wanted to see the crime scene? I can take you," he said and stopped. "You need to look over the case folder? I left it at my desk."

He's testing me… flashed in my mind.

"No, thanks. I wouldn't want to get too much information. It might interfere with my impressions."

He smiled. I'd passed the test.

"Good, let's go," he said as we walked around the side of the building. We passed a pair of large bay doors that I assumed housed the fire engines and headed for one of the cars parked in the lot. I looked up and noticed a storage company next door to the police station.

It was a much taller edifice, constructed from red brick, and it looked as if it was built at the turn of the century. As I looked up, I noticed that the side wall was unbroken by windows, except on the very top floor. There, several new ones reflected the morning sun.

There was a name emblazoned on the front of the structure, done in individual tiles to spell the word "LEACH."

We got into an unmarked car, a large white Chevrolet coupe with "City of Mountainview" on the license plates, and drove off. McGee turned on the street and aimed toward the more fashionable Upper Mountainview section, where trendy shops overlooked stately mansions.

In a short period of time, we pulled into a small parking lot behind several small buildings that housed shops. One of the buildings was cordoned off with yellow tape bearing the words "Police Scene – Do Not Cross."

McGee reached into his pocket and took out two pairs of latex gloves, handing one pair to me.

"Can you work with these on?" he asked.

"Won't affect me," I said. "Is this to help maintain my forensic identity?"

"The forensic team has been through the place over and over… but I wouldn't want to accidentally contaminate evidence from *either* of us touching something."

"I understand."

We approached the building tentatively. It was obviously the site of a fire. The windows on the first floor were gone, and large scorch marks rose up the walls above the empty sills.

"Was the whole building gutted by the fire?" I asked as we approached. I could see the blackened wood through the large openings but caught the glimmer of glass on the second and third-floor windows.

"No, the fire was contained to the first floor. But it was pretty devastating."

"Arson?" I asked.

"Why don't you tell me?" McGee snickered.

"Fair enough," I said and smiled back as we drew closer. "I can't promise empirical evidence. What I do isn't an exact science—yet. I don't know what I'll get, and at this point, I may not know what it means."

"Not what you were saying in your speech last night," he pointed out.

As we drew close to the building, I saw that a uniformed officer stood outside next to a heavy metal door.

"I believe I said the processes are being set up to make it more exacting. Imagine a hundred years ago with the art of fingerprinting. Energy reading is about at that point. We are only beginning to understand the applications," I said.

"Good Morning, Detective," the uniformed man said, and McGee silenced me with a quick hand gesture.

"Good morning…Hastings, isn't it?" McGee said.

"Yes, sir. Taking another look, sir?"

"Hopefully the last one. When will this building be secured?"

"They said this afternoon, but it was supposed to be done yesterday."

"Then I got here just in time," McGee said. He turned to me and added, "Shall we have a look, Doctor?"

"Thank you, Detective," I responded as I followed him in through the metal door, which Officer Hastings held for us.

We were in a storeroom. Everything was covered in black soot and still wet from the downpour of fire hoses. But I recognized a discolored Mr. Coffee in the corner on a desk with a fallen computer monitor. Built into the wall was a large vault.

"Jewelry store?" I asked.

"Psychic impression?" McGee asked.

"Simple deduction. Building doesn't look like a bank, it's in a fashionable neighborhood, and there is a safe built into the wall."

"That's what it was."

"Anything stolen?"

McGee nodded and gave a smile. "Fire to cover the theft? I like the way you think. We're still going over inventory, but it doesn't look like it. There was a witness, and no robbery attempt was made."

"So far we have a fire and a death. I will deduce that you believe they were connected?"

"I thought you didn't want too much information."

"Very well," I said and glanced around the room. From the smell of burned wood and dampness, I fought to suppress a sneeze. "The next step is to put myself in a light trance. I am going to tell you things as I see them. Would you mind writing them down?"

He pulled out a thin notebook and extracted a pen from his breast pocket. "Ready when you are, Doctor."

"Feel free to ask me questions—try to get as much information as you can. That will force me to describe things in more detail."

He nodded and I finally sneezed. I wiped my nose with a tissue from my pocket and leaned on my cane. Then I closed my eyes and focused on my breath.

I used the techniques Doctor Kohl had drilled me on again and again. Focus on the breath, shift the mind into an alpha state, then open myself up to what comes.

I slowed down my breathing and heartbeat until I began to slip into another level of consciousness. This would allow impressions in, and the residual energy could be interpreted by my mind. I heard my own heartbeat as it thumped slowly in my ears, and my breath rumbled with a roar like a giant set of bellows. In…out, in…out.

I opened my eyes; everything possessed a sepia hue as if I had suddenly awakened inside a black and white movie. At the same time, my every sense was heightened. I could smell the burned wood down into its very fibers. I could even detect the fragrance of a pine cleaner used in a nearby bathroom days earlier. I could hear McGee's feet make the floor creak as he shifted his weight.

What was more important, I could see the room, not merely the remnants as it was now, but as it had been. No soot, no water— just a clean little back room where a man put away his wares and ran his business.

I looked slowly around the room as I tried to decipher the impressions. Emotional situations leave an energetic imprint, a remnant that I can tap into while in this state. My vision distorted a bit, and I saw a heavy man standing in front of the vault, the door wide open as he placed sparkling baubles onto a tray.

"A man," I said aloud. "He spends a lot of time here—I think he's the owner. Average height, balding, heavy. He's wearing a suit that isn't cheap."

I took a step closer to the image, who seemed almost as solid as flesh and blood, but I knew from experience it was simply a projection in my mind. Something he did here had left an emotional impression.

"What's he doing?" I heard a voice ask.

"Putting away jewelry. He did this every night, at closing," I said, watching as the figure looked at each piece, and then placed the sparkling objects into their proper spots. I detected another figure out of the corner of my eye and turned to look.

"Someone else came in. A short man, dark hair. He has features like a rodent," I said, describing the scene playing out in front of me.

The newcomer began to move his lips, but nothing came out. In a vision, I sometimes receive full information, complete with sound as well as sights. However, on other occasions, all I get is the visual, like a movie with the volume off.

"They are talking. The first man doesn't like him. He's unhappy this man came by."

"What are they saying?" McGee asked.

"Their mouths are moving, but I can't hear words," I said. "It looks as if they are arguing."

"Any idea why?" McGee asked.

"No, but the owner is surprised—and he looks frightened."

The scene began to dim; the burned storeroom returned. Whatever emotional charge created this scene had faded.

I walked over to an area where the burn marks went up the wall.

"Did you find residue from an accelerant?" I asked.

"What do you think?" my cagey companion replied.

"I saw bottles and cans of something on wooden shelves over here. They looked like some kind of cleaner. From the way these burn marks go up the wall, I would say they were highly combustible."

"There were traces of flammable liquids—probably used to clean the jewelry."

I faced McGee. "He had a lot of them. Shelves and shelves. It seemed like a lot more than he needed for a small store like this."

McGee nodded. "Our fire chief came to the same conclusion."

I nodded. "Explains why the fire was so bad," I said and looked around the room. "That's all I get in here."

I walked through the open doorway and stepped into the remains of the actual store. Walking past overturned glass cases and burned carpeting, I craned my neck to glance at the discolored tin ceiling where paint had burned and flaked off from the heat. The walls had black soot that rose up in patterns resembling waves. In the middle of the rug was an unburned spot, but the sooty marks undulated outwardly all around it. I touched the rug and grimaced as images flashed through my head.

"What?" McGee said.

"Pain, burning," I said. I stepped back, and my clothes, hands, hair were all on fire. "I'm burning!" I yelled.

I beat my hands against the burning clothes. But it wasn't my body—it was heavier—dressed differently. I stopped, cleared my mind, and slowed my racing heart.

"Sorry, I'm not burning, he was," I said, regaining control. I looked at McGee who watched me intently. "Interesting experience, very intense. I got pulled right in."

"Any insights?" McGee questioned.

"Not yet. I need to try to stay disconnected. This was recent... last few days?"

"Yes," McGee said.

"And the man who burned was Philip Mishan?"

He raised one eyebrow. "So, you got that much?"

"Actually, it's printed on the glass," I said and pointed at the front door, where in spite of the soot, I could see "Philip Mishan, Fine Jewelry." Though backward to us, it could easily be read. The display windows had blown out, but the glass in the door was intact. "This guy burned to death?"

"What do you think?"

"I think you're not going to give me any information at all," I said and rubbed my eyes. "But I believe he burned to death. I also believe that you want me to tell you how."

Now both of McGee's eyebrows were up. "Why do you think that?"

I made eye contact. "Because that is the question going through your mind," I stated.

"Should I pick a number between one and ten?" McGee said, snidely.

"That won't be necessary," I said, and then broke eye contact to peer around the room again. "Three."

His mouth dropped open in shock, and I couldn't help but smile. "Relax, Detective. That's an old magic trick. Most people pick three."

He relaxed a bit and smiled. "So, you know magic tricks as well?"

"You did the research on me. You probably already know my brother is a professional magician. We used to do shows together, and that's how I bought my first car. He's in Vegas now."

"Vegas? In one of the shows with the feathers and the girls?"

"Yes, and more girl than feathers, I believe. You heard of Wizini?"

McGee frowned. "Yeah, he had a TV special, right?"

"Yes, his real name is Thomas Wise. He's my twin brother."

"Identical?"

"Except both his legs work," I said. "It's helpful to know magic tricks. It makes it easier to discover clever trickery masquerading as psychic ability."

"You can understand my concerns. There are a lot of frauds in your line of work."

"Yes, there are also a lot of self-deluded people who believe they're receiving things that are actually projections of their own minds. That's the hardest part. I have to interpret what I sense with-out putting myself into it or getting lost in what I see."

"Like just now when you were burning."

"Exactly. Let's see if I can get more."

McGee nodded, and I shut my eyes, slipping back into the alpha state as I reminded myself to stay the observer. I wanted to watch what I saw and not plug it, or I would fall into the same panic Mishan did during his last moments.

I opened my eyes, and although in sepia tones, the store was restored to what it looked like before the fire. Clean, clear showcases with gemstones under glass. I gazed around the room.

"There is a woman…twenty-three, twenty-four standing behind that counter," I said and pointed. "Average height, very pretty, blonde hair, dyed. She looks…bored."

I turned to see the familiar balding man run into the store. He slammed the door with such strength that it shook on its hinges. He moved very slowly as the silent show played out for me.

"Mishan came in. He's in a panic about something—agitated."

I saw the girl reach for the cordless telephone.

"The phone, he wants the phone! Call for help, call the police!" I changed my position, tried to stand where I could look at his face as if he was really there. "He's sweating, scared—so very scared. He's taking off his jacket."

I looked over at the girl to see her eyes widen, and glanced at the coat in Mishan's hand in time to see it burst into flames that moved in black and white tendrils.

Don't panic, I told myself, *it's only an image of what happened.*

Mishan turned.

"He's looking out the front window," I said. "He's looking for someone out there." I walked toward the window that was now merely an open space. Glancing at the wraith that was Philip Mishan, I tried to see what he saw, know what he knew.

"'Coming to finish me off,' that's the impression I'm getting. He wants to get to water."

"Can you see who he is looking at?" McGee's voice came from out of nowhere.

I stared out the window and saw two eyes that burned with an unbearable hate.

I shook the image from my head, and I was back in the burned-out store. All the images were gone. I felt drained. And hot, so very hot.

"You're sweating," McGee remarked.

I nodded, loosening my tie. "Is there any water here?"

McGee led me like a child to a bathroom, where I splashed water on my face and drank several handfuls.

"Need water?"

"These experiences drain moisture from the body," I said, noticing that my hands were shaking. What did I tap into? What force had killed Philip Mishan?

Instead of answers to McGee's questions, I now had questions of my own.

FIVE

In the conference room, which also served as a data room at the Mountainview police station, I could hear the sound of computer servers as they whirred and clicked in the background. I sat with my eyes closed, focused on the memory of the rat-faced man I had seen in the back room of Mishan's shop. Across from me sat a police sketch artist named Chuck. As I described each feature the best I could, Chuck drew it. Then I would open my eyes and look at what he came up with.

"The forehead is a little weaker," I said, "the nose a bit larger."

Chuck nodded. With his close-cut hair and boyish looks, he obviously wasn't a cop. But he was good with a sketchpad, and obviously, a small town like Mountainview didn't have the computerized face-matching programs that larger forces use.

McGee looked at the face and fumbled with the file on his lap. He'd left the room several times and come back with a different sheaf of papers each time, which he'd put into a folder. Then he'd review the whole thing again.

That's what police work consists of, you get as many facts as you can, then go over and over them as you try it this way, then that, theorizing, deducing, then eliminating what doesn't work.

I could identify. A lot of the work I'd done in parapsychology investigations used the same techniques. Then sometimes you got lucky. I did, and it got me a lot of attention. But you can't depend on a fluke. You have to put in the work, and that gives the luck a chance to make a spectacular appearance.

Chuck showed me the finished sketch, and I nodded. It was the man I had seen with Mishan in my vision of the storeroom. He showed it to McGee, whose eyes grew hard.

"Two copies and bring me the original," he said. "Thanks, Chuck."

As Chuck left the room, McGee took his place across from me.

"So, Doc, you know this guy?"

"Not at all," I said. "But you do."

"Reading my mind again?"

"Just your face. Can you tell me who it is?"

He gazed at me, his steel blue eyes flashing as he carefully considered how involved he would make me. He sat in front of a nearby computer display, tapped a few keys on the keyboard, then turned the screen to me.

There on the screen was the mug shot of the man who matched my sketch. It was a full-front with a number under him and then a profile.

"Lonny Briback, aka Lonny the Match." McGee said. "When I saw where the sketch was going, I looked up his info."

My eyebrows shot up. "Arsonist?"

"Yeah, and a damn hard one to catch. FBI finally nailed him a few years back. I'm checking on his current whereabouts."

"FBI?" I said. "How does a local cop know what they're up to?"

He smiled and leaned back in his chair. "I wasn't always a local cop, Doctor."

"Tell you what, can you just call me Len or Leonard? I'm really not used to the whole 'Doctor' thing."

"Fair enough. Call me Bill," he said, then added with a warning finger. "In private…in front of anyone else, make it Detective or Detective-Sergeant."

"So, Bill, you were with the Bureau?"

"Twelve years," he said as his eyes focused on the tabletop. "And I was good at it."

"What happened?"

"I got married about eight years back. We had kids—two boys. I was away too much, working too hard. It was rough on Laura."

"Your wife?"

McGee nodded. "About two years ago, we had a bust—terrorist cell in Michigan—it went bad. Booby trapped, improvised explosives set to take us out. A couple guys I worked with ended up dead. Laura gave me a choice—change jobs or change wives. I decided to stick with the wife."

"So, you took a job here in Mountainview?"

"There was an opening for a detective. I go home to my family every night. It's better all around."

"So, what about this Lonny guy?"

"Lonny the Match," Bill said and turned the screen back so he could read it. "He's good. Studied with one of the old pros who never got caught. But he's hung up on electronics—builds ignition systems that can go off when he's a hundred miles away."

"Nice," I said sarcastically.

"Yeah, he was finally nailed for a little gizmo that was a stroke of genius. The whole thing was plastic. He sprayed a warehouse with a mixture of lighter fluid and grain alcohol—then this little plastic device used water to start a fire with sodium metal—ignited the accelerant and melted the gizmo."

"Leaving no evidence."

"Almost. But he screwed up. He had to use one small metal valve. It didn't melt."

"And that was enough to track him down?"

"It was a very special valve made by this one company and sold to three different stores in the whole country. From that one clue, the FBI found him and convicted him."

"Impressive," I said. "And considering how Mishan died…"

"Right. It certainly points to someone with the Match's skills."

"But how is he connected with Mishan?"

McGee looked at the screen again, then he grabbed a folder off the table and opened it. "Since this case came across my desk several days ago, I've done some digging into the life of Mr. Mishan." He glanced at the open pages. "It turns out that before coming to Mountainview, he had two previous stores."

I met his eyes. "Which closed due to arson?"

"Fires…yes. Arson couldn't be proven. But each time, Mishan came out ahead financially. His last place before Mountainview was in an amusement park on a pier on the Jersey Shore—mostly selling trinkets."

"So, you think Mishan hired the Match to burn his businesses?"

"I suspect an angry firebug might get involved in a murder if he felt he was cheated. You've pointed me toward a suspect."

"You'll need more hard evidence. My visions won't stand up well in court."

"If the Match did it, he left a trail. But to be honest, I didn't know he was out of prison."

"Any forensic evidence to point to a device?"

"Like you said, there was a lot of what could be considered accelerants on the premises of the building: High alcohol cleaners, acetone, and the like. Also, there was far more of them than there should be for a normal operation."

"Which I also pointed out."

"And forensics also found. Those are what really burned the place down, but the question is what set them off? There was no trace of fuses or timers."

"It also doesn't explain how Mishan caught fire," I said.

"No, but if Lonny perfected his technology—y'know, made something that burned Mishan and then burned up with him."

"As well as set off everything else in the store."

McGee nodded and looked at the file again. "I don't know. But, anything is better than what the coroner suggested."

"What was that?"

"Spontaneous human combustion."

"You're kidding!" I said. "Your ME said that?"

"To be honest, Dr. Latrell may have been making a joke at the time," Bill said. "Then again, he didn't have another explanation."

"I can't buy that."

"Really?"

"Yes, and I actually believe in ghosts. After all, I've met a few. But even so…"

"I had trouble with that theory as well. But Casey found nothing on the body that could create such a powerful fire in such a short amount of time. Hell, for all I know, Lonny had a giant magnifying glass and fried Mishan like a bug."

"Do you think that's a reasonable theory?" I smirked.

"Probably not, but I'll look into any idea right about now. Lonny the Match is the best lead we've got," McGee said, glancing at his watch. "How's your time?"

"I'm fine. If I can do anything else…"

"You can, Len. I have a witness coming in, the girl who worked in the jewelry store, Wendy Wallace. Could you be here, see if you get any insights?"

"Sure," I said, and rose with my cane as McGee got up.

I followed McGee out of the large data center. We turned left up the corridor. As we walked, there was a door to the left that led to the processing area, and I could see three empty holding cells through the open doorway. We turned right and into the detective's bull pen. The detective's desks were against the wall on the left side of the room. Bill went to a desk in the corner near a divider that separated the other half of the room. To my right were two small rooms marked Interrogation A and Interrogation B.

Bill picked up a second file from his desk, which was covered with piles of similar cardboard binders. He led me into a third room marked Interrogation C. There was a desk, several chairs, and a large pane of glass that showed the table in Interrogation B quite easily. I decided it was a mirror in the other room that was actually one-way glass.

"Can I get you coffee, Len?"

"That would be nice."

McGee walked through the room and out a second door, which appeared to go directly into the squad room. I sat at the table and checked my phone for any messages or alerts.

As my screen lit up in front of me, I considered the situation. Bill's theory about Lonny and the victim made sense—good cop sense. So why did I feel like he was wrong? I'd only seen a few pictures in my head, but he said they helped. I should let him do his job while I figured out where I would be going after I was done here.

I could return to California. Dr. Kohl wanted to continue work on Scudder House, the famed haunted house we researched near San Francisco. Then in the fall, I could work with him, teaching— now that the pressure of writing my doctoral thesis was over.

But somehow, when I received my PhD, I felt that it was time to move on. Doctor Kohl was like a second father, but I wanted to go out and make my own mark. Scudder House, although considered a victory, was an upsetting experience. The idea of returning there made me uneasy.

Then again, I didn't have a lot of offers. Good thing I was staying with the Baines's. Until I got the check from Jon, I didn't have money to afford a hotel.

My father the neurosurgeon was happy to pay for my college and medical school when I zoomed through my bachelor's degree and premed at GSU in an astounding two years. Then off I went to study at Johns Hopkins for three years, where I graduated first in my class. I could've completed that four-year course in two instead of three.

But then I met Cathy, and my priorities changed.

Then she died, and my world fell apart.

When I told my father I was moving to California and changing majors to psychiatry, he cut me off. We weren't speaking when, two years later, I met Doctor Kohl and shifted to parapsychology. Fortunately, I got paid as Kohl's TA, and with odd jobs, I didn't starve.

Once I was paid for this lecture at GSU, I'd have enough money to bum around the country for a few months. But where would I go, what did I want to do?

"Who the hell are you?" a gruff voice demanded.

I sat up, shaken out of my reverie, as I saw a balding man at the door that led to the detective's offices. He was thin and hawkish, with beady eyes focused on any move I might make.

"I-I'm Doctor Leonard Wise," I said, and rose from my chair. "Detective McGee called me in as a consultant."

"Oh, really?" the man said, duly unimpressed. "Well when his highness deigns to return, tell him Sergeant Tice is sitting with his witness."

"Oh?" I said, trying to act like I knew what to do. "You can send her back."

"No, I can't," Tice said, not any happier. "All witnesses have to be escorted. And where the hell is *your* visitor badge?"

I patted the breast pockets of my suit as if one might mysteriously appear. But I knew I didn't have one. McGee just brought me in a side door near the locker rooms.

At that moment, McGee walked in the opposite door with two cups of coffee.

"What's going on, Tice?" he asked.

"Your witness is here," Tice said, maintaining his bad disposition as McGee put the coffee on the table. "And where is his visitor ID?"

"He's forensics, he doesn't need it," McGee said, leading Tice out of the detective's bullpen. "Tice, you have to relax."

"Why the hell didn't he tell me, or flash his creds…" Tice said as they went down the hall. I sat back down and noticed that McGee had left the Mishan folder. With a quick glance toward the door, I picked it up and opened it.

It fell open to a page that listed information about the jewelry store, with names of employees, partners, corporations, and the like. The names were nothing more than a short laundry list, totally meaningless to me, but I felt inspired to read each one.

When I reached the Nova Corporation, an odd pain went through my head, like a migraine behind my right eye. I closed the folder and put it down, suddenly feeling warm. I loosened my tie.

"You all right?" McGee said, walking in with a pretty young woman at his side. I recognized her from my second vision of the jewelry store.

"Fine," I said, as I stood at the table and offered my hand. "You're Wendy?"

"Yes!" she said, taking my hand and shaking it. Then she looked at me as if to see if I was anyone famous. "You're some kind of doctor?"

"Yes, I'm Leonard Wise. I hope you don't mind my sitting in."

"Anything that helps," she said.

"I'm glad you were able to get out safely," I said.

She nodded. "Just in time. It was terrifying."

I sensed something that she wasn't expressing. "Yes, it all burned so quickly."

"Please sit down, Miss Wallace," McGee said, the perfect host. "Can I get you anything?"

"A diet soda would be great—whatever you have," Wendy said.

McGee nodded and strolled off.

"So," Wendy said to me, her tone conspiratorial. "Are you like a headshrinker? Did they call you in to find out if I'm crazy?"

"Do you think you're crazy?" I asked.

"I'll tell you, I'm not sure. I mean, it was impossible. He was just standing there one minute, the next he's on fire."

Can't tell…

A buzz tickled the back of my mind. She wasn't telling what she knew—in fact, she didn't want to.

"And you're sure you didn't see anyone?" I said as I tried to reach out and sense what was bothering me. "Maybe someone threw something in through a window? Except for the door, the windows were shattered."

"No. Y'see, I'm standing in the shop, like every day. Things had been pretty slow lately, the economy and all. And in comes Mr. Mishan like a bat out of hell. He's all red and out of breath, and he says he's got to call the police."

"Did he tend to be excitable?" I asked.

"I've never seen him so upset, maybe once or twice. He has— uh—*had* high-blood pressure, and made it a point to stay calm."

"Really?" I said.

Just then, McGee came back into the room with a can of diet soda and a plastic cup full of ice, which he placed in front of Miss Wallace. She poured as we all sat, and McGee slid my cup of coffee over to me. I sipped it and scowled.

"It's not very good," McGee said.

"No argument there," I said.

"So, Detective, why do you think I need a psychiatrist?" Wendy asked.

McGee looked puzzled for a moment. "Oh! No, the doctor isn't a therapist, he's forensics. I thought if he could be here it might help everything make sense. Did I say he was?"

"No, I'm sorry, I just assumed," Wendy said.

"My fault," I said. "I should have out and out denied it when you asked me."

"No, I'm just glad you don't think I'm nuts."

"Miss Wallace," McGee said, "you've been a big help already. And I hate to bring you down here and bother you with more questions…"

"No, it's OK."

McGee pulled the folder in front of him, opened it, and took out a piece of paper.

"Now, is this your statement?"

She glanced quickly at it. "Yes, it is."

"Do you want to double-check it?" McGee asked.

"No, I know what I wrote," Wendy said and flashed a smile that could melt hearts. She was very aware of how attractive she was and knew how to use each movement for its best effect. "I was telling the doctor, I don't know what I could add. It was all so weird."

Can't tell…

There it was again, the niggling feeling on the back of my brain. It was as if what happened wasn't weird, but may have even been expected.

"Was there any kind of smell—I mean before the fire?" I questioned.

She grimaced, then looked at me. I made eye contact, slipped in to just the outer edges of her consciousness. The memory of the smell of Mishan burning was so fresh in her mind that I could experience it across the room.

"Just his coat burning," she said.

"Could you smell gasoline or lighter fluid—perhaps even alcohol?" I asked.

"Nothing like that," she said.

It was true, I could sense the memory in her mind.

"He was standing there, and his coat started burning. Then he began to yell that he had to get under a shower—or into a tub of water, then—poof!" she said, shutting her eyes from the painful memory, and our contact was broken.

I had no reason to try to go deeper, so I didn't attempt to reach in when she looked back up.

"You ran out immediately?" I said.

"Yes, there are cleaners in that shop that were flammable. I was afraid the whole place would go up," Wendy replied.

Which it did, but she had enough time to get out, I thought.

"Did you know of anyone who might want Mr. Mishan dead?" McGee said. Standard police question.

"I told you, everyone liked him. And I didn't know all that much about the business. He could've been in hock to the Mafia for all I knew."

She changed subjects—cleverly.

"Did you see anyone milling around outside or perhaps someone suspicious in the store around that time?" McGee queried.

She looked up at the ceiling as she tried to remember.

"There were a couple of people in that morning," she said. "A couple getting wedding rings, a man who got earrings for his wife—oh yeah, a funny dark-haired man who met with Mr. Mishan." She paused for a moment. "He left carrying a shoulder bag, like for carry-on luggage. I don't think he came in with it."

The bag...

Another buzz tingled in the back of my brain.

"He was funny, you say," I confirmed. "In what way?"

"Well, I don't like to make judgments about people being unattractive, but he had a face like a rodent."

McGee reached into his file folder and extracted the drawing his sketch artist had made.

"Is this the man, Miss Wallace?"

Her eyes brightened. "Yes, that's him!"

McGee and I exchanged a glance, knowing each other's thoughts. *Lonny the Match.*

. . .

The rest of the interview was tedious as McGee went over everything again with Miss Wallace. After an hour, we were done, and both of us rose as she collected her things.

McGee met my eyes. "I've still got some legwork on this one. Doctor, I'm done with you for right now."

"That's great," I said. "You have my cell number, right?"

"Yes, but give me the number where you're staying just in case," McGee said, and I quickly wrote the Baines's phone number on a piece of paper. "You need a ride?"

"That would be nice," I replied. "I don't have a car here in town."

That was only half-true. I didn't have a car at all, either here or California. I hadn't owned one since the accident. And to have a custom one with the special controls I needed was beyond my meager means.

"I'll give you a ride," Wendy said, as she stood at the door.

I gave Bill a shrug. "That would be lovely," I answered.

Bill escorted us through the corridor, then we went to a door with a square panel to the left of it. Bill waved his ID badge in front of it, there was a sound, and we went into a short hallway that led to the lobby.

The lobby had several chairs lined along both walls. Directly across from the main entrance was an elevated desk that had a low banister with a section that opened. As we went through the gate, I saw Sergeant Tice seated behind the elevated desk. He looked down upon us.

"Hey, McGee!" Tice said as we passed. "I called Doug Milbank and they don't have anyone on staff in forensics named Wise."

"He's from out of town, Tice," McGee said without even turning toward him. "Some of us actually know people beyond Passaic County."

Tice muttered something unintelligible under his breath, and we stepped outside. McGee shook both our hands, thanked us, said he'd be in touch, and disappeared back into the station.

I followed Wendy. The view of her tight rear end was even more pleasant than the spring scenery.

"So, what happened to your leg?" she asked as we ambled toward her car.

"Car accident. My knee was fused. I'm lucky I didn't lose the leg."

She sucked in breath at the thought.

"Here's my car!" she said and pointed at a small sports car at the far end of the lot.

"Very nice!" I commented, looking at the fire-red sports car, one of those two-seat jobs with a roof that probably folded back. "Rather pricey for a girl with a job at a jewelry store."

"It was a present," she said with a shrug. "People like to give me things." She stopped cold. "Oh dear! Can you fit? I mean your leg and all?"

"I can manage," I said as I opened the door, slid the seat back as far as it could go, and manipulated my six foot four frame into the vehicle.

I ended up sitting on my left side, with my right leg crossing over my body. Diagonally, I was able to fit with my legs on the passenger side of the car. This did put my face very close to her shoulder as she sat in the driver's seat.

"This is cozy," she said, giving another of her dazzling smiles. I felt myself turn red. My relationships since Cathy's death had been limited. And here was a very good-looking woman giving me all the signals.

I gave her the address and we took off.

"So, where are you from?"

"Originally Copeland, New Jersey, but I've been in California for years," I said, trying to make sure I didn't blow my cover as a forensic expert.

"Are you here just to work on this case?"

"I've been lecturing at Garden State University," I said. That was true enough.

"How long are you in town?"

"A few more days. It depends if Detective McGee needs me."

"Oh?" she said and raised her eyebrows. "Well, it seems to me if you've been away for a while, you could use someone to show you the sights."

"That would be nice," I said.

"What are you doing tonight?"

"Not a thing."

"Neither am I," she said and then bit her lip. "It's only Wednesday night, and I never thought I'd miss my job, but it gave me something to do. How about I pick you up at eight?"

"Well…"

"Problem?" she asked. Her eyes still watched the road, but she wore a look of disappointment. "You're not married, are you?"

I gave a hearty laugh. "Nothing like that. I'm afraid I don't have much money on me…" I said, a bit embarrassed.

"That's not a problem. We can go dutch, and I'll pick some spots that don't cost a lot."

"Sounds great!" I said with a smile.

We pulled up in front of the Baines's house, and she turned to face me.

"Until later, then," she said, her eyes bright.

"How should I dress?" I asked, realizing it had been a while since I'd dated or been out to any kind of club or night spot.

"Casual. Definitely no tie," she said, smiling as I rose carefully to extract myself from the tiny car. She gave a wave and drove off.

"I have a date," I said aloud, surprised by the sound of my own voice.

SIX

At six-thirty, the three of us sat down to a meal that Jenny threw together as if by magic: Fresh bread, salad, and pasta primavera. It all tasted wonderful.

"So, how did it go with your old friend?" Jon asked. "And how is it you have a friend I don't know?"

"I actually have a few you haven't met, Jon."

"I'm more interested in your date," Jenny said.

I told her when she got home that I was going out that night. She offered herself and Jon to come with me, and I finally admitted it was a date.

"I can't tell you much. She used to work at a jewelry store until it burned down."

"Burned down?" Jon said. "Oh, yeah, I read about that! Mishan Jewelers, only about twelve blocks from here."

"You don't have to tell me about it," Jenny said as she swallowed a forkful of pasta and cheese. "I'm on the case."

"Case?" I said.

"Yes, the insurance on the place. Part of my job is finding out if arson was involved."

"But I thought Mishan had no heirs. Who would put in the claim?"

"His business partners, and there are several of them," Jenny said, as she pushed a small leaf of romaine lettuce into her mouth and then spoke while chewing. "Hey, how did you know he had no heirs?"

"I heard about the—uh—whole thing, from Wendy."

"Is that the girl you're going out with? Wendy Wallace?" Jenny said, still chewing.

"You know her?"

"Know her? She's one of the claimants on the insurance."

"I thought she just worked there."

"She was one of the investors," Jenny said and sat back while she sipped a glass of the red wine Jon had poured with dinner. "Through a corporation called Nova, of all things."

I stopped chewing and looked at her as a chill went up my spine. The exact name that had elicited a response when I'd read it!

Jenny went on. "She's been calling me every day about when the policy is going to pay out. Can you believe it? The guy isn't even cold, and she's wondering why she can't get her money."

"What kind of policy did this corporation have on Mishan?" I asked.

"The partners had key man insurance on Mishan. It makes sense, if anything happened to him, there goes the business. Then there is an overall policy on the business for fire, theft, and all that. It pays out to each partner depending upon their original investment."

"Sounds intense," Jon said.

"Nova invested pretty heavily in that little store, and if she gets a portion of the money, she could come out of it pretty well off."

Jon smiled at me. "Wow! Available and soon to be rich. You know how to pick them, Len."

"She isn't too hard on the eyes, either," I said as a flippant answer. But I was troubled by the connection between this corporation and the mysterious Miss Wallace.

. . .

As I waited in the cool spring air, I had a new point of view on the girl about to be my date.

At eight oh five, the little car pulled up and stopped. I opened the door and held out a single red rose I had bought at a florist within walking distance of the Baines's.

"Ooh!" she said, taking it and bringing it to her nose as I juggled my body into the passenger seat. "It's lovely."

"Not as lovely as you."

"That's sweet," she said and smiled broadly.

"So where are we off to?"

"An eclectic mix of sights and sounds that can be enjoyed cheaply. First on our agenda is a place in the center of town."

We drove for about ten minutes, making small talk, until she pulled into a lot and parked.

"Watching you get in and out of my car is entertainment in itself," she said without scorn as we walked to Bloomdale Avenue—the main drag in town.

"It's good training for the limbo championships," I replied.

"Glad I could help you practice," she said. "Here's our first stop."

I looked where she pointed. In the middle of the block was a small place with an open door. It had a hand-painted sign over the door that read the Halfway House. We walked into the dimly lit room crowded with overstuffed chairs and sofas in various stages of decay. The room was about half-full as people talked, drank coffee, and ate desserts. A glass case on our left displayed cakes and pies. From behind the counter came the *whoosh* of cappuccino machines as milk was frothed to make lattes and other coffee drinks.

"Starbuck's it ain't," I remarked.

"Starbuck's doesn't have live music," Wendy said as we found a place to sit. There was a woman behind the counter who walked over with a notepad. She was tall and well groomed, her hair short, and her manner brusque. She gave a smile of recognition to Wendy and flashed knives at me.

"You want a latte, Len?" Wendy said, oblivious to the waitress's attitude toward me.

"I'd love one," I said, and tried to read the waitress's energy. She was very unhappy that I was here with Wendy, and I didn't have to be psychic to know it.

"Two lattes," Wendy said with a teasing smile to the waitress, who wrote it down and wandered off.

An African-American guy was standing next to a stool holding a guitar and sipping coffee out of a porcelain mug with a crack on one side. His hair was long with lines of gray in the kinky mass, and he wore a thick moustache. Dressed in a denim vest and no shirt, showing off his good physique, his face lit up with recognition and he rose and walked over.

"Wendy," he said, and bent to give her cheek a peck. "It's been a while. I thought you'd given up on us."

"No, I'm still around. I just can't be everywhere," she said, then she turned to me. "This is *Doctor* Leonard Wise. Len, this is Char."

"Char?" I repeated.

"It's a nickname," Char said. "Short for something, but I've forgotten what."

"Char plays here most nights," Wendy said. "He's really good."

"That's what I tell her, anyway," he said, glancing at his watch. "I guess I'd better start the next set."

"We'll talk during your break," Wendy said.

Char went back to his guitar and leaned against the stool. He set a microphone to his mouth and started to play.

He sang in a mellow baritone and had a slight rasp that came from too many nights in too many bars. His fingers slipped up and down the guitar as he sang his way through "In Your Eyes" by Peter Gabriel.

Wendy was right. He was good, really good.

Our lattes arrived in large mugs—like the one Char drank from—except ours possessed no cracks. We sat and listened, enjoying the ambience.

"This is nice," I commented.

"Yeah, I've always liked this place."

"Sorry about bringing you in about Mishan," I said. I felt a need to try to pump her a little for information, to see if she would tell me anything about her true business relationship with the deceased. I didn't want to go so far as to invade her mind—after all, it was a date. But I wanted to be aware of anything she might be withholding.

I felt a momentary flash of guilt. Here this attractive young lady was going out with me, and a part of me wanted to grill her as if she was a suspect. But if she was an investor, wasn't she a suspect? Could she have been an accomplice to murder?

"Yeah, well, I was lucky I ran when I did, or I'd be dead right now."

Lucky or good planning? I thought. "I'm glad you weren't hurt," I said and gave my best disarming smile.

We sat and chatted quietly while Char played. I tried as artfully as I could to ask her questions to open the door as to her level of involvement, but she didn't bite. In fact, she started to ask me about forensic procedures. With my medical background, I handled it as well as I could. I began to realize that perhaps her interest in me might be based on a desire to learn more about the evidence the police found. I almost started to laugh at an inopportune moment when it hit me that while I was trying to probe her for information, she was doing the same to me.

Finally, I changed the subject, just in time for Char to sit down with us.

"So, how y'all doing?" Char said as he sat.

"Good, Char," Wendy said. "That was a great set."

He shrugged. "Wish we had more people. Business has been a bit slow."

"It'll pick up," she said.

"You being here would bring 'em in," Char replied. "You always had a magic touch with this place."

"So how do you know each other?" I asked. Char looked older, certainly not a high school chum of Wendy's.

"She used to manage this place," Char answered.

"I did not," Wendy said, momentarily flustered. "I just played hostess and sat people on busy nights. There was no money in it."

"I don't know," Char said. "Looked to me like you were telling people what to do."

"Oh, come on, Char," she said and turned on her charming-but-brainless blonde routine like she'd hit a switch. "I was just trying to keep this place open in my small way. I didn't do much."

"Heard that jewelry store you worked at burned down," Char said.

"Yeah, I'm lucky I didn't get hurt," Wendy replied.

"You could come back here," Char said. "We'd love to have you. Besides, you could watch out for your investment."

My ears perked up. "Investment? Wendy, you have money in this place?"

"Now stop!" she said, a little too cheery. "I just helped out. You guys don't need me. But, it's nice to hear you say that, Char. I've been feeling low since the fire. I'm glad there are people who want me."

Char glanced at both of us, suddenly aware he'd said too much. "Yeah, we do, kid. Hey, I gotta grab a smoke and hit the head. Nice meetin' you, Doc."

"Likewise. I love your playing."

He nodded to us both and walked toward the back of the room and out of sight.

Wendy sat and watched him, and I could sense an anger inside that she was being very careful not to let show.

"You're pretty popular," I said.

"I always have been." She gave me another dazzling smile. She regained her composure, the lapse had been fleeting. "But, I have other places to show you."

"Do tell?"

"This is show, not tell. Come on," she said, getting up and heading for the door. I followed.

"Shouldn't we leave money for the—"

"Don't worry, I'm an old friend," she said, as she gave a wave to the tall waitress, who waved back, her expression still stern.

"Well," I said, as we stepped out into the warm night. "You certainly kept your word about going out cheaply."

"I know what it's like to not have money," she replied, her mouth a tight line. "My parents didn't have a lot, and what they did have, they didn't share. I grew up with very little."

"I'm sorry," I said.

"But you're a *doctor* and all. I figure your current financial condition is just temporary."

"I am about to get paid for a lecture I gave. I would be delighted to take you out to a good restaurant," I said.

"See," she said, putting her arm through mine. "It's just temporary."

"Wendy, I'm a researcher," I said, measuring my words so they would be true. "I don't know that I'll ever be the kind of man who can buy you a sports car."

She let my arm go. "Is that what you think? That I'm just interested in money?"

"I didn't mean to make it sound that way. It's just that I want you to know, right up front, that even though I'm a doctor, I'm really just a glorified investigator. Like an archaeologist; I dig up information. It's not glamorous, and I could be the top of my field and still just get by."

We walked on in silence, her face getting a hard cast to it.

"I've known men with money," she said and pulled her jacket tight. "It doesn't make them any better than anyone else. Sometimes, it makes them worse."

She turned to me. "I don't need anyone to take care of me. I know how to take care of myself."

The evening did improve after my faux-pas, and we visited a bar where Wendy had a kamikaze, and I drank soda. There was a piano player—quite good—who also knew Wendy.

After that, we walked over to what looked to be an old church, but upon entering, I discovered it was a dance club. The music was unbelievably loud, and no one looked older than nineteen. But it was fun in a Bohemian way.

We danced as well as I could with my leg and cane. Wendy drank, and I enjoyed observing the people as they wandered, danced, and posed. The energy of the place was intense. I was aware of a negative current that ran through the room, but I stayed the observer. Fortunately, the loud music dulled my psychic senses enough so I didn't get pulled into the thoughts of the patrons.

At about midnight, we made our way back to the car.

"Pretty wild place," I said.

"This is nothing. Some nights, people are all but doing it on the dance floor."

"I suddenly feel old."

"How old are you anyway?"

"Twenty-nine. And you?"

"Twenty-seven."

"Really? I thought you were maybe twenty-four."

"I'm in good shape." She shrugged, then added with a smile, "And besides, how would you know? You're really old."

I laughed. On the drive back, we told jokes, laughed, and enjoyed each other's company. Once I stopped playing detective, I was aware that she really was charming, intelligent, and with a ready wit, despite the dumb blonde persona she slipped into when it suited her.

She pulled in front of the Baines's house, and we both paused. I was sitting practically in her seat because of my leg, and our faces were close.

"Well," I said.

"Well," she repeated.

"I had a wonderful time."

"So did I."

"Could you give me your number? I'd like to go out again."

"You did promise to take me out to a good restaurant," she said with a smile that could melt any man's heart.

"That I did. I try to live up to my promises."

"Give me your phone," she said.

I pulled out my mobile phone and unlocked it. She quickly typed in her name and number.

"Here you go," she said and handed it back as I pulled close, and our lips met. It was a soft, almost chaste kiss. She shifted, and we pulled closer and fell into a more passionate embrace, our mouths opening and our tongues touching.

I saw fire—burning—a body bursting into flames with a howl of pain and fear. I shuddered.

"What's wrong?" she asked.

"Wha—"

"You pulled away. Did I hurt you?" she asked, concerned. "Was it my tongue stud?"

"No, no," I said, as I tried to drive the blazing image from my thoughts. "It was…my leg, it fell asleep."

"Let me give you a hand," she said, and got out of the car, holding out a hand to help me up.

"Thanks," I said, and moved close to kiss her again.

She turned her face away. "Not out here on the street, Len."

"Sorry. I'll call you tomorrow."

"Good night," she said, as she got back in the driver's seat with one last smile to me before driving off. I waved and touched my lips.

The vision I saw when we kissed had seemed so real. Was it a memory or a prophecy? I wasn't sure who was on fire. It might have been Mishan.

Or it could have been me.

SEVEN

I woke up Thursday morning a little past eight and stumbled into the kitchen for coffee in time to see Jenny, dressed and ready for work, as she finished her cup.

"Well, well," she said, as I grabbed a mug and wrapped my bathrobe tighter. "How did the date go?"

"It was nice…puzzling. Miss Wallace appears to be a financial investor in more than just one business."

"Really? Did she diversify with you?" Jenny said with a naughty smile.

"I don't get pecuniary and tell," I said.

"Only if you get fiscal?"

"Ouch!" I said and feigned an injury as I filled my mug with coffee. "I surrender."

"So, what was so puzzling about Miss Wallace?"

"It's not anything I can pin down. If the police wanted to check the insurance policy she has with your company, what would be required?"

"They'd have to file a warrant. But how are the police involved with Ms. Wallace?"

"Well, it's a suspicious fire and a possible homicide."

"And how, Leonard Wise, are you involved?"

Her body was in a pose I knew so well I could almost have drawn it from memory. It was the one Cathy would assume when she caught me in a bit of misinformation. I never really lied to her in our time together, but I would neglect to tell her about nights out with friends and the like. She caught me every time and made sure to make me squirm when she did. I soon stopped trying to wrangle and just told her the truth.

Seeing Jenny in that pose, I suddenly wanted her far more intensely than Wendy Wallace, even when I'd been kissing the latter.

"You're turning beet red, Len," she said. "Embarrassed that I asked?"

Embarrassed that I felt a bad case of the hots for my best friend's wife.

"I-I was asked t-to keep it a secret," I said, my mouth stumbling over the words. "The police—well one policeman—called me in on the case."

"Called you in?"

"As a parapsychologist. He heard my lecture and wanted to know if I could do what I talked about."

"This is great!" Jenny exclaimed. "We have to tell Jon!"

"No!" I said, my voice firm. "The detective wouldn't want any publicity about it. That would be the worst thing."

"Why? I mean, if it helps the university…"

"It's a murder case! If I can show the police that a psychic can actually be helpful—without drawing attention to himself—it could help to make parapsychological techniques more accepted."

"Could you tell Jon when you're done?"

"Afterward, he can post billboards. Right now, well, let's just say that so far, I haven't been much help."

"Are you finding things they didn't know?"

"I think I may have given them a lead. Can you give me your business card? That way, I can have Detective-Sergeant McGee give you a call."

"All right," she said and extracted a card from her wallet. "But he has to have a warrant."

"I understand."

"You'll be here for dinner?"

"Should be."

"See you later," she said, giving me a quick peck on the cheek as I kept my robe wrapped tight.

She walked out the door, and I sat with my coffee and breathed a sigh of relief. It's said that an average man thinks about sex at least once every ten minutes. I've been in relationships and had an active sex life when I did. But in the last few years, I just didn't think about it. Women were around, some interested and available. But I was too wrapped up in trying to master my gifts, meditation, visualization, learning to relax and focus my mind—as well as following the course of study to complete my PhD. It had been grueling.

There was also the drinking, which promoted the desire but took away from the pursuit. My sexuality was sublimated. To have it come back now so strongly and in such an inappropriate circumstance was disquieting. Perhaps being sober and kissing Wendy opened the floodgates.

No, it was Jenny standing in that pose, looking every bit like Cathy.

I decided to meditate for a half-hour and see if I could rearrange my thinking.

Two hours later, I strolled in the front entrance of the Mountainview police station and approached Sergeant Tice at the elevated desk. I'd shaved, showered, dressed, and walked to the station. It felt good to stretch my legs—make that leg.

Sergeant Tice gave me a quick glance. "He ain't here," he said and returned to his paperwork.

"Ah," I said.

"Don't know when he'll be back," he said as he wrote. "So, where are you from, Doc?"

"California. I've been working out there for years," I said.

"Forensic Unit is pissed that you showed up out of nowhere," Tice said. "I hope you're not planning on stepping on any toes."

I stayed centered and didn't let his attitude bother me.

"I just want to help," I said.

"Yeah, help McGee, the hotshot," Tice said. "He doesn't go by the book. You'd better make sure *you* do."

"Yes, sir, I'll do that," I said, and headed for the door. "Please let Detective McGee know I came by."

I stepped back out in the sunny day, feeling as if a weight had come off my shoulders. What an unpleasant man, and the only person he hurt with his attitude was himself. Still, in my precarious position, I didn't want to make an enemy.

I headed for the university, only about two miles away up Valley Road. I hoped I could find Jon there and maybe get access to the school's Internet and Wi-Fi. It wouldn't hurt to have a little more knowledge about arson. It might give me a better idea what happened to Mr. Mishan.

The vision I'd seen had been very real and very intense. I didn't know what he thought except for the perception of the unknown man outside the window. The odd sense of being watched by malevolent eyes when he was about to burn—that pointed to murder. But who watched, and how did he do it?

As I walked onto the grounds of the university, I passed buildings I remembered from my own time there, when I was a premed student who frantically finished a four-year course in two years.

I had a lot to prove back then.

As I walked, the beauty of the day filled me. Roads for vehicles led to concrete paths snaking through the grass that linked the buildings together.

I passed Williams Hall, constructed to be one of the larger buildings, erected on an artificial hill so that it loomed over the open court below. I glanced up at the carved stone steps and the waist-high walls that ran at the level of each flight. With five levels, the stone wall went from ground level all the way up the hill to the front of the building.

I recalled those short stone walls fondly, as at night, they served as a place for romantic encounters, though nothing much beyond necking occurred due to the proximity of university police.

In my time here, I was dating a girl from high school, Julia Tannenbaum, although we never availed ourselves of the amorous locales. By the end of my first year, our relationship had ended. After that, I focused entirely on my studies—until I met my Cathy.

The image of Cathy hanging upside down in the wreckage of our car, blood on her face, flashed into my mind.

I focused on my breath, pushed the memory away, and put my attention on where I was walking. I approached College Hall, the original mansion on this former estate, which stood three stories high and had a large domed roof. Since I'd been a student, they had done a renovation in which the entrance was fronted with glass all the way up. At night, with the lights on inside, you could see the two huge curved marble staircases as they rose up from the marble floor and traveled the rotunda in the gleaming brilliance of the polished white stone. Of course, in daylight, the glass reflected like a dim mirror, and I saw a smoky version of myself as I drew near the glass and brass door.

I entered and walked between the staircases toward the offices on the first floor. I passed a regal office with a fine oak door—that was for Dean Walters. I continued down the hall to a less extravagant doorway that bore a nameplate: Jon Baines – Associate Dean.

I walked in as a woman rose from behind her desk. She was thin, in a fashionable pants suit, and her dark hair had begun to go gray at the temple, which she allowed unashamedly.

"May I help you?" she asked.

I smiled gregariously. "Leonard Wise to see Dean Baines."

"Oh! You're Doctor Wise," she said, a smile on her face. She came up to me and shyly put forth her hand for me to shake. "I'm so glad to meet you!" she gushed as I took her hand. "Dean Baines has said so much about you! And everyone is talking about the lecture you gave."

"Thank you, and you are?"

"Trisha Heywood," she said. "I'm Dean Baines's personal assistant—I'll let him know you're here."

She went to the phone, pushed a button, and announced that I was there. In less than a second, Jon burst through the door and grabbed my hand. "Hey, Len! Come on in!" he said. "Can you hold my calls, Trisha?"

"Of course, Dean Baines," she said, still smiling.

The office wasn't opulent, but it was paneled in a good blond wood, and he had a desk that was big enough without being imposing.

"Not bad digs, eh?" he said.

"Not at all."

"So, did Jenn send you?"

I blushed red as the mental image of Jenny in the pose that inspired my morning lust appeared in my mind unbidden.

"No, I just wanted to maybe get some computer time here at the university."

"Sure, no problem. Want to check your e-mail?"

"I figured the library would—"

"Not the library, Len. We have a room just down the hall. You can use that."

"I don't want to put you out."

"C'mon, I'll set you up." And like a whirlwind, he took me down the hall and into an office that was empty except for several computer stations. He booted up a machine.

"Jon, I hate to be vulgar, but do you know when my honorarium will be paid for the lecture?" I asked.

"Not a problem, Len. I'll have a check for you tomorrow."

"Check?" I said. My heart sank.

"Yes, and I'll go with you to the bank—you can convert it to cash or a prepaid debit card—or, I dunno, traveler's checks."

I relaxed. "Do they still make those? It would be a help. I'm pretty much broke."

"You won't be after tomorrow," he said and slapped me heartily on the back before he strode out of the room.

I sat at the computer, manipulating the chair until I could sit with my paralyzed leg sticking out and still see the screen. I watched the monitor as the machine flashed information in its self-analysis. Finally, the main screen arrived with all its icons. I quickly opened the browser.

I retrieved my e-mail, sorted out and erased the offers of copyright infringement (COPY ANY MOVIE), free pornography (WILD BARNYARD SEX), and get-rich-quick schemes (YOU CAN BE WEALTHY IN THIRTY DAYS!!).

There was something from my sister—and a note from Doctor Kohl, which I opened immediately. It read:

> *Dear Leonard,*
>
> *I hope your lecture went well. There is no need to rush back as funding has been held up on Scudder House. Stay in touch. I'm trying another source, but project is put off at least three months—and more likely until next summer.*
>
> *Enjoy your time in New Jersey. I hope you find what you need there.*
>
> *Your friend,*
> *Fritz*

I felt a twinge of regret that I wasn't there. Scudder House had been Fritz's pet project for years. Doctor Kohl parlayed our successes at other sites to secure a chance to visit that house, considered a major source of phenomena.

We'd only been able to do a few days of work when we—well, I—made a discovery of such significance, Scudder House had to be cordoned off until it could all be categorized and photographed. It made celebrities out of both of us, and even Doctor Janis, a thin, studious sort of fellow who had the permission of the estate to run the research there.

Doctor Kohl wanted to do more work at Scudder House. He then planned to write a book—his definitive work on parapsychology with Scudder House as the central theme. After the previous success, it looked like it was finally coming together with a combination grant from three universities.

He wanted to spend the summer to chase whatever ghosties, ghoulies, or things that went bump in the night might reside there. After the last time, I didn't want to ever go into that house again. But he was my mentor and my friend. If he wanted me there, I would go.

At the same time, I was pleased that there was no rush—there was a lot I wanted to do in New Jersey. There was this case, if McGee wanted to keep me involved.

I now had *no* possible work until the fall, when I could go back to Doctor Kohl as his assistant. But I'd done that for four years. And right now, I was doing what we'd both talked about for years: acting as part of the investigation team.

So far, my results were pretty paltry.

I closed the e-mail and did a web search for "arson and investigation," then sat back as the computer gave me a list of possible choices.

I bounced around several sites—they were not very informative. Then I found a site working in conjunction with a university of criminal law, and there I found a complete profile of arsonists.

It was fascinating.

I discovered that very few arson cases are for profit, most fires are set for revenge by young white men under the age of eighteen, who are misfits with below-average intelligence and who had no sense of remorse. The young men usually had an absent or abusive father and a bad relationship with their mother, were poor students, and tended to veer into subservient jobs or positions.

Only five percent of the national total for arson cases were for profit, and those were where the profile changed—dramatically. It went to a select group who bordered on the genius level.

I printed the profile on the nearby laser printer, went back to the main site, and found another article on explosives. It not only listed the different terms used in arson cases but also the different types of explosives and accelerants.

I hit print.

In my pocket, my phone began to ring its odd musical tone. I quickly retrieved it.

"Hello?"

"Hey, Leonard, it's Bill McGee," his deep voice intoned. "You were looking for me?"

"Yes, I was out last night with that young lady we spoke to yesterday. I may have some information that you'd be interested in."

He chuckled. "On the case one day and you're already interrogating people."

"I thought it might help."

"I'll take what I can get. Come on over and we'll talk."

I grabbed the sheaf of pages fresh from the printer and headed back toward the Mountainview police station.

. . .

On the way, I must have looked the classic image of a professor in my tweed jacket and long hair, reading a sheaf of papers as I went. I tucked my cane under my arm and limped along as I studied the downloaded information.

It was very helpful, as it gave the principles of combustion, different explosives, and burn patterns that could be observed in arson cases. I whittled my way through the five or so pages and finished just as I arrived at the station.

Tice was behind the elevated desk in the police lobby.

I exhaled deeply and put my best face on, trying in my mind to send him love and hell—and maybe a couple dozen roses while I was at it.

He raised his head and said, "He's waiting," jerking his thumb in the general area of the interrogation rooms.

I took advantage of his good mood and walked past Tice's desk down the short hall and through the door as he hit a buzzer that opened it. For a moment, I wasn't sure where I was since McGee had brought me in through a different door the previous day. But I made a right and followed the sign for processing. I knew the detectives were across from the holding cells, so that seemed the right choice. I found McGee in the same room as yesterday, going over papers of his own.

He rose to shake my hand. "So, what have you got?"

I sat as I folded the papers and put them in my breast pocket. "Our Miss Wallace is not quite what we thought she was."

"How so?"

"I assumed she was just an employee at the jewelry store, but it appears she was an investor in Mishan's business—and I believe a few other places here in town."

"She told you this?" McGee said.

"It was observation, mostly. I do know she's listed on the insurance—she's been trying to get a payout for the Nova Corporation."

McGee shuffled the papers to the laundry list I had seen the day before and nodded. "Yeah, that rings a bell. Here it is, Nova Corporation." He raised his head to meet my eye. "How did you know that? You read her mind or something?"

I smiled. "No, the people I'm staying with—the Baines's. Jenny is an insurance adjuster. She also happens to be the investigator on the policy."

McGee sat back and exhaled heavily. "She's not supposed to say anything about a case."

"I just wanted to let you know so you could look into it."

"Tracking down the names listed on any policy is standard procedure," he said. I could tell he was getting annoyed. "And I put a warrant in for the insurance records two days ago—Damn it, I should have it by now."

"Bill, I'm only trying to help."

"I know, Len," he said and calmed a bit. "It's just always difficult when an amateur starts nosing around. I'm not a big fan of people who've read too much Agatha Christie."

I smiled and put on my worse Belgian accent. "Wood you like the eminent 'Ercule Pierrot to explain le murder?"

This made him break into a series of guffaws. But he quickly got over it and became serious. "I just want you to know, your involvement is on a limited basis."

"Bill, I'm here to act in any capacity you want, as little or as much as *you* decide. I just got this information by accident, and I thought it might help."

"Just don't start thinking you can play detective…"

"I have enough trouble playing parapsychologist," I assured him. "But what comes is what comes. Sometimes through visions or flashes and sometimes through meeting the right person—what one might call coincidence."

"That is what this is, right? A coincidence?"

"Carl Jung would call it synchronicity. I mean, look at all the situations. I arrive here to give a lecture, and all around me, people are involved in your case. It's more than luck."

Bill nodded. "Just don't think you're Sherlock Holmes. Last thing I need is you getting hurt."

"I'm not even Doctor Watson, and I've been hurt enough for one lifetime," I said, tapping my stiff leg with my forefinger. "Now, about Miss Wallace…"

"So you went out with her. Was it a date?"

"A casual one, and I didn't do it for information. In fact, she's very closed-mouth about her finances." I retrieved Jenny's card from my wallet and handed it to him. "Jennifer Baines is in charge of the insurance investigation. If you call her, maybe it would speed up your warrant."

McGee took the card and looked it over. "It would. If Wendy is on the insurance, I could push for a warrant of her financial records.

She *is* the only witness. Perhaps she knows more than she's saying. If there was monetary motive…"

"I don't think she's a murderer—if that's where you're going."

"Why?"

I shrugged. "Just my impression—but she knows more than she's telling."

"About what?"

"I don't know," I said, as I got clumsily to my feet. "But I'll let you know if I find out."

"Remember what I said—and that you are not *officially* on this case."

"I know, Bill."

I left the building and began walking north in the direction of Route Three. It was a beautiful day for a stroll, and in California, I was in the habit of walking several miles every day. I found it good for my mind as well as my body to move along and feel my breath and muscles stirring.

I pulled the papers from my breast pocket and reread the information. I wanted to have the terminology down so that if I actually came face-to-face with a *real* forensic expert, I would at least use the right words.

I began reviewing the concept of burn patterns and how all fires blaze in an inverted conical style, from point of least damage to most damage. I remembered that the store area had such a pattern, everything rising out of the place where Mishan's body fell.

But the amount of energy and Wendy's claim of just getting out before the whole place went up suggested something that set off the cleaners in the back, and then they acted as an accelerant. Even

Wendy seemed puzzled by how much there was at the store. And how did they combust so easily?

This suggested the idea of a bomb of some type, with a design that would be called "rich" by an investigator. A rich range explosive is a combination of chemicals in a sealed container, with ten percent oxygen or less in the container. This fit the bill because when it went off, it would create a vacuum, sucking in the surrounding air, and the damage would be more fire than explosion.

This could be manufactured out of homemade materials, with the use of a vacuum pump to bring the oxygen level low enough. Of course, the device could have been made to smolder first, which would explain Mishan's coat smoking before the fire started. This could have created the necessary heat to set off the chemicals and destroy the shop.

But the makings of any kind of bomb should have been detected by forensics as well as the fire chief. Right now, it was nothing but a theory.

I stopped and realized that I had reached my destination. A memorial park along Route Three. It is beautiful and grassy and on some of the most expensive real estate in the state. The roadways and walking paths crossed each other under the budding trees. Despite traffic nearby, it was oddly quiet.

I strolled through the gates, which bore a metal plaque with the words "Endless Vista," as I put the papers back into my pocket and tried to focus on what I was there to do. The energy was very peaceful as I walked past headstones, some of which dated back a hundred years. The place had changed since my last visit. Trees were taller and fuller, but the grounds were still immaculate.

I walked the same route I had taken years earlier to finally reach the familiar stone. Time and the seasons had darkened the light granite, giving it black lines like trails of tears. But chiseled into the stone were the words:

CATHERINE CYNTHIA GARBER
BELOVED DAUGHTER

It always strikes me how simple that tombstone is for a woman who was so much more. I would add, "promising doctor", "beautiful fiancée", and "enthusiastic lover". She didn't just embrace life, she ripped the hell out of it and pulled as much sensation out of each moment as possible.

Until that night…

We had been at a party, a simple party that Jon Baines had thrown together to celebrate my graduation as well as Cathy and I getting married in a few months.

At the party someone pulled out a Ouija board and as a joke, we played with it. However, it only worked when I touched it and the answers it gave were stunning. Specific names, parent's birthday, things that only the person asking could know.

Then someone— I think his name was Jeff, suggested we conjure a demon.

Silly, ridiculous, and though I only had one beer, I agreed. We got into a circle and hands were held as he chanted strange words, and I felt an energy all around us.

An energy that scared me.

He finished with something like "Come forth. Fiat, Fiat."

There was a flash of light and we all were pushed apart as if thrown. At first, people were shocked, but quickly suggested the flash was from the storm outside and laughed it off.

A part of me was not convinced.

Shortly after, we said our goodbyes, even though the night was still young, and I drove with Cathy up a mountainous road towards Mountainview, where she was staying with her parents. We'd always found it funny, the two of us met at John Hopkins in Maryland, yet we were both a pair of kids from New Jersey.

"Still want to get married so soon?" Cathy said. "Before we start our residency?"

"The sooner the better. I love you, Cathy."

She gave me that smile, the one that owned my heart and I glanced over at her for the briefest moment.

When I returned my eyes to the road there was a figure ahead in the rain.

It was a red-skinned demon with a huge, muscled body and horns on its head the size of a bull's— it stared right at me with yellow eyes. I screamed and pulled at the wheel to avoid hitting it. The car screeched as it slipped from my control and we careened through a guardrail and over the edge of the mountain. We spun through the air and down the summit rolling end over end.

We finally came to rest upside down, all the windows smashed. My eyesight was clouded by flashes of light, as I fought to stay cognizant. I tried to push my body free, away from the steering wheel, but there was terrible pain in my legs, especially my right one. I could barely move, but I could see Cathy dangling upside down in the passenger's seat, blood dripping from her head.

It was then I had my first true psychic vision. I saw a life, the one Cathy and I were supposed to share. I saw each making sacrifices to help the other achieve their dreams. I saw resentments towards each other for a minor disagreements. I saw her give birth to one of our children, and us pull together in times of need. I saw us holding hands into our old age, more in love, because we stood the test of time in a world where marriages don't last.

"Cathy, don't go," I croaked.

But she was gone.

I heard someone outside the remains of my window. I thought there was still a chance, that somebody saw us crash and there would be an ambulance. I shifted to see that red face stare at me, its horns rising from his brow.

The creature knelt inches away from me. His long, narrow face twisted into a smile, the white teeth shining against the deep crimson of his flesh, as he leaned against our broken car and said:

You have to be careful what you conjure, boy!

Mercifully, I blacked out.

And now, years later, I fought to drive the memories out of my mind as I focused in on what I came to say today.

"Hi, honey," I whispered, as tears stung my eyes. Where could I begin? It had been so long since I'd even allowed myself to focus on her. And here she was in her final resting place, which opened the wound once more.

I sat, all but falling down on my one good knee, and was overcome. I began to weep, a pain in my chest as I heaved and sobbed. There weren't words for my loss, just the knowledge that she was gone and there was nothing I could do to touch her again.

"Why did you have to die?" I said, aware of how stupid this question was, and at the same time, I knew it was the question of all those who grieve. My grief was years old but was still a hard lump in my throat.

I began to get control of myself, thankful I'd remembered a handkerchief, which I pulled from my pocket and used to wipe my face and blow my nose. I sat for a few minutes, allowing the grief to pass, and tried to enjoy the peace of the place, although traffic roared a few hundred feet away. It was good to be near what was left of her on this earth. Just being close to her in some way—any way—calmed me.

"I came back to help Jon Baines," I said, as I found my voice. "Actually, it's more like he's helping me. He got me a lecture—I'll even be paid."

I reached out and ran my fingers over the letters carved into the stone. "I'm a doctor now. Remember, that's what we talked about and worked for. The day when we would be doctors…"

I turned away and blew my nose.

"Not the way we planned it, I guess. Then again, we planned to both be alive, didn't we?" I said, a grim smile on my face—humor in the midst of sorrow—that was one of my traits she loved.

"I'm at a crossroads, sweetie. Don't quite know where I'm going or how I'm getting there. But if you can keep an eye on me, maybe help me out, I'd appreciate it," I said, and then closed my eyes and sat in silence.

There was a quick breeze that caressed my hair, and for a moment, I felt a touch, like a pair of invisible lips giving my cheek the lightest of kisses.

Then it was gone.

I opened my eyes and smiled, a real smile this time. If I'd learned one thing over the last few years, it's that we don't die—we merely change form. A part of us endures. Sometimes, that part gets fixated on its last moments, which can lead to a haunting. But most of the time, we just move on to another plane.

I got up feeling younger, freer. She was there, and she would watch over me, as she probably had all these years. I had just never taken the time to listen.

I kissed my fingers and lay them to the stone. Then I headed to the gate to make my way back to town.

EIGHT

After I arrived at my guest quarters, I showered off the sweat from my walk and called Wendy Wallace.

"Hello?" she bubbled on the other end of the line.

"Wendy, it's Len."

"Wow! A man who calls the next day like he said he would."

"It has been known to happen."

"So, what's the latest on our case?"

"I didn't know it was 'our' case," I said, taken aback.

"Well, I want to know what happened—I was there, for goodness sake!"

And there is the insurance, I thought, but pushed it aside. "Still running tests," I said to dismiss it. "By the way, did you hear any kind of sound—perhaps an explosion or even just a whoosh of air?"

"Yeah, there was a kind of sound, like wind, when I got out the back and slammed the door." She paused, and then there was a light gasp. "Do you think my opening the door did anything?"

"It's hard to say. Anyway, the reason I called is to invite you out for dinner tomorrow night, my treat. I'll even wear a suit."

"Not the same one you wore yesterday…" she said.

"What was wrong with it?"

"It was too big on you!"

"I have others," I lied.

"That's good. You dress nice for me, and I'll dress up for you. Believe me, you'll think it's worth it."

"You always look good, Wendy," I said.

"I work at it. Pick you up at seven?"

"Great, see you then."

I hung up the phone and had to admit, I was about as enthusiastic as if I had just been hired to clean the bathrooms in Grand Central Station. I felt stupid. Wendy was actually an interesting woman. She was beautiful and intelligent, with a remarkable figure. But it all seemed so meaningless, especially after the visit to Cathy's grave.

However, Cathy was dead and I was alive, and a few hours with Miss Wallace would be enjoyable and might help me shake my inappropriate attraction to Jenny. Jenny was so much more like Cathy than just looks. She possessed the same spirit, that internal energy that gave her a glow that just filled the room every time she entered…

Or was I projecting that? Reading things into her I wanted to see? This was all frustrating on many levels. After Cathy's death, I took years of psychoanalysis, both with a therapist and as an academic course of study. If I couldn't be an MD, then I figured I'd be a shrink. That didn't work out well as my unique abilities wouldn't shut down. A guy who hears voices and peeks into other people's brains is not the best candidate for therapist of the year.

That's when the drinking increased. During that time, I lived with a woman—Susan Haring—whom I treated poorly. I didn't strike her or do anything grotesque, but I played games with her mind. It was a terrible thing for her to be with someone who always knew what she was thinking. It scared her and made me feel like she was somehow less, as I possessed the ability to say the things that would hurt her the most.

She was only safe when the alcohol turned my abilities off. But then she dealt with the depressed drunk. Talk about a lose–lose for her. She finally left to preserve her own ego. At the time, I hated her for it.

But in retrospect, I don't blame her one bit.

I wanted a drink, just a little one. I must have made enough progress where I could just have a little to put me to sleep. Jon has a liquor cabinet somewhere…

But, no, if I start again, I can't stop. That's how bad it got; I drank from the time I got up until I went to sleep. Not falling down intoxicated, but never sober. It shut off the noise in my head. Then again, it affected everything—and now I was involved in something important, something more than just myself. I sighed and decided I needed a nap. I headed to my room, undressed, and slid between the sheets. I focused on my breathing until I began to doze.

I was dreaming—drifting free—or was I?

I was in the jewelry store as I had seen it, burned and damaged. The windows were streaked and covered in soot. There was a smell, one I could recognize.

Gasoline.

I walked to the window in the door and wiped the pane, leaving streaks of soot on my hand, but clearing it a bit. There was a man outside just beyond the window. He watched me through the dirty glass, a figure dressed in black. I could see his ebony hair and his thin face with a Roman nose—but the eyes—they glowed a bright red.

He could see me.

I was afraid, so very afraid, and I turned from the window and tried to run, my legs and arms pumping, but I moved so terribly slowly.

Fire began to spit forth from different places in the room—the counters, the floor, the remains of the cash register—like little erupting volcanoes that shot fire into the air, spreading the tongues of yellow and orange to the ceiling and walls.

I ran to the back room, but it was alight as well. It was blisteringly hot, yet I leaned away from the intensity of the inferno and kept running for the back door. Reaching for it, I felt the metal against my palms. I grabbed the doorknob—and yelped as I pulled away. It was glowing, red-hot. I looked at my hand; it was scalded.

I turned from the door, and could see the figure still there. The blaze grew higher as I threw myself against the door with all my might. I pounded it again and again, and finally, I heard it give, and the door flew open.

To a scene from hell.

All around me, the parking lot was on fire, burning away. It shouldn't be possible, but the pavement itself was aflame, and the asphalt melted and bubbled. There were two cars that would probably explode once the fuel tanks caught…

"Len?"

I jumped up, breathing hard. It was dark, and there was a knock at my door.

"C-Come in," I said.

Jenny walked in the door, causing the light from the corridor to shine into the darkened bedroom.

"You'd better get up, sleepyhead. Dinner is in a half-hour." She flicked on the overhead light, and I pulled the blanket up over my naked form.

"It's nice I'm not the only one who sleeps in the nude," she said, a grin on her face.

Then her smile froze, and she approached me. Concern appeared on her face. "My God, Len, what did you do to your hand?"

I looked down at my right hand. The fingers and palm were seared, white blisters forming on my flesh.

"What the Hell did you do?"

My mouth was dry, my throat tight. "Jenny," I croaked, "can you get me some ointment?"

"Of course," she said and left the room.

I grabbed my underwear and dove into my pants and shirt as well as I could with my stiff right leg and my right hand now burned. Jenny came back into the room just as I, barefoot, went to the chair where I had left my jacket.

"A phone!" I said. "I've got to get my phone."

"But, Len, you're hurt!"

I looked at my damaged hand as well as the gauze and tube of medicine in Jenny's hand. "Can you bandage it while I make a call?"

She nodded as I pulled my phone out of my jacket pocket. I was thankful I could operate it with my left hand. I touched the screen and brought up McGee's number.

"Let me look at that!" Jenny said. She touched my hand and I flinched.

The phone rang in my ear.

"This is not good," Jenny said, delicately rubbing the cream on my hand. "How could you burn your hand lying in bed?"

The phone rang again.

"You've heard of psychosomatic illness? When you think you're sick, so your body starts to hurt?"

"Yes—but this…" Jenny said.

The phone rang a third time.

"This is called a psychogenic effect. It's when you believe something in your mind with such clarity, you experience it physically."

"McGee," the voice boomed in my ear.

"Bill, it's Len. Don't ask me how I know this, but get a fire truck over to Mishan's Jewelry store right now."

"What the hell?" he said.

"Bill, I'm serious—"

"And a bit late. There are trucks already heading there. The place starting burning about ten minutes ago, big time. The whole block might go up. But how did you know, are you there?"

"No, I'm at the Baines's house," I said, releasing my pent-up breath and feeling a bit dizzy. "But I was at the store—in a dream, I guess—a vision."

"And your hand is burned," Jenny said, as she pulled a gauze pad out of her pocket.

"Bill, you should get down there!" I said into the phone. "Whoever did this might still be there. He's dressed in black, tall, thin, Roman nose…"

"What are you talking about?" he said, not convinced.

"I was there, in the building—I saw him outside, just like the day Mishan died. He's there now, watching the fire."

"All right, I'm on my way. I'm going to want to talk to you later. You'll be in?"

"Yeah. I'll be here all night."

I gave him the address and hung up as Jenny finished binding my hand with tape.

"Are you all right?" she asked.

"I'll be fine. Thank you—I don't want your food to burn."

"Dinner!" she yelped and ran toward the kitchen.

I went back to my room and put on my socks, shoes, and my well-traveled tweed jacket. Then I went to the bathroom and, using my left hand, splashed cool water on my face. Haggard eyes stared back at me from the mirror.

. . .

Jenny's quick work saved the broiled salmon from becoming ash. At six, Jon, Jenny, and I sat down to vegetables and fresh bread that Jenny, with great modesty, claimed she just "threw together in the bread machine."

"No end of excitement today," Jenny said. "I woke Len up and saved him from burning alive."

"What?" Jon said with a glance to me.

Jenny related the story from her point of view, while I added very little. Just as she finished, there was a knock at the door.

"I'll get it. It's probably Mrs. Kinney from around the corner."

As soon as Jenn left the room, Jon moved close and whispered, "So, how long can you stay?"

"I should leave soon. I don't want to wear out my welcome."

"Len, I've barely had any time with you. Tomorrow is Friday. At least stay through the weekend so we can hang out together a bit."

"Sure, that will be—"

Jenny walked into the room, pale and stiff.

"It's a police officer, Len. He asked to see you."

I brightened. "Oh, that's Detective McGee. It's all right, he's the one I called."

I got up, but Jenny still looked worried. I could sense that there was something about the situation that made her uneasy.

I hobbled out to the hall. Not an easy feat as I was not accustomed to using my cane with my left hand. There was McGee, flanked by a uniformed officer I had not yet met. The officer was average height with features I would expect on a movie star. Strong chin, high cheekbones. He was well-built without being too pumped.

"Doctor Wise?" McGee said, his eyes tight and his attitude stern.

"Detective McGee, I'm glad you—" I started.

"I have to ask you your whereabouts this afternoon between three and five p.m."

"My whereabouts?" I asked, puzzled. "I was here, asleep." Out of the corner of my eye, I saw Jon and Jenny come into the room behind me.

"Do you have any witnesses to confirm that you were here?" McGee said in the same flat tone.

"I woke Len at five-thirty," Jenny said.

"And where is your room, on the second floor?" McGee asked.

"No," I said. "On the ground floor, back near the garage." I could see why Jenny was so nervous about McGee's arrival. He was acting totally different, hostile.

"So you could have climbed in through a window or entered through the garage without Mrs. Baines knowing it?"

At this, I couldn't suppress a smile. The image of me with my bad leg climbing through a window was beyond comical—it was practically Three Stooges material.

"That would be impossible…" Jenny said.

"What is this about, detective?" Jon said, ever my defender.

"I understand, Doctor, that you received a burn on the palm of your hand," McGee said, fixing his intense eyes on my bandaged hand. "May I see it and have Officer Galland photograph it?"

The uniformed man next to McGee nodded, and I saw the camera in his hand. It was a high-quality digital one with a large lens and an attached strobe. They'd come prepared.

I paused for a moment. "Of course," I said, and began to loosen the bandage.

Jon raised his hand. "Len, if they are accusing you of anything, it would be better to have a lawyer present. I could make a call…"

"That won't be necessary," I said. "I honestly have nothing to hide." I unwrapped the tape, and the bandage fell away.

I heard Jenny draw in breath, and then move over closer to me.

"But—it was burned. I saw the blisters…" she murmured.

McGee grabbed a flashlight from Galland's belt and shone the bright light in the palm of my hand.

There wasn't a mark.

I looked over at Jenny. "I told you, it was psychogenic—all in my mind. Once I accepted that I really wasn't burned…"

"That's amazing," Jenny said, her eyes wide.

I turned to face Jenny and Jon. "I think Detective McGee and I should talk. Detective, may we step outside?"

McGee still looked at my hand, puzzled. "Of course, Doctor," he said, his manner less cold.

We stepped out on the front porch and shut the door to the house. It was cooler, and I pulled my jacket tighter.

"I'm sure Officer Galland has a report to fill out," I said.

"Yes, I'm sure he does," McGee said with a nod to the man who returned the nod and walked away, playing with his camera as he went.

I looked at McGee and wiggled the fingers of my right hand. "You thought I started the fire."

His eyes followed Galland as he headed to the car. "Look, Doctor, think of it from a detective's point of view. You call me about a fire, and I overhear a woman saying you got burned—what would you think?"

I turned to watch Galland as well. "Probably what you thought. Here I am, this guy you don't know, wanting to be involved in the case. Then I call you raving about a fire—I'd be suspicious, too."

I could see McGee shift uneasily. "There are people who do things to get attention..."

I nodded. "Agreed, especially people claiming to be psychics. They seek a lot of publicity to try to validate their abilities." I faced McGee. "Look, Bill. I'm only here because you asked—and somehow, some way, I'm involved in this case on levels I don't completely understand." I gazed off down the quiet street lined with houses. "That dream was so real, and to be honest, it scared the hell out of me. It's odd, it's like I'm being pushed to find the truth. But, if I'm in your way, then I'm out of here and headed back to California."

Bill nodded. "You actually have been a help. I found out Lonny the Match is out of prison."

"For how long?"

"A few months, and he skipped out on his parole officer. He's had plenty of time to make his way to New Jersey."

"Where was he living?"

"California."

I accepted the coincidence of my own arrival. "And I show up around the same time, from California, and conveniently point suspicion on him. If I were a detective, alarm bells would go off."

"Can you see why I ran out here?" McGee said.

"If it's any help, you can have forensics go over me and my belongings. I can assure you I do not have any residue of accelerants on anything I own."

"That's not necessary."

"But if it becomes necessary, I won't take it personally, Bill." I sat down on the steps, my leg stretched out. McGee followed suit.

"How bad was the fire?" I asked.

"Bad. The fire department called in squads from other towns. We may lose that entire block."

"I hope everyone got out."

"Still people unaccounted for."

"Damn!" I said.

"And we lost any possible chance of going over the site again. Anything left will be far too damaged."

"Damn!" I repeated. A faint breeze came, carrying the slight odor of gasoline, I guessed from the fire since it burned only ten or twelve blocks away.

"In my vision, I smelled gasoline. Like someone doused the place with it."

"That's for the fire department to find out. Then I'll see if there are any witnesses, see if anyone was walking around with a gas can."

"The oddest thing for me is that I saw a face," I said. "It wasn't Lonny, it was different. It was someone with a presence…" I exhaled heavily. "There I go, ranting again. Look, I'd better let you go. But my offer stands. Any way I can help or if you want me to just leave, let me know."

"Do you think you could look over some mug shots tomorrow? See if anyone on the books matches this new face you saw?"

"I could try."

"Then come on by in the morning. I'll see you then," McGee said, standing and taking my hand in a firm handshake. As he left, I knew we were still friends.

NINE

The evening was spent reassuring Jon and Jenny that everything was fine and that I wasn't going to be arrested or develop stigmata. Jenny spent a lot of the evening surreptitiously taking peeks at my hand. I probably stared at it a bit myself.

I have seen phenomena similar to what had happened to me at hauntings, though I've never been a big fan of physical mediums. The term applies to a clairvoyant who speaks with spirits—and causes physical manifestations. This includes table raps, movement of objects, and materializations—the sudden appearance of an object or person.

The problem with such displays is that the effects are usually accomplished through subterfuge. There was a strong spiritualist movement in the Victorian era in America and England, and although there were several truly gifted psychics in the mix, the vast number were clever manipulators, much like the modern "manifester" Uri Geller, with his spoon and key bending trickery.

That was the advantage of working my way through high school as a magician with my brother, who'd made a career out of illusion. I was familiar with many of the manipulations that fraudulent characters use. I have also recently witnessed events that I would call miraculous. You can find the truth if you look for what the psychic is attempting to accomplish. I'm trying to help people and keep my ego out of the equation. The people who can do the real stuff try not to draw attention to themselves. If you see a psychic making television appearances, he's probably a fake.

My suggestion to such people who promise to connect you with your lost loved one on television every day at four PM is that they should switch to home cleaning products and let people work through their grief without them.

"So, Len, are you able to stay the weekend?" Jenny said as she sipped on a brandy.

I could smell the sweet odor from my seat, the aged cognac—my favorite tipple—and it was like smelling ambrosia and my own demise at the same time. You can't get enough of the thing you don't want, and I really didn't want a drink at that moment, and I *did* want it with every fiber of my being.

"Yeah, as long as I'm not imposing," I said.

"I hope you and Jon will get out of my hair this weekend and let me finish a book," Jenny said. "I intend to spend most of the day with my butt on the sofa."

"No problem, Jenn," Jon said. "We'll go out and do manly things."

"Home Depot?" I said.

"Be still my heart," Jon replied.

"Sounds fine to me," Jenny said. "What do you gentlemen want for dinner tomorrow?"

"I'll cook," Jon said.

"Just not your chili. We want Len to like us," Jenny remarked.

"I love Jon's chili," I said.

"There, see," Jon said.

"But," I interjected, "I'm going out tomorrow."

"Miss Wallace?" Jon asked.

"So you should plan a romantic dinner for just the two of you," I said.

"If Jon's cooking, then I'm already feeling romantic," Jenny said, giving him a wink.

"If you two will excuse me, it's been quite an evening, and I would like to get some rest," I said as I grabbed my cane and rose.

"You slept this afternoon," Jenny said. "You can't be tired again."

No, dammit, I just have to get away from the smell of the cognac. You would be drinking my favorite brand, I thought with annoyance.

"Been a busy few months with my doctoral dissertation and all. I guess I'm finally unwinding," I said.

"That's fine, Len. Good night," Jon said.

"Good night," Jenny added as I trudged out of the living room to my guest bedroom.

I was tired. The nap I'd had earlier had not refreshed me as it was troubled by the vision. I undressed, lay down with a book, and was out in about a half-hour.

· · ·

The next morning, I followed McGee's suggestion and dropped by the police station. Tice wasn't at the front desk, which made the day rosier right at the beginning.

I gave my name to the officer on duty, and McGee came right out, all smiles. He shook my hand and took me back to Interrogation

Room C, which I found out was also called soft interview or observation, where several large ledgers sat on the table.

McGee rubbed the back of his neck as I sat down. "Look, Len,
I hope there's no hard feelings about last night…"

"It's fine, Bill," I said. "I really do understand. I'm just glad
you're still willing to work with me."

He slid the mug books in front of me, then paused. "I've been
able to get some information on that Nova Corporation."

"And our Miss Wallace is listed on the board?"

"As a matter of fact, yes, along with several other names I want
to look into."

"I have a date with her tonight," I said.

"Then I should tell you, I have filed paperwork to get a warrant
for her financials, including her taxes."

"And you're telling me this why?"

"We are probably going to execute the warrant tomorrow. So, if
you have a date tonight and, well—how do I put this?"

"If I get lucky," I suggested with a stupid smirk on my face.

"You get the picture. Just be sure to be out of there by morning,"
McGee stated with a somber expression.

"I don't know if it's that serious, Bill."

"My one suggestion, Len. If a woman like that offers, don't
say no."

I nodded lamely and opened the book in front of me.

Bill headed out the door, saying, "If you need coffee or anything, I'm right in the next room."

I got down to the business of looking at the faces. Time passed
and I recognized not a one. By noon, I'd worked my way through
all three books and still hadn't seen a face that was even close to a

match. In my memory, the most outstanding feature was the red, glowing eyes. Did they distract me from the rest of his face?

I got up with my cane and walked through the open door and over to Bill's desk, which sat out in plain sight at the false wall that subdivided the detective bureau. His desk was neatly piled with folders, but the concept that there was a specific order to his system was beyond me.

McGee lifted his head. "Any luck?"

"Not even a nibble," I said. "I have the additional problem that I can't focus on him in my memory. I concentrate, and he gets fuzzy."

"At least you know it's a him, that eliminates half of the population."

"He's white, thin, Anglo-Saxon I think," I said.

"Getting closer all the time," Bill said, as he pawed through some papers.

"I guess. I should take off. By the way, don't let Wendy think I had anything to do with—y'know."

Bill met my eyes, an eyebrow raised. "More serious than you thought?"

"I don't know," I said, suddenly flushing. "I just don't want her to think I was using her."

"Hold on a second, Len," Bill said and signaled me to sit next to him.

I did.

"There may be more to Wendy Wallace than you think. I'll probably sort it out when I get hold of her records, but this Nova, it appears to be an entire dummy corporation. Miss Wallace is the only real person I've been able to locate."

"Real person?" I repeated, surprised. "But you said…the names…"

"While you were going through mug books, I was looking into them. They appear to be mostly fake, and one I haven't located, Denny Kalhaskalwicz, has almost too many letters to be real," Bill said. "Once I bring Wendy in for questioning, I'll figure it out. But if not, I may have to call in some old friends."

"FBI?"

He nodded and held up the papers. "This Nova is a pretty handy little creation. Dubious names, the addresses listed are empty lots, the only one to take the fall is our Miss Wallace. I don't think someone would have gone to all that trouble just to invest in a jewelry store."

"What do you think it is?" I asked. "Drugs? Money laundering?"

"Slow down, cowboy," Bill said. "Just be aware that she might not be what she appears to be. But don't say anything to her."

"You afraid she'll slip me a mickey?" I attempted with my best Humphrey Bogart impression.

His blue eyes flashed steel. "Things like that do happen. Just be aware—and be careful."

. . .

I made my way to the university. It was raining, with a slight nip in the air. I wore my rumpled raincoat and tried to stay dry as I trudged along.

Trisha got Jon on the intercom, and with great ceremony, Jon pulled out an envelope containing my check with all the flourish of a prestidigitator.

I opened the envelope and noted that the check was for a thousand dollars more than my agreed fee.

"Jon," I said, "this is more than—"

"Relax, Len," Jon interrupted. "It was in the fine print. You get a larger percentage if we sell out, and your lecture did."

My head spun, and feeling every bit flush, I rode with Jon to the bank. We took my first real fee and converted it all to traveler's checks and a debit card. I now could keep going longer than I had planned, and my dinner with Wendy wasn't going to be a problem.

But she did say she didn't like my clothes.

I thanked Jon and had him leave me in town, where I made my way to a local men's store, one that advertised designer suits at reasonable prices. There, I bought a new suit, forty-two long, very fashionable. It helped make my skinny form look more proportioned. I waited while a little old man who looked like he was just shy of a hundred hemmed the pants. I also bought a colorful tie and a few good dress shirts. Maybe I had worn denim just a little too long. I also bought a new raincoat, and my salesman was happy to throw away my ratty one after he gave it a look that compared it to roadkill.

I paid with my debit card and got some cash back from the transaction for walking around money. Then I headed off toward my temporary abode with several plastic bags in tow. On the way, I passed a barber shop, a quaint old-fashioned throwback to ones my father would have taken me years ago. A couple of chairs were mounted on a tile floor as middle-aged men snipped with scissors and buzzed with an electric razor.

I went in.

"What would you like?" the barber asked, standing up from one of the chairs.

"Can you give me a corporate look?" I asked.

"Shorter all around, longer on top," he said, as I sat in the chair and undid my ponytail. "But not as long as this. Mother of God! When was the last time you got a haircut?"

"Seven years."

"Don't worry, I've got this."

And he did. As he carefully snipped here and cut there, cascades of my long hair drifted to the floor. After about twenty minutes, he used a set of electric clippers and buzzed the back of my neck, which felt odd being so exposed. But when he was done, I wore a short and certainly more respectable haircut.

I paid him with my cash from the clothing store and made my way back to the Baines's, where I showered, shaved, and dressed in my new suit to get ready for my date.

Jenny arrived at five, and I decided to show off my new look.

"Hey, Jenny," I said, coming up the hall. "I've got something I want you to see."

"That's a dangerous line coming from a man," she said.

I stepped into the kitchen, and she turned, a carrot in her mouth. She stopped chewing as her jaw fell open.

"Len?" she asked.

"Yes, I'm not some well-dressed stranger who broke into your house."

"Or maybe you are," she said, circling me. "God, you are gorgeous!"

I felt myself burn with embarrassment from the tips of my toes to the top of my newly trimmed head.

"You are turning so red!" Jenny said with the glee of a child who has done something naughty and is pleased about it.

"You're making me feel like a piece of meat," I said, as I tried to smile, but it felt crooked.

"That's how I treat all my men," she said, and as she walked by me, she playfully smacked my rear end with her free hand.

That didn't help the situation for me at all, and I turned even redder. "I've got to finish getting ready," I said, trying to maintain what little composure I had left. "Big date tonight." I moved swiftly toward the guest room, sat on the bed, and focused on my breath.

Seeing Jenn with that admiring look in her eyes was tough enough, but the physical contact of her slapping my butt, even as a silly gesture, was too much for my suddenly overactive libido.

My "friend" was in a state of arousal. By sitting on the bed, it hid the fact within the folds of my trousers, but if I'd stayed in the kitchen, I would've been mortified in a whole new way.

I thought only about my breath, on being the observer, on being detached—dammit—detached.

There was a knock at the door.

"Come in."

Jenny opened the door and peered in. "It is all right?"

"Sure."

She came in delicately, like a mouse walking into a cat's room to get some cheese. "I feel I should apologize…" Jenny said. Now it was her turn to be flustered. "I didn't mean to embarrass you like that."

"Ass being the key word," I said and smiled.

She giggled naughtily again. "I guess I'm just bad. Jon is always telling me I have to behave more like a dean's wife."

"Or associate dean's wife, anyway."

"Jon is sure he'll be running the whole university before long."

"I don't doubt it, he's a good man," I said. She looked contrite, which again reminded me so much of Cathy after we'd had a fight. My heart ached with a strange longing that I worked to keep from moving to my loins.

"But all kidding aside, you do look good, Len," she said, walking over and touching my hair in a move that was meant as friendly, but was incredibly sensual at the same time.

"Thank you," I croaked.

"I love Jonathan," she said and sat next to me on the bed. "But ever since he became assistant dean, he's just been so…stuffy."

"He does seem more mature than when I knew him last."

"You know he asked me to marry him repeatedly before I said yes?"

"Jon told me."

"He thinks it was because I was planning to never marry. But the reason was just because I knew if he settled into something, he'd turn middle-aged in a year. And he has, Len. He's so stoic, controlled, and busy—all the time."

She rose from the bed and leaned her back against the doorframe.

"When he was pursuing me, he couldn't get enough of me," she said. "Now that we're married, sometimes, I feel like an afterthought. I mean, Jon offered to make dinner tonight. Yet, here I am doing the cooking while he works late."

I was filled with a desire to rise and take her in my arms.

"I know he loves you, Jenny. He's working hard to be responsible."

"You're right," she said and stood straight. "And speaking of responsibilities, I've got to start dinner. Because that's what little wifey is supposed to do."

"But you don't regret marrying him?" I asked.

"Not at all," Jenny said with a sigh. "I just wish he'd be a little more spontaneous and a little less proper sometimes. So, you're going out with that Wallace *person*?"

She made "person" sound as if she'd said "slut."

"She's actually a nice girl."

"For a suspect in a murder case. I got the warrant today and turned all of our paperwork over to that rather large detective who was here last night."

"That's McGee."

Jenn exhaled heavily. "Get ready for your date, and we won't leave a light on for you. Looking like that, you're bound to get lucky," she added with a smirk and closed the door on her way out.

I considered it lucky that I hadn't acted on my impulses with Jenny.

• • •

By seven it stopped raining, and I was waiting out front when Wendy swung by in her little car. I limped out to meet her, and she got out of the car and gave a reaction similar to Jenny's.

"If it weren't for the cane, I wouldn't have known it was you. My God, you're gorgeous!"

"Just a haircut and a new suit," I said, not nearly as embarrassed with her. "Besides, your dress is a killer."

"You like?" she said, giving a twirl and opening the jacket that matched the dress, revealing a large gap in the back. There were no bra straps. The entire dress was black, silky, and stretchy, and looking like it was poured onto her, with a few touches of sparkling black beads in appropriate places. The small jacket went to her waist and covered her bare arms—to make the dress look more formal and in case the spring weather became chilly.

"Wow," I said quietly. Perhaps the night had grown cool, because her nipples appeared to be erect through the dress, and she didn't try to hide them.

"I take it you approve. Now, where are we going?"

"The Manor," I said.

Her eyebrows lifted and an "ooh" escaped from her lips. "You do have good taste."

"I also can afford it, at least this one time," I said, as I tried to be nonchalant. "You know the way?"

"No problem," she said as we got into the vehicle and sped off.

The drive was pleasant—hell, pleasant wasn't the word. She was wearing some scent that was subtle, yet inviting. I observed her face as we drove, with me sitting sideways in the seat. She was wearing some blush and lipstick, and I was sure she even did her nails. All of it with the skill of a professional so that she didn't look made up, yet every one of her features was improved.

We got to the Manor in a few minutes, and the valet took her car, thrilled that he got a chance to drive such a machine.

We went in, I gave my name and we were brought to our seats. As I planned, we were in the room where a pianist played classical music on a large ebony grand.

The only downside was that like any other place with lots of guests, I began to sense the mental leakage that permeated the room. The background chatter swelled in my mind. I carefully constructed my imaginary walls to limit what came to me.

"This is very nice," Wendy said as we sat. "I'm impressed."

"Well, you showed me a nice time the other night, and I felt I should return the favor."

"More than repaid," she said and picked up the wine list that lay on our table. "How about a nice merlot?"

I remembered how in AA, they told us this would happen. You would be out with a friend or on a date, and a drink would be suggested.

"Sure, get what you want," I attempted to sound casual.

"You'll have some?"

I looked at her, not sure how to reply. "I'll…uh…have a glass," I said with a smile.

Danger…

In the back of my mind, I heard the buzz warn me, and I ignored it. It had been an odd week, and my latest encounter with Jenny upset me. I would have to avoid being alone with her, as unbidden desires arose.

What made tonight difficult was that Wendy looked so good, everyone noticed her and therefore, me. To have other peoples' minds focused on me makes it harder for me to block them out. I needed to keep a handle on it. As I sat, I decided that if I had just one glass of wine, it would dull my psychic edge and I could relax, really relax, and be myself.

I examined the menu as Wendy ordered the bottle of wine, and I decided on my choice by the time two glasses appeared filled with the ruby liquid.

"A toast," Wendy said with a twinkle in her eye. "To old friends and new lovers."

"May they never meet," I added with a smile.

That first sip had all the shading and texture of the finest wine I have ever tasted. It slid down my throat, and the warmth felt like it kept going all the way down to my toes. I looked at the glass like a lover I'd missed with all my heart.

"You're really enjoying that, aren't you?" I could hear Wendy say, as if from a distance.

You have no idea, I thought. "It's a…really good wine."

We ordered dinner, and soon the waiter created a Caesar salad dressing at table side using oil, vinegar, lemon, spices and anchovies. He mixed the creamy liquid with romaine lettuce and croutons and placed portions in front of us both.

She refilled my glass, and I didn't stop her. After all, if one glass was so wonderful, it could only be better if I had a second. That made sense.

Our dinners were exquisite, a filet mignon for her, and a black sea bass with tiny potatoes for me. It was prepared perfectly, and we drank, ate, and chatted about life, goals, people we'd known. I gave her the rough outline of how my leg was crushed, and she gave the vaguest hints about her relationship with a man who had money but never treated her well.

As the dinner plates were cleared, I requested a cognac. I had smelled the damn stuff all week, and with my inhibitions deadened, I decided I would have it. After all, if the wine had made me un-aware of all the *thinking* around me, a cognac would be even better.

"I can't believe you can drink more!" Wendy said as she sipped the remains of her last glass of wine.

Like many alcoholics, I could hold my liquor so well you would never know I was the least bit intoxicated. I had fallen into the trap alcoholics face. We think we can just have only one and then stop.

But I couldn't, and after a year away from it, I felt remarkably jolly. "Are you all right to drive?" I asked.

"Yes, you've had twice as much as I did."

"So, you were telling me about this man…"

"Aren't you bored of hearing about it?" Wendy said.

"It seems like he's on your mind. Recent breakup?"

She looked at the red liquid in her glass, swirling it as she spoke. "Recent enough. About a year. But I have to see him—y'know, business stuff."

"Which you've told me nothing about."

She leaned back in the chair. "Got to keep you guessing. Gives you a reason to stick around."

"And you have to be around this man, but…"

"It's all so dreary. He acts like he *owns* me. He watches me like he's an owl and I'm a mouse. He checks up on me—phone hang-ups—but I know it's him."

I frowned. "Maybe you should talk to the police."

"I can handle him. That was the problem, possessiveness. But here I am, out with you and having a fine time."

I clinked my snifter to her wine glass. "To a fine time," I said.

I paid the check with pleasure. It had been one of the finest meals of my life. I had taken Cathy here a day or so after I proposed to her. It was nice to see the food was just as good years later. As we went to valet, I had the strangest feeling, as if the fact that I brought Wendy here was in some way being unfaithful to Cathy.

"What's wrong?" Wendy asked.

I jumped. "Oh? Nothing, I was just thinking about the last time I was here."

"Well, the night is young, Doctor," she said, getting on her tip-toes and kissing my cheek. "If you don't pay attention, you might miss something."

Her kiss was warm and inviting. So why was my mind filled with thoughts of Cathy—and worse, Jenny?

She tipped the valet and got into the car. I leaned, grunted, and manipulated myself in, and we were off.

"So, would you like to come over to my house for an after-dinner drink?"

"Sounds lovely." Yes, like the one thing I needed was another drink. I couldn't help but notice that the secondary level of aware-ness that disturbed my nights and days was dulled by the liquor. I saw her only with my eyes, and any background impressions didn't touch me.

We drove back to Mountainview, and then up in the hills to Upper Mountainview, the fashionable part of town.

"Nice neighborhood," I remarked.

"It has its perks," she said and smiled.

We pulled into the driveway of a house that was slightly smaller than its neighbors, but still large enough for a family of seven. The garage door opened and she drove in. As soon as we stopped, she darted out of the car and shut the garage door, leav-ing me in darkness.

"Hey! Where are the lights?"

A moment or two later, fluorescents flashed on overhead, and I pulled myself from the car.

"Sorry," she said, as she breathed hard. "It took me a minute to turn them on."

I looked at the garage doors and noticed black curtains covered the glass windows, attached by curtain rods. Were they open when we pulled in?

"Come on, silly," she said, and walked toward the door to the house, her rear end swaying almost hypnotically.

I followed her through the neat garage, which had an empty space for another car, and into a laundry room that then led us into a living room decorated completely in white.

"Wow!" I gasped.

"Yeah, I know, it's pretty amazing," she said. "But I have to admit, it's totally unlivable. I'm always worried I'm going to spill something. Take off your shoes."

I stopped, pulled off my shoes and left them in the laundry room.

"See, I'm already getting you out of your clothes," she said as she pulled off her heels.

She took me through a dining room with a twelve-foot ceiling, and then into a large kitchen. The house appeared to have had an amazing remodel at some point, because just past the modern stove was a dining nook, where the ceiling went up twenty feet, with skylights and open space.

She sat me down at the small counter and opened a cabinet, pulling out two beautiful cut-glass snifters and a crystal decanter of amber liquid.

"I noticed you like cognac," she said, pouring us each a knock. "I have the XO."

I gave a small whistle of appreciation. XO is the top of the line and pricey. I gazed around the kitchen and breakfast room. The cabinets looked new, with matching woodwork on the refrigerator and the trash compactor. Two sinks, new, and a collection of shiny pots and pans hanging from a wrought iron rack suspended on chains over the stove.

"You must do a lot of entertaining."

"Actually, I don't cook at all," she said and handed me the glass of cognac. "The pots are for show, and everything else was already here."

She removed the short jacket from her ensemble, moved closer to me, and loosened my tie. "Actually, I've been living like a nun for the past year."

"Now *that* is a pity."

"Well, maybe it's time for a change."

She pulled close to me, and our lips met, first as gentle as a whisper, and then harder. Finally, our mouths opened, and our tongues began to explore each other. I felt the hard nub of her tongue stud and heard small moans in the back of her throat. Meanwhile, visions of Cathy and Jenny both danced naked through my brain.

Her hand gingerly stroked my leg, and my hand touched the naked flesh in the opening on the back of her dress. I delicately traced her spine with my fingers, touching her so softly that I created goose bumps as I caressed my way to her neck.

"Mmm!" she said, then pulled her head away and took a sip of brandy. "You have a great touch."

"So do you," I said, the image of the other women still in my mind.

She kissed me, and her hand slid down to my crotch.

"Looks like I got the desired effect," she said with a smile.

She wriggled out of my grasp, grabbed her drink, and took my left hand. "Why don't we continue this upstairs?" she said and pulled me to my feet.

She went up the stairs ahead of me as I hobbled up one step at a time.

"Second door on your right!" she said, as I braced myself with my cane and plodded up.

I reached the top of the stairs, and the hall was dark except for a flickering light past an open door. I stepped in to see about ten different sized candles illuminating the room. The bedroom was huge, with fabric covering the walls and arcing like a tent to the center of the ceiling. In the middle of the room was a huge round bed, where Wendy sat under the covers, her drink in hand.

"I feel like I'm walking into the *Arabian Nights*," I said.

"And I'm your Scheherazade! Come on, it's not nice to keep a lady waiting."

I left my cane at the door and limped to the bed, tossing my jacket aside as I went. This made her giggle and hide deeper under the covers, which appeared blue, though it was hard to tell by candlelight.

I sat on the bed and kissed her, my hands going under the covers to discover that she was naked.

"You're not wearing anything," I whispered.

"See, you do catch on," she kissed me and began to unbutton my shirt. "Why don't you join me?"

I all but leaped out of my clothes. I threw my socks, shirt, and pants to the floor and got under the covers with her. We kissed and clung, touched and tasted, moved our fingers to the other's most sensitive regions, tantalized our bodies as if we were one creature that fought to pleasure itself in a hundred different ways at once.

But I couldn't have that much alcohol without it affecting me. My extra senses were shut down, but my imagination played havoc with me. With my eyes open, I saw Wendy, her naked pert body soft under my touch. With my eyes closed, it was a jumble of Cathy and Jenny. The mental images didn't match the physical, and I had to keep bringing myself back to Wendy, her room, her bed.

She took me into her mouth, and I moaned, the images confused as they collided with memories of Cathy doing this same act and then an imagined Jenny giving me her wicked smile as she swallowed me.

We kissed more, touched, and turned, and all at once, I was entering Cathy, as Jenny moaned with delight and Wendy sighed. We began the most ancient of dances. We writhed with each thrust and parry, as the woman under me changed and transformed, caught between the reality and my fantasies.

Our tempo increased, then slowed as she moaned words of encouragement. I groaned and gasped, while sweat glistened on our skin as our pace built and built. Finally, we were both overwhelmed with pleasure, cries ripped from each of us as the moment of release was achieved.

We lay in the dim light and looked up at the ceiling. It was so much like a tent, I expected a trapeze to be hanging down from it. My heart still pumped fast. I was drunk, sated, and still not sure which woman I was in bed with.

"Hmm," she said, her cheek against my chest. "That was even better than the meal."

"I'm honored," I said, turning to look at her. It was Wendy, without a doubt, though her makeup was a bit smeared and her hair was a mess. But seeing her a bit askew only made her look sexier. I kissed her and only her, hoping the illusions were gone.

"I've never…" she said. "I mean, I thought I made noise, but you *screamed* when you—y'know."

I nodded and held her. "Guess I had a lot pent up. It's been about four years."

She raised her head. "Four? Jesus, I thought my one year was tough enough. How did that happen? I mean, you're an attractive guy."

"Just didn't have the interest, I guess," I replied.

"Oh, yeah, your dead fiancée."

"There were a couple of women after that, but I was a mess—I mean psychologically. I threw myself into my studies."

"Oh, right, forensics. That must've taken a lot of books."

My rational mind quickly was brought back to the lie McGee told her, that I was with forensics, and I let Wendy go on believing it.

I ran my fingers through her hair and felt guilty for my deception. And I also realized that she was actually quite a woman. My time of study was over, I'd earned my PhD, and now I'd met a charming girl who was an exciting lover. Maybe it was time to let go of the past, and that included getting involved with someone who wasn't a mirror of my lost love, who was instead her own person. But you can't begin a relationship with a lie.

"Wendy, there is something I have to tell you…"

"Can it wait until morning? You wore me out, I'm ready to snooze."

Morning would bring McGee and the warrant.

"No, it can't. Look, that day we met, I wasn't entirely honest with you…"

A candle sputtered out on the nearby dresser.

Wendy rose up from the bed, her eyes wide in fear. She stared at the dresser.

"Oh God!" she whispered. "No."

I followed her frightened expression, but all I saw was the candles.

"It's all right. A candle just went out," I said, but I could feel her trembling.

Another candle winked out. No flutter of the flame, no sizzle or movement of a wick in hot wax, it was just gone. Then another went out.

"Get your clothes!" Wendy whispered harshly, throwing the sheets off and looking at the floor for her dress. "Now!"

I stumbled out of the bed, my body tired from the exertion and uncoordinated from the booze. I clumsily pulled on my underwear as another candle, then another, went out, leaving only one burning.

"HURRY, HURRY!" she said, as she pulled the spandex over her head in one motion, and I pulled on my pants.

The one remaining candle began to burn brighter, emitting a light as bright as all the other candles combined. The wax began to melt, and all at once, a flame shot out from the center of it, rising at least a foot into the air.

"Jesus," Wendy yelled as she bolted barefoot for the door.

The flame ignited the cloth hanging all around the bedroom, and the fire climbed up it as if there were gasoline poured on it.

"Wendy!" I yelled as the flames crawled up the wall. I followed her out the door.

She didn't stop in the hall. "Come on, come on, we have to get out of here!" she said, as she ran for the stairs.

"Have you got a fire extinguisher?" I asked.

She looked up at me and let loose a maniacal laugh that bordered on madness. "That won't do any good! RUN!"

Down the stairs she went as I followed. Clambering down is faster for me, but the air was already beginning to cloud with smoke. She met me at the bottom with both pairs of our shoes in her hands.

"We can't get to the car! The garage is on fire!" she shouted as she pushed my shoes at me.

"Then we have to go out the front door!" I said, coughing, as I slipped my feet into my loafers.

"No, no, we can't. That's what he wants," she said, the haze thickening.

"Who?"

"Go out a back window, try to sneak out."

I grabbed her arm. "Who is it? Who are you afraid of?"

"The m-man I used to go out with—he did this."

"Is it Lonny?" I asked as we moved toward the back of the house.

"W-who's Lonny?" she stopped talking and fell into coughing.

I knelt on my good knee and pulled her closer to the floor. "Stay near the floor. You go for a back window, I'm going out the front!"

"He'll kill you!" was the last sentences she ever spoke to me. I crawled toward the front of the house, pushed with my hands and one good leg, and dragged my stiff leg behind, my cane under my armpit. If there was someone waiting for us, the sword inside might be my only weapon.

It was easy to lose my bearing in all the smoke, but I could think more clearly. The adrenaline pushed away some of the effects of the liquor. Now I wished I hadn't had anything to drink. If not, I could have *sensed* the danger before it got here and we ended up trapped in this fire hazard. I found the main stairway and crawled directly across. Then I reached up to feel the handle of the door.

It was cold to the touch.

I turned it, and nothing happened. I pulled myself up and undid the locks. The door opened easily onto a vestibule of some kind, where stained-glass windows let in light from outside.

I fell into the vestibule and shut the door, letting myself breathe the fresh air. I couldn't believe how quickly the fire engulfed the house. And how did that one candle burn so hot that it set an entire room ablaze?

I stood up, my cane at the ready. I didn't know what was behind this front door, but I might be in for the fight of my life.

I turned the handle, then pushed at the door. It didn't open, so I tried pulling it. I searched for a lock. Nothing. The door was jammed. Whoever did this had wanted us to try this way out and be trapped. I looked back; smoke was beginning to seep in under the first door.

The stained glass was two enormous windows on either side of the door. I examined them. It wasn't real stained glass, just ordinary glass covered with a plastic decorative wrapping, which created the illusion of stained glass and kept prying eyes from looking in. I stepped back and smacked the glass with the metal head of my cane. It made a cracking noise, and I hit it again. Now the glass bowed out, still held together by the plastic. This was my one way out. I backed up, took whatever space there was, and with my hands over my head and face, leaped against the glass, shoulder first.

The glass gave, and I could feel myself flying through the air. I was up and over the bottom of the short windowsill, and I rolled as I hit the front porch. But I was still drunk, and my coordination was off. I couldn't get my feet under me, and I kept tumbling. I struck stone or brick steps with my back as I went down a short flight of stairs. When I unrolled onto the sidewalk, my head struck concrete with a "thud" I could hear inside as well as outside my body.

I was reeling, but the air felt fresh and cold in my lungs. I wanted to reach out with my befuddled brain, but the alcohol dulled any of my abilities. I raised my head and looked back at the house. There was fire coming out of the windows on the second floor, and flames flickered behind curtains on the first.

I fell back and felt something wet at the back of my head. I wanted to reach up and touch it, but I knew what it was: blood. I lay there bleeding, and unable to move, except for my eyes. And I fought to remain conscious.

Just then, Wendy came out through the hole in the glass, coughing as she went. She stumbled, then pulled herself to her feet. She saw me on the ground and took a step toward me, to the top of the stairs, then her head snapped up. She looked at something out on the street that I couldn't see.

"JACK!" she shrieked.

I wanted to raise my body, look at who she yelled at, but I just lay there, helpless to do anything but watch.

All at once, Wendy burst into flames with a scream. I could feel the intense heat from where I lay. She howled in pain and anguish as her hair became lit strands of fire, smoke rolled off of her, and the orange light consumed her.

Her hands went to her face, which was turning as black as burned wood. The thin outer layer of skin fried away as the flames danced over the surface, and her screams faded into a strangled gurgle. The lifeless corpse, still ablaze, fell to the porch and smoldered, black smoke rising from it.

I could hear sirens in the distance as I blacked out.

TEN

Shiny steel rails were around my bed as I opened my eyes. My head was in such pain that I fought to remain conscious. Slowly, I raised my right hand to my head and felt a bandage wrapped around it. I lifted my left arm to discover I was handcuffed to the railing.

When I tried to sit up, a female voice spoke. "You're all right, just lie still."

"Where…?" I tried to ask, my voice faint and faraway.

"You're in Mountainview Medical Center. You should rest."

I lifted my left hand to show the manacle.

"Why?" I gasped.

"That was the policeman's idea, though I told him you weren't going anywhere. He's outside, wants to ask you questions, but I told him—"

"No," I said. "I'll talk…"

"I don't think that would be a good idea. I really should ask the doctor."

"Sit me up," I said. My voice became clearer, as did my thoughts. It must be McGee out in the hall, but why would he cuff me to the bed?

She handed me a control, and I pushed one of the buttons and began to rise into a sitting position. It made my head ache more, but I wanted, *needed* to tell McGee what I'd seen.

A man came in the door, standing just outside the radiance of the light so that I couldn't see him. For a moment, there was something familiar in a shadow just beyond where I could see, and I was suddenly afraid.

The man, the man with the red eyes…

The figure walked closer and spoke. "OK, Nurse, you can leave us alone," he said.

It wasn't McGee. I looked hard at the man who spoke.

Tice.

"I'm staying here until I'm sure that Doctor Wise—" the nurse began.

"If that's even his real name—" Tice interrupted.

"—Is all right," the nurse went on, ignoring him. "You chain him to the bed and post an officer at his door. What has he done?"

"Murder, lady. Maybe even two. Now, why don't you take a coffee break. I'm not going to beat him, I'm just going to ask some questions," Tice said.

The nurse's lips grew tight, but with a sympathetic glance to me, she left the room.

Tice sat on the edge of the bed, all chummy.

"So, you want to tell me about it, Doc? If you really are a doctor. Forensics, my ass, they never heard of you. You know, you came in with your blood alcohol at point one-six."

"Didn't know I was driving," I croaked.

"Yeah, funny. So, you were hitting the sauce pretty good. I don't know why McGee was working with you, helping you. But if you tell me how he fits in, maybe we can make the charges manslaughter instead of murder."

"The house," I said, my memory returning to the strange images. "Wendy…"

"The house is burned beyond repair, and the broad is dead. But you should know that. You killed her and burned the body, thinking we couldn't figure out how she died."

"No."

"Pretty neat job. What was it, you killed Mishan, and then the girl wouldn't share the insurance money with you, so you had to kill her too?"

"No," I insisted.

"You might not be forensics, but first thing this morning, our forensic guys got on that house like ants on an anthill. They're going to go over every inch of it, and what's left of her, until they find out what you used to make it burn so fast. Then it'll be my pleasure to arrest you."

"I didn't do anything…"

"So you say. What were you doing at her house?"

"Date—we went out on a date. We had dinner at the Manor—there—has to be—witnesses."

"Yeah, but once you were alone at her place, what happened?"

"We—we made love," I said. "That was all. I didn't kill her."

"Sure, sure. Did you know she was getting served with a warrant in the morning? If so, you had to remove her then and there."

The door blew open as if an explosive was behind it, and into the room came the hulking shape of Bill McGee.

"Tice, what the hell do you think you're doing?" McGee barked.

"I'm questioning a witness," Tice replied icily, his eyes still on me. "One who appears to have too many ties to the local police."

"Uncuff him, for Christ's sake," McGee said in a low and menacing voice.

"He might make a break for it. After all, he's connected to two murders, and he's been getting information from you…"

"He wasn't even in town when Mishan died. I have witnesses who saw him on the train. Of course, if you want, read my report."

"Oh, believe me, Detective, I will. And I'm gonna find out everything there is to know about this guy. Then I'll bring anything I think is important to the lieutenant—and Captain Harris," Tice said.

"In the meantime, until the lieutenant or the captain say otherwise, this is still *my* case. So uncuff *my* witness and get the hell out. And take Hastings with you."

Tice pulled out his keys and opened the cuffs in one well-practiced motion. As I rubbed my wrist, he faced McGee and rose defiantly. "Yeah, go ahead, give orders while you still can. Let me tell you something, Mr. FBI, this whole case is going to blow up in your face. Then we'll just see who gives orders to who."

"Whom," McGee said.

"What?" Tice said.

"It's 'give orders to whom,' not who. Syntax," McGee said.

"Yeah, and fuck you," Tice said as he headed out the door.

McGee came over to my bed and sat in the same place Tice had just vacated. He looked at my head.

"You OK?"

"I've been better," I said with a vague smile. My face felt puffy—had I landed on it as well?

McGee's shoulders relaxed. "Been quite a night. And Tice is right. If I don't make some headway soon, I'll be walking a beat."

I smiled. "They don't have foot patrol in Mountainview."

"So, worse, they'll stick me on a bicycle," McGee muttered. "What can you tell me?"

Stumbling as I went, I related the story to McGee, from the candles extinguishing and the one becoming a blowtorch, to the immolation of Wendy on the front porch. Bill wrote it down in a long, thin notebook he pulled from his jacket pocket.

"Could her dress have caught fire? Or she spilled something on herself?"

"No," I said, "she just burst into flames, and it was familiar, like I'd seen it before…" Then it struck me. "Like Mishan in my vision."

"What?"

"It was the same way that Mishan burned in my vision. The same technique, whatever it is."

I sat up, which caused pain to wash over my head again. "She said her old boyfriend was very possessive. Jack. She yelled the name Jack just before she died."

"Jack…huh," McGee said. "I'll do some legwork with her picture, see if anyone recalls her going with a guy by that name."

"They broke up about a year ago. And there were places in town she was known." I quickly related the coffee house and club she'd taken me to on our first date.

McGee dutifully took down the information, nodding as he wrote.

"I have something that might interest you," he said, with a glance to the door. "Maybe a lead on how this was done. There is word, in a certain marketplace, that you can purchase an incendiary launcher."

"A what?" I asked.

"An incendiary launcher. From what I've heard, it's a small unit that uses CO_2 to fire sodium metal projectiles. When it hits a person, the water in the body is enough to set it off, causing a fire that keeps burning until every bit of water in the victim is used up."

"My God. Who came up with that?"

"I only have rumors, but the inventor is one Lonny Briback."

I jerked, causing another wave of pain with the addition of nausea. "Lonny the Match?" I said, shocked.

"You have it. I am—if you'll pardon the pun—hot on his trail. I have to go. I contacted the Baines's. They'll pick you up when the hospital releases you."

"I could go now…" I said.

"Nope, they want to run an MRI on you, make sure your brain is where it belongs."

"I'm fine," I lied.

"You look like hell. Take the weekend off," he said as he got up and walked to the door. "I hope we're getting close, Len, and I wouldn't have even started looking for Lonny if it weren't for you."

"McGee!" I said, stopping his exit. "Wendy—when you run tests on…what's left, we made love."

"Did you wear a condom?" McGee asked.

"No."

"Are you crazy? Do you know what diseases are out there?" McGee said.

"It all happened so fast—I didn't plan…"

"So, you left a DNA sample *in* the victim. Great! I'll let Casey Latrell know, after all he's the ME. That is if there's enough of her left to test," he said, shaking his head. "What were you thinking?"

I turned red. "It's been four years. I was drunk…"

With a faint wave, McGee walked out the door. I lay there feeling stupid. *I was drunk.*

How much had I used that excuse over the last seven years? Sometimes on a daily basis. When I'd lived with Susan Haring back during my Psychiatry 101 classes, it was a mantra that I used almost daily to explain all my bad behavior. And here I'd fallen off the wagon again and immediately shifted into the gear marked "stupid."

But this was worse.

This time, my drinking allowed someone to die. I'd blocked out any of my talents that could have warned us. All at once, I could identify with any drunk driver who'd been in an accident where someone got killed.

If I'd been sober, I might have saved her, or a least done something. The image of her as she burst into flames repeated itself in my mind, and I was overcome by sadness and guilt.

I spent the day recovering from my first hangover in a year, which the drugs the hospital gave me only exacerbated. Then they insisted on a battery of tests, and my staunch defender, Jon Baines, told the hospital that I was covered by the university's health plan.

I saw a neurologist, and finally, they sent me to be scanned by an MRI machine, which I tried to talk them out of. I already knew what the results would show.

I was in my room with Jon when the radiotherapy physician came in with a laptop. He was a young man of about twenty-five, with glasses and perfectly cast in the role of computer nerd. His name tag read Doctor Robbins.

He introduced himself and went haltingly into an explanation that I would need a battery of tests.

"Thanks," I said, "but no."

The young man looked from me to Jon and back, as if unsure of what he'd heard. "But don't you see, you've got a very overactive amygdala. This could be a form of epilepsy or worse."

"Doctor, thank you for your concern. But my professor, Doctor Kohl, and I have done a series of tests using the MRI at Berkeley in California. My overactive amygdala is not a new condition, and I'm fine."

"But you don't understand. I have never seen anything like it. Your brain could expand some of our current knowledge—"

"The answer is no, Doctor. And I'm feeling much better. I'll be leaving today."

"That's against medical advice," the young doctor snapped, afraid that he was losing his guinea pig. "You should really have this checked out, for your own good."

"He said no, Doctor, and that's final!" Jon said.

The young doctor took the hint and retreated.

Jon turned to me. "This overactive…"

"Amygdala."

"I know—premed—remember? Is that why you're psychic?"

"Doctor Kohl believes there is a connection. It's the part of the brain that makes sense out of the things we perceive."

"So, if you perceive things other people can't, maybe your brain works differently."

I shrugged. "I don't know. When we did the tests, I was trying to find out why my…gift turned on all at once the night Cathy died."

"Any explanation?"

"Not a one."

Jon shrugged his shoulders. "Then we'd better get you out of here. Jenn wants to spend the day fussing over you."

It was after dark when we left the hospital, and once I got back to Jon and Jenny's, all I wanted to do was sleep. Jenny made clucking noises and got me some herbal tea. I drank it dutifully, if unenthusiastically, and went to bed.

ELEVEN

Wendy stared in horror at the distant figure and screamed as flames engulfed her body. Only this time, I could see him as well. In the distance, near some kind of car, he stood in the darkness. His eyes glowed brightly, like a pair of twin suns. Then he turned those eyes on me, and the air around me grew scorching…

I leaped out of bed, fully awake, as I panted in fear. It took me a moment to remember where I was. Yes, the Baines's house—it was—had to be—Sunday.

I was in a T-shirt and boxers. I retrieved my cane, which Jon had rescued from the hospital, and stood up. I had no idea where, but my new suit jacket was gone. I left the hospital in just the shirt and pants. Tice was probably out checking it for accelerants even as I lay in the hospital bed.

I grabbed the metal snake head of my cane and touched the latch just under the neck. With a soft *click*, the sword slid free of the stick and into my hand, two feet of stainless steel.

I looked at the gleaming blade, which I'd sharpened before I left California. I ran my finger along the edge. Only one side was honed, more like a saber than an epee. But if I needed to use it, it was there. Of course, I could probably just swing the cane and bop an adversary in the head with the metal snake—it would likely be just as lethal.

I put the sword back in its sheath, threw on the borrowed bathrobe, and made my way to the kitchen.

As I walked in, Jon was sitting on one of the barstools with his arms around Jenny, who was standing. They were kissing deeply, Jon's hands caressing her back. Jenny saw me and pulled away.

"L-Len!" she said, a bit red. "You're up."

"Did I arrive at a bad time?" I asked.

"Two minutes later might've been worse," Jon said as he stood, giving Jenny a lusty tickle.

"Jon!" she squealed, then broke into giggles. Jenny all but skipped to the stove and announced. "I'm cooking! Tell me what you want. Eggs, pancakes, I could even pull out the ol' waffle iron!"

Despite their bravado, I couldn't fight the notion that I'd intruded into their first chance for real intimacy since my arrival.

"Actually, Jenny, don't bother for me. I need to get some air. There's a café just a few blocks away."

Jon stood up. "I could drive you!" he said, too brightly.

"No, I need some time," I said. "Been a tough couple of days."

"Are you sure you're up to it, Lenny?" Jenny asked. "I mean, the hit on your head—and that poor woman."

I stood frozen for a moment. The full realization sank in. Once more, someone I'd been involved with, become intimate with, was dead. I couldn't help but believe it was my fault.

"No, I just want to be alone right now. Jon, you should spend a little time with your wife."

Jenny gave me a grin as if to say thanks.

"Take your cell!" Jon bellowed as I went to my room and put on my clothes. In a few minutes, I stepped outside, where it was a little chillier than the day before.

I had put on jeans with a sweater vest, a shirt open at the collar, and my tweed jacket. But it felt good after spending the previous day in the hospital. I still had the bandage wrapped around my head, making me look as if I'd just returned from a war somewhere. I put that out of my mind and focused on one foot as it moved in front of the other. I picked up speed and began to walk faster, headed toward town. Soon, I reached the café and headed toward the blocks of fashionable shops.

I was curious to see what was left of Mishan's place of business. No, it was more than that—I was fixated on seeing it, as if it was the most important thing in the world. I was going a different way than when I drove with McGee, but I was sure it was correct. It was like a giant magnet pulled me there. I trusted it to lead me correctly.

I walked past a supermarket, and up ahead was a block cordoned off with yellow tape. I slowed my pace. McGee had been right; the entire row of shops was badly burned.

I walked a few more steps and could see where Mishan's Jewelers had been the other day. Now it was an empty black pit, as the fire had burned away even the flooring. Peeking in the hole, I could see the safe had fallen into the basement, and black, oily water stood in fetid pools.

I looked past the store at the parking lot beyond, where the asphalt was cracked and broken. There were two cars, one burned but still whole, the gas tank on the other one must have caused an explosion because it was only a metallic skeleton that vaguely resembled a car.

"This isn't possible," I said out loud.

It would have taken an enormous amount of heat to do this much damage in such a short period of time. Even if McGee's rumor about a sodium projectile explained it—could it burn with that much intensity?

I looked across the street, turned, and began to walk again. I was almost hit by a car, but the driver sounded his horn, which stopped me. I waited until traffic cleared and crossed, as I sought *something* from the thread of the memory of my dream.

I'd seen a figure standing across the street. The man with the red eyes. Perhaps I could reach out, get a feel for him. I decided to occupy the same space where he'd occupied in my vision. It might have been an emotionally powerful moment for him, which could leave an energetic residue. I looked along the sidewalk and stepped carefully, attempting to place myself in his exact space. Then I reached out as best as I could, trying to focus on the remembered vision.

I needn't have worried. As soon as my foot was in the right location, I experienced a jolt like electricity climbing up my leg. I jumped back, stunned. Then I stepped back into the space, this time with both feet. My legs were quivery, and I felt almost as if I'd left my body.

I looked at the empty hole that was Mishan's Jewelers, yet in my view, it was recreated and was whole again, though it showed the ravages of the first fire.

Everything had moved into the sepia tones, and the building once again stood. Then I saw a face as it peered through the sooty glass of the door.

It was my face.

Then there was a flash of energy emanating from where I stood, like a tidal wave that undulated to the building, and as it hit, the structure burst into flames. It came from where I stood, from a presence filled with such *anger* that it couldn't be contained.

I spun in space, caught in that anger, so fiery, so hot with hate that I believed I could burst into flames as well.

"Are you all right?" I heard a voice say in my ear.

I had fallen to my good knee on the ground, holding myself up with my hands on the sidewalk across from the fire site. I was being helped up by a young African-American man, maybe twenty. He was large and beefy, and I immediately sensed that was a football player at GSU.

"Yes, I'm sorry," I said, as I forced my head to clear. My hand went to the bandage around my head to explain. "I must have passed out."

He assisted me. He was solid, with dark skin and the most amazing blue eyes. His hair was short and closely cropped, and he had arms that could've picked me up and carried me like a rag doll. He must have weighed 330 pounds, but all of it muscle.

"You need to get to the hospital, sir?"

It's exceedingly rare to hear a young man with manners who gives a hoot about some guy who fell down on the sidewalk.

"I'm all right," I said as he set me on my feet. "But thank you."

"Be careful around here. The sidewalk is a little broken up from the fire," he said as I got my cane under me.

"Do you know anything about it—the fire, I mean?"

His face broke into a grin. "I was here." He grew serious. "It was terrible, sir."

He pointed at a big and tall men's store just down the block. "I came out of that store, only place around I can get clothes."

He traced his route with his finger at the sidewalk. "I was about here when it started, flames shooting out like a firebomb went off or something."

"Did you see a man—white guy, dressed in black, thin nose?"

He paused for a minute, then a flash of recognition crossed his face. "You mean the dude with the sunglasses. Yeah, he was standing here, and when the sirens started, he took off."

I thanked the young man and assured him I was all right. But I felt drained. The psychic experience had worn me out, and I was desperately thirsty. I slowly trotted back to the café. It took about twice as much time as when I was going the other direction.

I sat at one of the small round tables, in a padded chair with a wrought iron back. I ordered a latté, some kind of egg sandwich that was on the chalkboard menu, and got a bottle of water, which I gulped down right away. That helped.

I reviewed what had just happened as I tried to keep the ideas clear in my mind. It was an unusual experience, yet had a familiarity to it. It was rather like the unstable energy I would tap into at the haunted houses, with Doctor Kohl.

Yes, that was it, the feeling of being lost in someone else's experience. This happened to me at Scudder House, where I went so deeply into the experience, I still had little recollection of the events. It was only when I heard my voice on the digital recording that I realized I'd even spoken the revelations that led to the discoveries that followed.

This occurrence was similar. Though I didn't lose myself completely, I got lost in a mental impression left by someone else. This didn't point to Lonny the Match or some type of physical explanation. This suggested someone who possessed a strong psychic ability, possibly equal to my own.

Or perhaps superior.

"When you have excluded the impossible, whatever remains, however improbable, must be the truth," Sir Arthur Conan Doyle said through the persona of Sherlock Holmes. But this was far too improbable.

Or was it?

Could the murderer be someone with a gift like my own? Perhaps his was the ability to start fires. It made sense of the two murders, where each fire blazed from nowhere at incredible temperatures. He killed Mishan for what—money? From the anger—was there a betrayal of some kind?

Betrayal—that could be the reason Wendy died. If the man with this power was indeed her former lover, sleeping with me would motivate him. Jealousy is described as hot, a burning desire. These words are common parlance, but what if there was deeper meaning behind them?

If so, why return and reduce what was left of Mishan's store to a black pit? If he'd felt betrayed, maybe Mishan's death wasn't enough. My research into arsonists suggested a certain immaturity, and revenge is the most common motive.

Pyrokinesis.

The ability to start and control fire with nothing more than the power of the mind.

Suddenly, I was lost in a memory.

Concentrate on the candle, Leonard.

Doctor Kohl and I tried many forms of extrasensory tests. We used cards with the five patterns: wavy lines, simple crossed lines, circle, square, and star. But we also tried esoteric forms: psychokinesis, telekinesis. There were several weeks when we attempted phenomena with match flames and candles.

I was in one of the lab rooms at the university, a clean, antiseptic place with a drop ceiling and small tables for experiments. It was Doctor Kohl and me, with the lights down low. On one of the tables, a candle was lit and acted as the light source for the room.

"Reduce the flame, Leonard," Fritz said.

I focused my attention on the flame, trying to not just observe it, but to become part of it.

"Remember," Kohl said quietly, "all molecules are patterns of energy from the air ve breathe to our own bodies, and energy is affected by vill. Place your intention upon the flame."

I nodded, focused so fixedly on the flame that I could almost feel the heat surrounding me. I became one with the burning wick and used my will to make it grow smaller.

The flame flickered and went down.

"Very goot, Leonard," Kohl said. "Make it brighter."

I am one with the flame, I thought. I focused on increasing myself, sucking in air and feeling myself become bigger.

The flame grew.

"Do you think ve are ready for the next part, Leonard?"

"I can do it. I can *feel* it," I said, totally out of my body. All that existed was the flame, and I was one with it.

"Goot! Then you know vat to do!"

I nodded and stared at the flame. This was the one thing in our weeks of experiments I hadn't been able to achieve, snuffing it out—and then restarting it.

I concentrated on the flickering orange and yellow flame with the blue at the wick and felt it/me shut down.

The flame died and the room darkened as a thin trail of smoke rose from the wick. But I held the flame inside me, I'd *pulled* it into myself, just as Doctor Kohl had instructed me to do on previous days. But this time, this day, I was doing it.

I stared at the smoldering wick and then let the fire out of myself, to return it to the candle. A small ember glowed, then flickered, and the candle re-lit. It wasn't dramatic; there was no burst of fire or explosion. It just started to burn again.

Doctor Kohl nodded. "Impressive, Leonard. How do you feel?"

"Tired," I rubbed my eyes.

"Zat vill be all for today…"

We soon moved on from work with the candle and focused on other mental exercises to strengthen my concentration and learn how to shut out the unwanted impressions that bombarded me all the time. However, it had been useful, as Doctor Kohl wanted me familiar with all of the different aspects of the mind's powers. He had named each capability as we practiced it.

Pyrokinesis. Could it be developed to the level I'd seen at the scene?

The realization was profound, because inside me, it felt right. There was a truth to this. A truth inside a man, like me, who one day discovered he could do things other people couldn't.

For years, I'd disliked my gift, fought it, shut it off with alcohol. Once I accepted and developed it, I used it to help at Scudder

House. What if this man used it for his own amusement and empowerment? That made him much more frightening than Lonny the Match because Lonny just did it for money, but my unknown stranger did it for the kick he got out of wielding his power.

He was struck with a desire to play God.

The problem was, without any kind of proof—other than my own internal knowing—there was no way I could bring this theory to McGee. Or anyone else. They would just say I'd read too many Stephen King novels. I would have to find this man and stop him before he could use his deadly ability again. Wendy had been involved with him, and it got her killed. Although not his equal, I was the only one who could track down her murderer.

The man Wendy called Jack.

. . .

I arrived back at the Baines's house refreshed from my meal and found Jenny and Jon as they finished eating waffles. They both seemed very pleased with each other, and Jenny was downright radiant. Apparently, they'd taken advantage of my absence to make love and restore their bond.

"Hi, you two!" I said.

"Len, did you have a nice walk?" Jon asked with a smirk to Jenny.

"Yes, thank you. Is the library open today?"

"The town library or the university one? There are both usually open on Sundays. After all, this is a college town, and students— well, they put off deadlines."

I smiled. "I recall you putting off a few deadlines back when we were premed, Jon."

"I'm on the other side of the equation, now. Doing research? You could use my computer."

"No thanks, Jon. I think I'm going to need to go through some microfilm, see some old newspapers—maybe go back ten or twenty years."

"Still on this arson case?" Jenny asked.

"Yes, but now it's personal."

Jon decided it was too far to walk to the library, and feeling a bit tired, I agreed. However, I asked Jenny to help me remove the bandage on my head.

"Would you like a haircut and a shave while you're here?" she asked as I sat in a kitchen chair with my back to her.

"Just the bandage would be fine," I said.

She trimmed away some of the tape holding the gauze in place, and pulled it carefully off, taking a look at the wound on the back of my head.

"Ooh! You got stitches," Jenny said.

"Only five," Jon noted.

"Am I bleeding?" I asked.

"No," Jenny said as she arranged my hair carefully over the area. "In fact, it's pretty much unnoticeable."

"You're lucky they didn't shave your head," Jon said.

"I'm not into that look," I said, getting up. "Ready to go?"

"Let's do it," Jon said.

"Seems like you've been saying that all morning, husband of mine," Jenny said and gave him a kiss.

I turned away. I was glad to see them happy, especially after our tête-à-tête of the other day. But another part of me felt jealous. I ignored my feelings as I rode with Jon to the library. I assured him I would call as soon as I needed a ride.

"I thought we could all go out to dinner tonight," Jon told me. "It would be a nice break for Jenn, and we could talk."

"Yeah, sorry to ruin your weekend."

"I'm just glad you didn't end up like that Wallace woman. Now you *have* to stay, at least until you get your stitches removed."

The situation with Jenny made me want to take off, but now with Wendy dead and my decision to track down her killer…

"Maybe a few more days," I said.

I got out of the car and walked into the Mountainview Public Library, a large and spacious building with an old-fashioned facade. The inside was totally renovated, which gave it a more clean and modern look. I immediately went to the reference desk and was directed to a basement where over a hundred years' worth of newspapers sat photographed on microfilm.

The question was: where to begin?

I thought about the man I saw. He was young, no more than thirty. If he'd played with this ability before…

I started with the *New Jersey Times-Ledger* ten years earlier, taking a reel of microfilm and threading it into the machine. Headlines began appearing, and I worked my way through the dates, keeping my eyes peeled for any references to mysterious fires or cases of arson.

I found several as the years went by, most of which seemed pretty ordinary: fires that took down warehouses and homes—most of it due to bad wiring or people who smoked while in bed.

One investigation led to a young, despondent man who torched his parents home and was put in Blackshale, the local asylum.

Then I reached a story three years ago where there was mention of a large fire at an old amusement pier down on the Jersey Shore, in Lavellette. It was suspicious because the owners had penned a deal to sell the site to be made into a mall, but there were some tenants who were using their leases to put the deal on the skids. My eyes lit up when I saw the listed owner as the Nova Corporation.

I put change in a nearby slot and hit the button on the machine to print a copy of the article as I read on. The image faded for a moment as the machine hummed and did its magic. As a piece of paper was spat out from the printer, I reached the middle of the article, and I almost leaped out of my chair.

Nova Corporation spokesman, Philip Mishan, was quoted as saying that this was a loss for Nova, as they had invested heavily in inventory for the upcoming summer.

Nova spokesman? Here was a clear connection to Nova and Philip Mishan. He might have been one of the mysterious members hidden behind the false names.

This was something I had to take to McGee—he wouldn't get it from another source. I checked the printed article and pulled out my cell phone, touching the screen to call him.

"Hello, this is Detective-Sergeant McGee with the Mountainview police. Please leave your name and number, and I'll get back to you."

Of course, it was Sunday. What was it he'd told me? He got out of the FBI to have a more normal life with his wife and kids. The phone beeped.

"Bill, it's Leonard Wise. I found an article here in the library about a fire three years ago. The owners were the Nova Corporation, and guess who is listed as the spokesman? Philip Mishan! Call me…"

I left my number and hung up, then went back to the microfilm. I'd found the first step to my mysterious Jack. I paused and considered what he might be doing as I went through reels of past records in search of him.

JACK'S DIARY: SUNDAY

I got up today, went into the living room naked, and looked at myself in the mirror. And I was again struck with how beautiful I really am.

My stomach is flat, even though I don't exercise as much as I should, and I'm really proportioned quite handsomely. I must consider getting another young lady. It is unfair not to share myself with the many women out there.

Friday night, I finally had to get rid of the bitch. I should've done it months ago, but I've always been sentimental. I suppose a part of me expected her to wake up from her error and return to me. She would've, once her money ran out, with the way she spends. No, wait, spent, past tense.

I'm just too tender. I showed extreme patience over the last year while she "found" herself. But when she took that damn cripple home with her and slept with the freak to boot! Well, even my patience has limits.

Did she really think I couldn't recognize from the lit candles and the dark house that she was having sex with him? And more than that, I could sense it. She never understood the full extent of what I can do—or how strong I have become. What I did to the jewelry store should've taught her that.

She looked so exquisite on the porch in that tight dress that hugged every curve. I almost didn't want to do it—but I could feel the cripple's jism inside her. That pushed me over the edge. She was never a bright girl. Except at the end, when she burned with a brightness that lit up the neighborhood.

Too bad about the house. But insurance does cover it. I will have to approach that insurance adjuster with more intelligence than dear Wendy did.

This cripple, he keeps turning up. Wendy met him at the police station and went out with him. I suppose she thought I wouldn't know. Then I thought I saw him in Mishan's when I torched the place. I was sure it was his face I saw through the window.

I should have finished him Friday when he crashed through the door and fell. But he was bleeding from the head, and I figured he'd done himself in. I thought it a nice touch to let him bleed to death on the steps.

But he lived! And he wasn't hurt all that bad. Head wounds do bleed a lot. Even so, they released him from the hospital the next day. It's so easy to check on these things.

Where does he live? How did he become involved? There is something I don't like about him—besides soiling my *Wendy. He'd better give me a wide berth because bad things happen to people who get in my way.*

TWELVE

McGee looked over the article printout. "This is helpful, Len."

He'd shown up at the Baines's house at about nine thirty Monday morning. Jon and Jenny were long gone, and our dinner the previous night had been a great success. They made goo-goo eyes at each other across the table, and I tried to keep the feeling of being fifth wheel to myself.

I brought McGee into the house and poured him coffee.

"So, I guess you're here because it's a bad idea for me to show up at the police station while Tice thinks of me as a suspect," I said.

"You're not a suspect," McGee grumbled. "But I figure if you're not there to annoy him, maybe he'll focus on something else."

I nodded. "I understand."

"And you're even less of a suspect because forensics can't find a sample of any semen."

"Too much damage?"

"You want to hear something crazy? Doctor Latrell says that Miss Wallace not only burned, but from the autopsy, it appears she burned from the inside out."

"What?"

"Her organs started to burn first. Casey says he's never seen anything like it, but I think it points to Lonny again. If he did build this sodium metal bullet I told you about, it would penetrate the skin, and the body would burn from the inside."

I nodded. "Any luck finding him?"

"I'm always about one step behind him. He's good at covering his tracks, but I've got an APB out on him. He's got to show up sometime."

I nodded. "What's the latest with Nova?"

"I spent part of the weekend trying to track down any possible lawyers who filed the corporate papers, but it seems that they were filed by the founders of the corporation."

"Can that be done?" I asked.

He shrugged. "Anybody can file legal papers it's just most people hire a lawyer. The deeper I get into this case, the weirder it gets."

If I told him my personal theory, it would get even worse.

Bill went on. "I understand the memorial service for Ms. Wallace will be tomorrow."

"Really?" I said and found I was standing. I returned to my seat. "I-I didn't know it would be so fast."

"Forensics should be finished by then," McGee said.

"Closed casket?" I asked, my mouth tight.

"Yeah," McGee said, and he leaned forward in the chair. "You OK?"

"I will be when we get the bastard who did this to her."

McGee's huge form rose from the chair. "OK, well, I will be there."

"In case Jack shows up?"

He nodded. "To see who does show up. Now I have to visit your friend, Mrs. Baines."

"Jenny? Why?"

"Turns out she is also the listed insurance adjuster on the estate of Wendy Wallace."

My mouth fell open. "Don't tell me—Nova was involved again?"

"Not sure. When I did research on Wendy Wallace, I found out both her parents are dead. Her mother died when she was born, and the father remarried, so she has a half-sister. The sister's listed as next of kin—the bulk of the estate will go to her."

Something bothered me. "How old is she?"

He went through the huge folder he carried. "Twenty-three. And about two years ago, the father and the stepmom went off the road up on Schooley's Mountain. The car exploded; killed them both."

In a fire... flashed in my mind. The same time Nova Corporation was building a fire of its own.

"So, who put together the funeral?"

"Don't know. I guess the sister. She lives here in Jersey, out in Mendham."

"Close by. Funny that Wendy didn't mention her."

"You want to hear something interesting? The sister, Janice, is married to a lawyer."

"That happens. Lawyers need love, too."

"His name is Jack."

I stood frozen on the spot at the mention of that name, the last word that Wendy ever said.

"Believe you me, I'm looking forward to meeting him," McGee said as he gave me his stern policeman stare.

I showed McGee out and took a few minutes to get dressed. I'd been wearing a jogging suit I'd borrowed from Jon. I didn't imagine

I would take up the sport in the near future. Then I made my way back to the Mountainview Library. The walk in the fresh spring air was invigorating, and I was beginning to feel less like a man who let a beautiful woman die because he screwed up.

Once sequestered in the library, I was able to find microfilm of a local paper, the *Bernardsville News*. Since it was a weekly paper, it was much easier to find what I was after.

"COUPLE FOUND DEAD IN CAR" the headline screamed, complete with a biography of the Wallace family and information about the car wreck. According to the account, the couple was on their way home after a visit to their daughter in Mendham. No one actually saw the car go over the edge, but the burned-out wreck was found the next day.

In the article, Jack Hoefler, the son-in-law, was quoted as saying what a tragedy it was.

Jack Hoefler, the sister's husband.

It could explain why Wendy was so close-mouthed about her old beau. Banging your sister's husband is not the sort of thing you want to share with someone on the second date, even if you *do* plan to sleep with him.

An image of her naked in my arms flashed through my mind. She lay there smiling and sated. Ten minutes later, she would be dead. I pushed the image away, swallowed the accompanying self-loathing, and focused on my work.

If Wendy was involved with lawyer Jack, it might explain how the paper trail stopped at Wendy. A crooked lawyer wouldn't have any trouble setting up the fake names and addresses for the corporation. If he had been Wendy's beau, and she stopped sleeping with him—she was the perfect patsy.

That is, once she was eliminated.

I looked forward to meeting Jack Hoefler myself.

• • •

I spent the rest of my afternoon on research of any other mysterious fires, going back further in other local papers. I uncovered a few that sounded like his style. They were major financial situations where insurance picked up the tab—but no mentions of anyone named Jack or Nova.

I then took a walk to the men's store I'd been to the other day and purchased a black suit and somber tie. I wanted to look good for Wendy's funeral, not borrow a suit from Jon.

In the dressing room trying on the suit, I felt a weight descend on me, and I had to sit on the small bench. I was overcome by uncontrolled tears, yet at the same time, I was detached and watched myself cry over Wendy—both inside and outside of the emotion simultaneously.

It occurred to me that the last few days had played havoc with my feelings, between the return to New Jersey and the terrible events. Until that moment, I hadn't allowed myself to grieve over her loss. It hit so hard because the added loss of a possible relationship stung me, pulling me back to when I'd lost Cathy.

Now I really wanted a drink.

"Hey, buddy, you all right in there?" I heard the salesman say.

"Yeah," I replied and wiped my eyes. I still felt enormous loss, yet a part of me just watched my body act it out. It was the oddest sensation, but after I completed the purchase and the alterations, I began to feel more myself—more *inside* myself than I had in the last few days.

I walked to the Baines's house with an overwhelming impulse to cook. I wanted something to keep me busy, to take my mind off of Wendy, Cathy, and any other losses.

In the kitchen, I went through the cabinets and found lasagna noodles and a bottle of spaghetti sauce. Then off to the refrigerator, where I located some frozen spinach and containers of ricotta and mozzarella cheese.

Perfect.

I started water boiling and laid everything out to make spinach lasagna, a recipe I can do entirely from memory. I worked away assembling the parts. I even found romaine lettuce, which I cleaned and made ready for a Caesar salad.

By the time Jenny got home at five twenty, I was baking the lasagna, had the salad and dressing ready, and was putting garlic and butter on a loaf of French bread.

"What smells so good?" Jenny asked as she walked in.

"I made dinner. I hope you don't mind," I said.

"Mind? I could kiss you!" she said.

I flushed red and focused on my bread.

"You get embarrassed more easily than any man I've ever known, Len."

"It's part of my subtle charm," I said.

"Subtle, yeah, right," she laughed.

At quarter after six, Jon arrived home to find the table set with a tablecloth and good china, Jenny's contribution to the meal.

"Wow! On a Monday?" he said as he came into the dining room and looked around. "Am I in the right house?"

"Don't get used to it," Jenny said. "This can only be done when there are two people making dinner."

"And one of them is unemployed," I added.

"Well, I could get a second wife, if that's OK with you, Jenn."

"Sure, if I get a second husband. I think between the two of us, we could afford to keep Leonard."

"This is my only recipe from memory, and I don't do windows," I quipped.

"Well, I know what Leonard costs, and only the university can afford him," Jon said as he slipped off his jacket and loosened his tie. "And Len and I have shared a lot, but I don't think I want to share you, Jenn." He gave her a quick kiss.

"There you go, spoiling all my fun," Jenny said, giving me her wicked grin. "I guess you'll have to do without the extra wife."

"The sacrifices I make," Jon said.

We sat down to the meal, and both the Baines's praised my cooking and fawned over how good it all was.

"So, Len," Jon said between mouthfuls, "what are your plans?"

"It seems Wendy's funeral is tomorrow," I said. "And I'm going to attend. Then I'd like to stay for another few days." I met his eyes. "I want to find her killer."

"Shouldn't you let the police do that, Lenny?" Jenn said, concerned.

"This guy killed her because she was with me. He could've killed me, too."

"So, instead you have stitches in the back of your head," Jon said. "I'm sorry, old buddy, but I don't see you as a superhero."

"Well, that puts the kibosh on my plans to be the next big action movie star," I said.

"Seriously, this guy has some kind of weapon—for all you know, it's a flame thrower," Jon said. "Do you have any training?

Self-defense? You've got good reflexes, but I don't see you taking out bad guys."

I sighed. "I promise I'll tell anything I learn to Detective McGee and let him take out the bad guys."

"Lenny, if this man saw you at Wendy's," Jenny said. "He might go after you."

"All the more reason that I need to be on the offensive," I said. "I'm hoping I'll meet him at the service tomorrow."

"The guy named Jack?" Jon asked. I'd told Jon about the entire situation while in the hospital.

"Jack?" Jenny said. "That's interesting. I got a call from a man named Jack. He said he was the lawyer for the Nova Corporation."

I tried not to jump out of the chair. "What did you do?"

She shrugged. "I took his number and called Detective McGee. He told me to call him if I heard from Nova Corporation."

I returned to my seat. "Was his name Jack Hoefler?"

Jenny picked up another forkful of lasagna and looked at the ceiling thoughtfully. "I—think that was it. I'm not sure."

Bingo!

Now I couldn't wait for tomorrow. It seemed my adversary wasn't nearly as clever as I believed.

$$\cdots$$

Tuesday was a beautiful day, with the sky clear and the sun warm, but not too hot. At 9:30 AM, dressed in my new black suit, I was dropped off by taxi at the Williamson Funeral Home.

It was the same location that Cathy's memorial service was held and far too reminiscent. I felt transported back in years, when I sat in a wheelchair and listened to the pastor of her family's church speak of what a gracious person Cathy had been. And here I was again. Another lover, another death.

I didn't even know if I could have made a relationship work with Wendy. We seemed very different. But to have even the chance of love ripped away—it made it very personal and the loss profound.

Funeral homes are tough for me. The mental energy of sadness and loss pervades the places, which can be difficult for my second-level senses.

But it's more than that.

At Cathy's service, my extra perceptions were new, and I was confused by them. I saw an old woman walking about, trying to talk to people, but no one paid her any heed. I was surprised that people could be so rude, and it seemed to frustrate the woman as well.

Finally, she approached me.

"Can you help me?" she said, clear as a bell. "I seem to have lost my way."

The pastor was in the middle of the sermon, but I turned to her and very quietly said, "I can't help you now. Maybe after the service."

The woman smiled and said, "I'll wait in the hall," and walked away.

Cathy's brother, Terry was next to me. He'd been the one pushing my wheelchair. He bent close and whispered, "Who are you talking to?"

"The old woman," I whispered back. "She was lost."

He gave me a look, then glanced around the room quickly. "What old woman?"

A chill went up my spine as it occurred to me that she was a ghost.

When we left the service, Terry pushed me. I kept my head down and my eyes closed, so as not to see her. I hoped people would assume it was my grief.

But that was then, when my abilities were new and such things frightened me. Since then, I'd studied, worked in haunted houses, and a lost phantom didn't shock me in any way. In fact, it's a walk in the park. The only reason I didn't want distractions today was so I could focus on finding Jack.

I used my training to suppress a certain amount of the ambient energy of the place and erected the walls so as not be overwhelmed by the emotions of sadness that pervaded the funeral home where hundreds had wept over their losses throughout the years.

The minister at Wendy's funeral was *very* different from any I'd seen. Long hair and beard, he talked in a rambling speech of the mother/father spirit and Wendy's specific path, with a lack of pre-paredness that made me think he'd gotten his ordination over the Internet and recently.

The group had several people I recognized from our first date at the Halfway House. Char was sitting there in a black shirt and pants, genuinely upset. Next to him was the angry-looking waitress who'd given me the evil eye. She wore a mannish black suit.

What was it about her that kept drawing my attention?

I looked around for anyone who could be Wendy's sister and finally found a young woman in the third row who I thought was a match. She was pretty, though not as stunning as Wendy. But she seemed to possess the same nose and fine bone structure. She had a different mother, so there were differences, but there were also enough similarities. She held a handkerchief to her eyes, dabbed them, and blew her nose.

Next to her was a man. He was about five foot five but broad, with powerful shoulders and hands that looked like they could pick up a bowling ball without the holes. He possessed a simian quality that made his arms appear longer.

I turned back to the preacher, who may or may not have been coming to the point. It was odd. If the man I just looked at was Jack, why didn't I get a feeling from him? Not even a little buzz.

When I'd stepped into the spot from where the fire was started, I received the impression of a very different face, not to mention the *feeling*—so intense.

I looked around the room a moment or two more, seeing if I could find the man in black from my visions.

"We will now listen to words from those who knew her best," the preacher said, encouraging people to rise up and speak.

The waitress rose and moved to the front of the room.

"My name is Denise, and I knew Wendy in many different ways. She was a person who loved deeply and freely. She could accept you for who you were, and yet she could push you when you needed it. She was a great soul," she said as tears overcame her and she returned to her seat.

The woman in the third row got up, still holding her husband's hand.

"I'm Janice Hoefler, and Wendy was everything anyone could want in a big sister. She was there for me all my life and did her best to protect me. She helped get me on my feet and taught me to live on my own. And she always helped me and Jack with our own struggles. She will be missed." She tearfully glanced at the ape-man and sat down.

A few others stood and gave glowing testimony to Wendy. I could only speak from the silence of my heart. I couldn't shake the feeling that I should've been able to do more to save her.

Finally, the service ended, and several of the men, including the one I decided was Jack Hoefler, acted as pallbearers and moved Wendy's coffin to the hearse.

There still was no one I could identify as the man from my vision, and I tried to get a reading on Jack. Janice seemed shy and very dependent upon him, but they appeared to be a married couple in grief over the loss of a relative.

I watched them get into their car and suddenly became aware I needed a ride.

"Can anyone give me a lift?" I said to the few remaining people.

"Yeah, I got a minivan," came a deep female voice.

Denise, who I thought hated me, waved me over. She was still with Char, and they both stood near a red van that looked fairly new. I approached, thanked them, and slipped into the back seat.

"Leg keep you from driving?" Denise asked as I got in.

"It makes it complicated," I replied, trying to be cheery.

Denise drove into place in the hastily assembled procession, and we ambled slowly from the parking lot.

"That was nice, what you said about Wendy," I said as I felt the silence lay heavily in the car. "She was quite a woman."

"You didn't know her very well," Denise said. "She was a collection of contradictions. Sometimes, I think she had the instincts of an alley cat in heat. Some of us wanted to see her settle down."

"Well," Char said. "*You* wanted her to settle in a specific way."

"Yeah," Denise said, "I admit it, I wanted her to move in with me." I saw her eyes looking at me in the rearview mirror. "What's your name?"

"Leonard, Leonard Wise."

"He's a doctor," Char added.

Denise nodded. "That was her type. Anyone with a title—anyone successful. Look, Leonard, you barely knew Wendy…"

"Now, don't go saying anything bad about the dead," Char chided.

"What does it matter?" Denise said. "I loved Wendy—and, yes, I slept with her—more than once, though we didn't do much sleeping, as I recall. I wanted her to live with me, but she wasn't sure what she wanted except for money. She always wanted money."

"There was more to her than that, Denise," Char said.

"Oh yeah? Well, she did end up with a lot of money," Denise said. "And she wasn't too keen on anyone knowing where she got it from."

"She invested in the Halfway House?" I asked.

"She kept the place going, especially in the beginning. She said it was the least she could do for an old flame."

Interesting choice of words, I thought.

"You own the Halfway House?" I asked.

"Own it, no—rent the space, yeah. It was my idea. It was supposed to be a place where gays, lesbians, and transgenders could hang out—but I have to admit, we're pretty mainstream. We mostly attract the aging Bohemian crowd."

"We do have a nice mix of folks," Char said.

"Yeah, the place is on the edge enough to be cool, but not so far out that people feel threatened."

"Wendy mentioned a boyfriend—broke up with the guy about a year ago, said he was possessive?"

"All men are possessive," Denise snorted. "Don't want your 'girls' wandering too far."

"I was just wondering, maybe she's dead because of that man. His name was Jack," I said.

Denise blanched but grabbed a pair of sunglasses off the dashboard and put them on. Char watched her, concerned.

"You know anything, honey?" Char said kindly.

"Don't honey me, I'll kick your ass," Denise said. Her covered eyes looked up at me via the rearview mirror. "She had been with so many men…"

"She said she lived like a nun for the last year," I said.

"So, she only got laid once a week instead of every night!" Denise said, turning red. "Look, I don't know anything about a Tom, Dick, Harry, or Jack. Maybe we should drop it."

"Of course—I'm sorry," I said.

"Don't mind her none," Char said. "This is how she deals with grief, by being pissy."

"Better than being pussy, you old fag," Denise said to Char.

"Don't blame me, you got the equipment—and I'm happy with what I got," Char said.

We rode on in silence. In spite of the gibes, they seemed to have genuine affection for each other as well as Wendy. They both suffered the loss, and it made me realize how little I really knew her.

I could tell from Denise's reaction that she knew exactly who Jack was—but she didn't want to say anything. What was it about him that scared people so much?

Perhaps the power to cremate you with nothing more than his will.

Pyrokinesis…

We arrived at the grave site, a huge place just off of Route Ten. In fact, I was surprised that such a large memorial park was hidden back in an area of warehouses and factories.

The grounds, however, were beautiful: manicured trees, green lawns, and well-groomed headstones. The procession stopped at a particular site where the dirt was excavated and piled into a small mound. The open grave would be Wendy's final resting place.

As we got out of the cars and assembled on the lawn, the pall-bearers took the coffin from the hearse and, with help from a man in a well-worn black suit, who I assumed was the funeral director, placed the coffin into position in the metal frame that supported it above the open grave.

I noticed an extra car that wasn't part of the procession and watched as Detective McGee walked over slowly to join our party. He gave me a silent nod.

The bearded man began again with a few more incoherent espousals of his unfathomable belief system. The driver of the hearse held a large bouquet of white roses that would soon be placed on the coffin by the guests.

Then—all at once—I felt *him.*

He's here…

It wasn't an overwhelming buzz like I often get at a haunted house, where the presence is just *there* and you grapple to understand your impressions. It was more like a chill that went down my spine. I could sense him, nearby, watching.

I turned slowly, trying not to draw attention to myself, as if standing six four in a crowd while leaning on a cane wasn't obvious. I wished I'd worn dark glasses, because then, at least I could pretend that I wasn't looking around.

I saw the mourners as I turned, Janice was now being supported by Jack as she wept noisily. There was Denise, Char, the preacher, McGee, many other people I didn't know. The group seemed to increase after we left the funeral home.

Then I saw him. Standing apart from the group, about twenty or thirty feet away. He was dressed all in black with a long black leather coat—looking like he stepped out of a movie. He wore dark sunglasses, but even at this distance, I recognized him. Roman nose, curly black hair, thin, lithe. But it was more than that. He radiated an energy, it seemed to pour from him.

I turned back to the preacher, and slowly, I tried to move in a way that wouldn't scare my rabbit. Rabbit, hell, it was more like an ocelot. I moved slowly so he didn't pounce, edging my way through the crowd until I was next to McGee.

"McGee!" I whispered.

"What?" he said, and bent to put his ear near my mouth.

"There's someone you should check out. Long coat, twenty feet away, by the grove of trees."

"What are you talking about?"

"He's the guy I saw in my vision."

McGee returned to his full height and scanned the group. He was wearing mirrored glasses, so I couldn't tell where his eyes were.

"Where?" he asked.

"Over there," I said, turning and pointing, keeping my hand close to my body.

"I don't see anyone," he said.

I turned quickly to look, and McGee was right. The man with the leather coat was gone.

. . .

The coffin was lowered into its final resting place, and flowers and dirt were dropped in upon it. I looked again and again for the man, but he was nowhere to be found.

Had I really seen him? Or was he merely another vision, a presence I was aware of, but not actually there, like the phantoms I see in haunted houses and funeral homes?

No, this was different, the energy was very strong. I *felt* him physically there, not just an apparition.

He must have noticed my movement to McGee, which took me several minutes, and left. I'm sure he could move fast, he appeared to be in good shape.

As the funeral ended, I saw McGee walk over to Jack and Janice Hoefler, flash his badge, and step a few feet away with Jack as Janice received hugs and handshakes from the guests.

A few minutes later, Jack returned. His face was ashen, and he appeared quite angry. He quickly went to Janice and led her to their car. She went along meekly.

"You need a ride, Doc?" Denise asked.

I turned to see Denise and Char, waiting for me.

"Oh! Thanks, but I think I have a ride back," I said with a smile.

Char returned the smile. "Well, you take care, and you can hear me play most nights at the Halfway House."

"I'll do that, Char. Take care, Denise," I said.

"Always do," she said. Her eyes watched McGee carefully as they headed for the minivan.

I walked over to McGee. "Give a fellow a ride?" I asked.

"This not driving thing of yours is a pain in the ass, Len. What if I was called to a crime scene? You couldn't walk to Mountainview from here."

"I'd call a cab. Besides, I might be able to give you more information."

"What did I tell you about playing detective, Len?" he said as we walked to his unmarked police car and he unlocked the door.

"That's why I tell you everything, Bill," I said, getting in the back seat.

As we drove, I brought him up to date on my talk with Denise. Not just the facts of what she'd told me, but what she didn't want to tell me as well.

"So, the major question is how Wendy went from wanting money to having so much of it," McGee said.

"And the time line seems to fit the burning down of that building at the shore and the death of her father and stepmother."

"Interesting. Did you get any feeling about Jack Hoefler? Read his mind?" McGee said, a gentle smile on his face.

"I didn't get much of anything. I don't think he's the murderer, but he's unhappy about something," I said. "He looked even more unhappy after he talked to you."

"I just mentioned I needed to talk to him alone at the police station. He asked why, and I suggested there might be evidence of an affair with his sister-in-law."

"Very diplomatically, I trust."

"I was the soul of tact," McGee said. "But it was his reaction that interested me."

"He was furious…"

"Yes, and if it weren't true, wouldn't he be, I don't know—surprised, shocked, maybe hurt?"

"That would be most people's reaction. But he was mad."

"Right, which says *something* was going on," McGee said. "Now, once I get him in interrogation, we might be able to clear things up. But right now, he's hiding something."

"Good luck with that," I said.

"I'll treat him with kid gloves and let him walk into a trap of his own making. Tell enough lies, and sooner or later, you trip up. I'll also stop by the Halfway House and talk to this Denise. Maybe a badge will get her to be more forthcoming."

"I don't know. You're male, and she has some serious anger toward men. If you know a policewoman, she might have better luck."

"Not a bad idea," he said as we pulled in front of the Baines's house. "Do me a favor, Len. I appreciate the information—but please, don't get involved more than you are. I really don't want to be going to a funeral for your charred corpse."

"Yes, sir," I said as I got out of the car and watched McGee drive off.

That was what he didn't understand. I was already far more involved than I should have been.

JACK'S DIARY: TUESDAY

This morning started off so well. I got out of bed, exited the total darkness of my vault, to look out the tinted glass of my aerie and see a day without a cloud in the sky.

I felt beyond benevolent as I had my breakfast and perused my iPad. I noted that my dear Wendy was having her funeral in the morning.

I thought it would be tacky to show up at the funeral home. After all, I did kill her. But to go out to the graveside, perhaps pretend to visit another grave. I would wait for the crowd of riffraff to leave, then go to her final resting place and say a few poetic words, perhaps a haiku.

I truly am a sensitive soul.

I phoned my driver and arranged a pickup time, then enjoyed my breakfast with my usual relish. Eggs, toast with lots of marmalade, and hot coffee. I prepared them all myself and ate every bite.

I suppose I could get help, a cook or a butler, which would make meals easier. But then again, they would be around, be aware of my comings and goings. As it is, I never see the cleaning staff. They come in and do their work when I am out or asleep. It is better that way. They can stay in awe of their young master.

So, I was in a fine mood as I rode out to the memorial park, even though it was in a seedy part of the state. Well, what of it? Where you stay once you're dead doesn't matter. At least there was a place I could visit my lost love if I felt nostalgic.

I had the driver park well away from the rabble and walked until I was in view of the ceremony. Some preacher said words about Wendy. It was all so touching, I could almost feel a tear. Poor Wendy, why did she have to bring this all upon herself?

Then I felt it—felt him. I looked hastily around to try to locate where it was coming from, but none of the group looked in my direction. Then, slowly, he turned.

The goddamn cripple.

I could sense him reach out the same way I do. He actually probed me and then glanced at me, sidelong, as if I didn't know.

I saw him start to move slowly through the crowd, and I recognized that tall police detective from the jewelry store in the crowd. The cripple limped toward him, undoubtedly to tell him I was there.

I moved quickly—I have the reflexes of a cat—and ducked behind trees, then crouched and slid around gravestones until I was well out of sight.

I made my way back to the car, but dammit, I got mud on the knees of my pants. I hopped in the car and ordered the driver to back out of the graveyard, so we wouldn't go past Wendy's mourners.

I cleaned my pants with some wipes I make sure are always in the car, but the brown coloring stayed. I would have to change at home and shower again. I breathed deeply to submerge the anger that flared within.

It appears this cripple has some kind of ability, not as powerful as mine, but there. It is possible he could reveal me, take away my precious anonymity.

This was unplanned. I have no wish to reveal myself to the world. My abilities are best used in the background. The choice must be to get the insurance money and leave town. Perhaps return to the Bahamas? I may have to call in money from some of my other sources.

I knew I didn't like the cripple, but now he is more trouble than he's worth. Who does he think he is playing with?

I will consider my next steps with care.

THIRTEEN

With the afternoon free, I decided to walk into town. There was nothing I needed to buy, but I wanted to do something physical to get out of myself a bit.

I walked to a small park that wrapped around a lake with a majestic bit of statuary rising from the center, and sat on a bench. I closed my eyes and relaxed, putting myself into a light trance. I hadn't been regular with my meditation since I arrived. I would change that starting today. I needed to keep my mind sharp.

After twenty minutes, I opened my eyes and rose from the bench. I felt very relaxed, and the chatter of my own thoughts and any around me had been quieted.

I walked toward the center of town. I felt light, as if my body weighed nothing. It was just a pleasure to put one foot in front of the other as my cane pushed me along. As I got closer to town, my eye became focused on a particular building which bore large letters reading "Associated Insurance" in a fanciful logo that intertwined the A with the I.

I must go there…

I found myself headed toward the building, aware that this was where Jenny worked. Bad enough I had the hots for her, now I was stalking her at work. But that was my rational mind, and my instincts told me to keep going.

Another twenty minutes, and I was at the security desk. I signed my name on a page as they phoned Mrs. Baines. I was given an adhesive "Visitor" patch and told to go to the tenth floor.

As I rode the elevator up, I had the oddest sensation, as if I was part of a play, and that I was making my entrance just a moment later than I was supposed to.

I walked into the tenth-floor lobby and approached a woman at a desk.

"Jenny Baines, please," I said.

"She's right there, sir," the bespectacled woman said, pointing at Jenny as she walked down the hall toward us.

"Jenny!" I said.

"Lenny? I got the call you were coming up. Isn't that the oddest thing? The lawyer from the Nova Corporation just left."

A chill went up my spine. "Was it Jack Hoefler?"

"No, I got the name wrong, it's Hallman—Jack Hallman. He just left."

I looked over at the elevators. "What did he look like?"

"It's weird. He was dressed all in black, with a big leather coat and sunglasses."

"Which window faces the entrance?" I asked frantically as I pointed at the walls of glass on either side.

"That one," Jenny said, pointing to my right. "But what does—"

Before she could finish, I moved quickly toward the glass wall and wove my way past a few cubicles until I arrived at a place with an unobstructed view. Jenny followed me as I went to the glass and stared down to see a figure in a black leather coat turn the corner.

"I missed him," I said, leaning against the wall of a cubicle.

"What are you doing?" puffed Jenny, who now was breathing hard as she tried to keep up with me.

"This man, this Jack—he was at the funeral this morning," I said in hushed tones. "What did he want?"

"He came in with an affidavit, making a claim on the insurance money from Mishan's store," she said and opened one of the files in her arms. "I was about to copy the paperwork for Detective McGee."

"What did you tell him?" I asked.

"The truth. That it was still under investigation, and I couldn't release funds until the inquest was completed. Then for a kicker, I told him that there were questions about his corporate papers."

"What did he do?"

"He got angry, but I told him that if he wasn't polite, I could make it more difficult to get his money," Jenny said, her chin jutting out sternly. "That shut him up. I mean he was really strange, and he never took off those sunglasses…"

"Jenny, if you make a copy of the affidavit, I'll take it right to McGee," I said, and took her arm protectively. "And listen to me, you are never, *never*, to see that man alone."

She smiled and extracted herself from my grasp. "Calm down, Lenny. I can handle guys like him. It comes with the territory. Come on, you can help me make copies."

I followed her into a small vestibule with a large copy machine. She was all sweetness, and asked me about the funeral. I couldn't get past the fact that she'd been alone with that creature. She didn't understand how dangerous he was, even in an office filled with people.

The only saving grace was that he still needed her for the money. But if he felt that dealing with a replacement would be easier…

I stood nearby as she finished running the papers through the machine, then she handed me four or five sheets.

"I really should do this through channels," she said. "But I do want Detective McGee to have them quickly."

"Anything in particular I should point out?"

"Yes, the paper is signed by one of the names McGee claimed was faked," Jenny said, as she pointed to a signature at the bottom. "But it says that he's a resident of the Bahamas, which may have been misleading when McGee tried to track down names."

"So, McGee might be able to find this guy in the Bahamas?" I said.

"I don't know, Lenny," Jenny said and took a look at the original. "It just lists him as a *citizen* of the Bahamas. He could be right here in New Jersey."

"What is his name?" I asked, studying my copy of the affidavit.

"John Gingold," she said at the exact same moment I saw his signature on the bottom of the paper.

A flash of recognition ran through me, yet it was a name I'd never heard before. His signature, even on the copy I held, seemed to glow, as if a highlighter had been used on the round, firm script that clearly spelled his name.

"Gingold," I repeated, staring at the handwriting as if mesmerized.

"Are you going to stand here all day or take the papers to the police?" Jenny said.

I jumped as if shocked. "O-of course," I said, and pulled the papers together before heading for the elevator.

"So, now you know where I work, maybe you can meet me for lunch," Jenny said.

"That might be nice," I said, but my mind was elsewhere.

John Gingold. Why does that sound so familiar?

"See you later," Jenny said as I pushed the button for the elevator.

I waved and mumbled something incoherent as Jenny walked away purposefully. I waited, and found my gaze again returned to the signature. The door opened, and I rode down to the first floor, then left the building in the direction of the Mountainview police station.

It took about a half-hour, but I got there, relieved to see that Tice wasn't at the front desk. Instead, there was a heavyset man with white hair and a dark gray moustache. He was in uniform, and his eyes carried heavy bags under them.

"Detective-Sergeant McGee, is he available?" I asked.

"He's with a witness, can't be disturbed," the desk sergeant answered. He did not look up from the paperwork piled in front of him.

"Can I leave something for him?"

"As long as it ain't a letter bomb," the sergeant said, deadpan.

"Do you have an envelope?"

The sergeant met my eyes. "Yeah, I guess," he said and opened several desk drawers until he pulled out a stained number ten envelope. He held it out and looked hard at me.

"You've been here before, haven't you?" he said.

"I'm doing some…research for Detective McGee," I said, attempting a new lie. "I'm from Garden State University."

"Oh?" he said, leaning back in his chair. "'Bout time you academics did something for us for a change."

He began a tirade about how much the police did for the university, with little appreciation or help. I stood there and nodded my head like one of those toy dogs people put in the back window of their cars.

As I placed papers in the envelope, I looked for a break in the officer's one-sided conversation where I could make a run for it—well, a quick limp away at best.

At that moment, I saw ape-man Jack Hoefler as he walked from the back and made his way for the door without noticing me. Behind him, McGee followed his egress. He saw me and raised a hand as he approached.

"Not to mention the end of the year, when we have to keep a watch on the graduation parties…" the sergeant was saying.

"Tony, are you blaming Doctor Wise for everything wrong with this town?" McGee interrupted.

"He said he's from the college…" Tony said, a bit surprised.

"I don't think he has the dean's ear," McGee said.

Just the associate dean, I thought. I kept it to myself to avoid him going off again.

"I brought you that research you asked for," I said.

One of McGee's eyebrows went up. "That's great. Join me in the back, and we'll take a look."

I followed McGee dutifully, and he took me to the conference room, where he poured some coffee into a Styrofoam cup and rubbed his eyes with his free hand.

"You want some?" he offered.

"No, thanks. I prefer my stomach lining intact. I have the most recent papers from Associated Insurance."

"Renting yourself out as a messenger?" he quipped, as he sat heavily across from me and took the envelope I held out. "I'd advise a bicycle, or at least a golf cart."

"I want to maintain my amateur status," I said.

He opened the envelope, took out the papers, and read them quickly.

He grunted. "John Gingold? He's one of the people who formed the corporation. I wonder why he didn't turn up in my database?"

"According to one of those papers, he's a citizen of the Bahamas," I pointed out.

"Which is like having money in Switzerland. It's there, but no one can trace it to you," he said as he went through the pages. "Neat little scam. This guy could be an American, but if he transferred his passport—it might be hard to track him down."

"His lawyer was at Mrs. Baine's office," I said. "And he fits the description of the man I saw at Mishan's—and today at the funeral."

"You sure you saw this guy, or was he just in your head, like the fire?"

"It was a vision when I saw him at Mishan's. But at the memorial park, he was quite real."

"So, he's an arsonist who can vanish into thin air. Good skill set."

"He didn't disappear at the insurance office. I saw him walk away."

"Same guy?"

"Absolutely."

"Might be a lead," McGee said as he read the affidavit. "This lawyer, he's Hallman?"

"Yes."

"Well, I might have news when it comes to firebugs. I think we've located Lonny the Match."

"Really?"

"Paramus police spotted him and should be picking him up within the hour."

"How do you suppose he's involved in all this?"

"I dunno. Maybe that invention of his. You said you had a vision where he met with Mishan…"

"Yes," I said with a nod. "What happened with Hoefler?"

Bill shrugged his massive shoulders. "He's weird, even for a lawyer. I began asking questions about Wendy Wallace, and he claims that he was *her* lawyer. So any discussions were privileged."

"Convenient," I said, "considering the only one who can verify that claim is dead."

"Yeah, I wasn't getting anywhere. So, I asked him about the death of his wife's parents…"

"And he had nothing to say?"

"No, get this! He says, 'I had nothing to do with that.' Now, that got my attention. I ask him if their deaths were not an accident, and he just says 'It was an accident, you can check with the police in Mendham,' stuff like that."

"So why say he had nothing to do with it?" I mused. "Odd choice of words."

"He wasn't sure how much I knew. But he backpedaled after that, trying to tell me he didn't mean anything. But I say the hell with that! I caught him off-guard and glimpsed a moment of truth. He knows something about their deaths."

"Can you reopen the case?" I suggested.

"I'll exhume the bodies if I have to. But I think I'll have a talk with Mrs. Hoefler next."

"Think she'll be forthcoming?"

"She won't be as practiced a liar, after all, she doesn't do it for a living. She can't testify against her husband, but maybe she might point me in a new direction."

"And maybe she knows something about Wendy's boyfriend."

"Provided it isn't her own husband. I still didn't get the answer to that."

"I don't think so," I said. "When I saw him at the funeral, I didn't get any kind of insight about him. I think if he was the man who killed her, alarms would have gone off in my head."

"You only get those for our guy in black."

"Which makes me want to find out who he is."

"I thought you said he was the Nova lawyer, Jack Hallman."

I shrugged. "What if there is someone hiding under all of this that doesn't want to be found? I mean, people living abroad, a corporation with no officers? It all points to someone trying to stay in the shadows."

"I'll go to this lawyer, Hallman and try to get some answers."

"What do you think the big picture is?" I asked.

McGee shrugged. "Arson for hire, hidden money, insurance fraud? Len, I just don't know." A broad grin spread on his face. "Isn't that why I brought you in?"

"I guess," I said. "So, am I helping without exceeding any boundaries?"

"You're a help. But, please, stay away from any more fires or anyone who dies."

"I'll try," I said, thinking of Jenny's visit from the man in black and how uncomfortable it made me feel.

• • •

I wandered back to the Baines's house and found myself bored. I looked around and discovered an ancient stained copy of *The Joy of Cooking*. I decided to attempt another simple dinner from what I found in the refrigerator and cabinets. On Jenny's arrival home, I received a grateful hug for the cooked meal, and it made me melt.

I was still worried about her, wondered if there was any way that the man in black could get to her, and it bothered me that it kept coming into my mind repeatedly.

The next day, I got up very early, put on my usual tweed jacket, and asked Jon for a ride to the university to use their computers. He readily agreed, drove me to GSU, and after he said "Good morning" to his assistant, Trisha, he put me in the same computer room I used before.

My first action was to e-mail Doctor Kohl:

Fritz,

Need any and all info about pyrokinesis and any possible protection or suggestion as to how to confront it.

Doing field research.

Len

I then put the word "pyrokinesis" in the search engine, but only got several sites littered with characters in role playing games who possessed pyrokinetic "power" which was worth a certain number of points. These points allowed you to defeat an enemy through additions and subtractions that bordered on numerology and were all but incoherent to me, despite my PhD.

Upon deeper study of the web selections, I also found a Japanese movie released on video bearing the same name, with a plot that turned and twisted around a lead character with pyrotechnic powers. I didn't feel a need to know more about it or purchase it.

I was busy living it.

After about an hour, I was ready to give up. Just in case, I checked my e-mail again and was pleased to find a response from Dr. Kohl.

Leonard,

A surprising request. Research in the field, you say? A very esoteric choice.

Might I suggest you consider cryokinesis if you are after a counter-effect? This is the ability to slow molecules down. You are familiar with the effects of it. Cryokinesis is what causes hauntings to be cold. Encountering paranormal phenomena slows down the air molecules, and the atmosphere in the room becomes colder.

Remember how cold it became in Scudder House? Same effect. There is a correlation between haunting and telekinetic experiences—cryokinesis being the most common.

There is information out there, but I'll keep it simple. Recall our candle exercises. That might be a good place to start.

Your friend,

Fritz

Yes, I could remember how cold it was in Scudder House. The one evening we did research, one machine registered a change of forty degrees in the room when I acted as a medium.

Odd, it's the one place where I did my best work, and yet the presence I felt there made me want to blot it out of my mind, as I try to do with the memory of the night Cathy died.

I'm attracted and repelled by it at the same time. I would have to think about the Scudder House because there might be something I learned that could help me. What I remember most is the feeling that I only touched the surface, that there was a presence there—another personality—that was strong and *hungry*.

Fritz was right; I distinctly remembered how *cold* I'd felt, chilled to the bone by whatever was there. If I could think of a way to do the same thing—create frigid temperatures—I could use it as a weapon against a pyrokinetic.

I shut down the computer in disgust. Yes, there were measurable temperature changes at the Scudder House. But I had no idea how to do it unless I could find a helpful ghost willing to follow me around and chill the room on command like a trained puppy.

I pushed myself up with my cane and walked back to Jon's office, where Trisha Heywood looked up from some paperwork she was filling out.

"I'm taking off, Trisha. Thank Jon for me."

"That's fine, Doctor," she said, smiling in her unassuming way. "Did you find what you were after?"

"No," I said. "There doesn't seem to be anyplace on the Internet to look up metaphysical studies."

"Oh? I imagine not. Most universities don't have programs for that."

"That would be something I would be happy to change," I said. "I'm telling you, parapsychology departments at major universities would make a huge difference in available information. Personally, I think there is a tremendous interest nowadays."

Her eyes widened. "Do you think so?"

"When I began my course of study, the only place I could go at all was to Southern California University of Health Sciences to work with Doctor Kohl. It's the only school of higher learning in the country with a parapsychology program. And there's a waiting list to get into the program."

"That's really very interesting."

"Yeah, but it doesn't help my research. I'm going to the campus library. Maybe I'll have better luck there."

"All right, Doctor. See you later," she said and gave me a little wave.

I tapped my way out of College Hall and headed towards the huge Templeton Library building, only a few dozen yards away. But, in spite of the enormous collection on hand, after an hour of research I found less than on the Internet. All I located under 'pyrokenesis' was an old scary novel and the *Encyclopedia of The Occult* that listed the ability as a variation on PK—psychokinesis—and telepathy.

Finally, a little before noon, I decided a lunch with Jenny would be a better choice. I quickly extracted her card and tapped the number into my phone.

"Jennifer Baines," she said, picking up.

"Leonard Wise," I said. "I didn't know Jenny was short for Jennifer."

"Lenny, just stick to Jenn or Jenny. I only use my full name for business," she said.

"I wanted to see if you were free for lunch."

"I thought you were busy doing research."

"It's not panning out. Are you free?"

"Sure. You'll be walking—can you be here by twelve-thirty?"

"On my way," I said and hung up.

It was another beautiful day. The chill from Tuesday had given way to a sunny Wednesday with temperatures in the sixties. I still needed my tweed jacket, but I was comfortable, and the air was filled with the fresh scent of life as it renewed itself from the New Jersey winter.

It was a pleasure to breathe through my nose, and it invigorated me. There was also a feeling of belonging, like I was home. I grew up experiencing shifting seasons. In California, the perpetual warm weather and the desert shrubbery and palm trees never quite looked right. Here, as I walked along streets lined with maples, oaks, and pines, I was in my environment, the one from my childhood. Suburbia and small towns, spring in the air, it was—comfortable.

I wandered back to the Associated Insurance building, and after filling out the book and getting my badge from security, made it up to the tenth floor.

The same receptionist sat at the desk, wearing a pink outfit that bordered on the ridiculous. I approached carefully, not wanting to be blinded by the neon shade of her attire.

"Leonard Wise to see Jenny Baines," I said.

"She's with—a client," she said, her voice interrupted by muffled shouts down the hall.

Danger…

"What is that?" I asked as I felt the buzz far in advance of a raised voice in an office.

"That might be the man who came by to see her. He was very agitated," she said. As she rose from her chair, her hand went to her hair, primping it unconsciously.

I faced her. "The man from yesterday, all in black—with sunglasses?"

"Yes, but I…" she said, uneasily, as the loud voice spoke again.

"Where are they?" I demanded, already in motion down the hall.

"Third room on the right," she said.

I moved down the hall and could see other people as they stood within their cubicles. They were also alarmed at the loud voice in the usually quiet domain.

The hall was decorated in wood stained a reddish color, and I passed two solid doors with long rectangular windows in them, which gave me a quick view of the offices behind them.

The third door also contained a glass section, and in it, I could easily see Jenny as she stood and confronted a tall, dark shape.

I pushed the door open and stepped noisily into the room. Apparently, Jenny was speaking, but she didn't shout. My entrance into the room stopped her and left her agape, her mouth open and slack.

The man turned to face me. Still wearing black, but this time a very well-tailored black suit. He wore a maroon shirt so dark that it was only a little lighter than the suit itself; a black tie finished the ensemble. He carried on his arm the black leather coat I remembered from the funeral—and wore the same sunglasses, reflective and angular, giving his eyes the look of a bug.

But worse was the feeling like a hundred alarm bells going off in the back of my head. I've had buzzes by the score, and I've undergone visions, hunches, and even the occasional out-of-body experience. But this was like someone set off a dozen small firecrackers at the end of my spinal cord, and they were each popping and sending explosive energy up into my brain.

I was not only aware that *this* was the man, but that my sudden entrance may have been the worst possible choice.

It was my turn to gape.

"L-Lenny," Jenny stammered.

"You know him?" the man said, his expression stony. He wobbled a little bit on his feet—could he be as affected by my presence as I was by his? He gathered himself and stood up straighter.

"I should have known," he said. "So, this is why my personal business is of such interest to the police. You are conspiring together."

He wasn't yelling this time, but his words were tinged with an anger that I *felt* as well as heard.

"Nonsense, Mr. Hallman!" Jenny said, trying to regain her own composure. "The police are involved because it was a suspicious fire. You do want people to find out how Mr. Mishan died, don't you?"

Clever, I thought. *She's turned it around, made it so that it was in his best interest to have the police involved.*

I started to recover and put up my imaginary walls to seal myself off from him.

"I heard yelling…" I said, as best an explanation for my arrival as I could come up with.

"Yes, Mr. Hallman was getting a bit loud," Jenny replied.

"My office was overrun with police!" he said, forcefully, but without raising his voice. I'd left the door open on my entrance, and that helped him maintain his composure.

"They are investigating a possible murder," Jenny said.

"Murder! How ridiculous! This is all an attempt by your company to avoid paying on our insurance. After all, the store burns down—there are no bombs—no spilled fuel—and no evidence of a murder. It was probably faulty wiring!"

"Hard to tell now that the building is a blackened hole," I blurted out.

His face turned toward me, and I could feel his gaze through the lenses. I wondered if the glasses were removed, would I see a pair of flaming red eyes?

A small smile played on his lips, and he spoke quietly, even politely. "Which proves my point. If it were bad wiring, that's what caused the fire to start again and destroyed the property."

"I cannot release funds during a police investigation," Jenny said. "It's the company's position, and you can read it in your policy. As a lawyer, I'm sure you know how to read fine print."

He turned back to Jenny and jabbed his first finger in the air. "This isn't over."

"It is until there is a final determination by the coroner as well as our own investigators. You must be patient."

"I'm very patient. But it is wearing thin," he slid toward the door and stopped next to me. "Our paths keep crossing."

"It seems that way," I said.

"I do hope *you* carry insurance, Mister…?" he said, one eyebrow raised above the glasses.

"*Doctor,*" I said, a little louder than necessary. "Doctor Leonard Wise. I'm glad we could meet face to face."

The smile returned. He enjoyed mocking me, and he had a high opinion of himself—smug, condescending. "I think you would prefer to avoid me in the future."

"Or I'll end up like Wendy Wallace?"

The smile became broader.

"I only knew her in passing. A tragedy—her death," he gave one last look to Jenny. "Probably faulty wiring as well."

"Or things she was connected to?" I snapped.

His mouth became a hard line. "I'll be in touch, Mrs. Baines." He sashayed out the door and down the hall toward the elevator.

His leaving changed the energy in the room and I leaned against my cane, dazed.

Jenny walked over and shut the door. "What an unpleasant man!"

"A very dangerous one," I said.

"Only his wardrobe."

"Come on, Jenny. I'm serious."

"Look, Lenny. He was here because Detective-Sergeant McGee showed up at his office, and I was the only connection. He came here to yell at me."

"And I show up to give credence to the idea that you're working with the police."

"Insurance companies *always* work with the police when arson is suspected. It's nothing new."

"He just takes it very personally, and he doesn't like me."

Jenny frowned. "You know him?"

"Actually, this was the first time we've met. It's complicated."

"Dealing with him is complicated."

"Does he ever take off those sunglasses?"

"He can't," Jenny said. "I asked him about it the other day. He's got something called uveitis. It's a sensitivity to light."

"We should go to the police."

"Jeez! He annoys me, and now I lose out on lunch, too?"

"Did he threaten you? You could file charges."

She shook her head. "No, just yelled. He has a temper, but he chooses his words carefully. He implied that if I didn't start helping him, I would be the one needing help."

"Sounds like a threat to me."

"He said it better. He could deny any threat easier than a politician with his hand in the till."

"I should let McGee know."

"You could try the phone. I hear it's even faster than walking."

I smiled and pulled out my cellular phone. "All right. Besides, it's probably better if I only show up when I'm invited these days."

"He hasn't tried to arrest you again, has he?" she said as I pushed the speed dial.

"That was merely a misunderstanding…" I said.

"McGee," came the voice over the line.

"Bill, it's Leonard."

"I was just thinking of you—you must be psychic."

"I won't touch that," I said. "I'm at Jenny Baines's office at Associated Insurance. Jack Hallman was just here, raising hell about the police being all over his place of business."

I heard a chuckle over the phone. "Yes, we asked him a lot of questions, and he was pretty sore about it. We can do more once we have a warrant."

"He's the man I saw at the graveyard."

"Really? You gave me the impression he was taller," McGee said.

"No, he's the one, and the same as in my visions. I'm worried about Jenny, Bill."

"Did he threaten her?"

"Not exactly—more like it was implied."

The phone on his end was silent for a moment as he gathered his thoughts. "Well, if she wants to sign out a complaint, I could assign a man to her."

"Hold on," I said and hit the mute button on my phone. "If you sign out a complaint, Bill says he can get you protection."

"Lenny, I can handle this."

"Jenny…"

"I'm not filling out anything," she said, crossing her arms in that Cathy way of hers. I knew there would be no way to convince her.

I touched the button and was live with Bill again. "She's not sure she wants to go that route…"

"Then there's little I can do, Len."

"Can you have a car go by the house at night, maybe, once in a while?" I said.

"That's not necessary," Jenny argued.

"Sure, I can arrange that," McGee said. "But I have something more pressing. Can you be here in an hour? Don't worry about Tice, he's still off."

"Sure, what do you need?"

"Two of my men are picking up Lonny the Match from Paramus and giving him a ride here for questioning. I want your impressions."

"Do I get to grill him?" I asked.

"Very funny—grill an arsonist. You're a regular comedian."

"Actually, I'm not a regular. I'm an extra large. I'll be there."

"Thanks, Len. Don't bring the jokes when you come," McGee said and hung up.

I put the phone down and looked at Jenny. "Lunch is still on."

"Goody!" she said, getting her jacket. "You're treating, right?"

"Yes, but I wish you'd change your mind about the police. I'm telling you that man is dangerous. I believe he killed Wendy."

"I can handle myself, Len. Come on, there is a place just a few doors down from here…"

Off we went.

JACK'S DIARY: WEDNESDAY

So, the cripple has a name—Doctor Leonard Wise. Oh, and he made damn sure to stress the Doctor. *An overeducated oaf, who has to impress you with his doctorate. As if that makes him better or smarter than me.*

I'm educated more than enough. Besides, once I knew of my talent, it was much more important to learn how to use it. I built my small financial empire by using it cleverly. Of course, I live comfortably, not grandiose. Well, not yet.

The cripple has to be the link between Mrs. Baines at the insurance company and the police. He feels like a cop, and yet, not. And every time I'm near him, I sense him. Being so close to him was almost pain-ful. I think he felt it, too. But if he has any abilities, of course he'd sense my power.

I've drawn a bit of suspicion with the three fires so close together. Mishan and his shop were enough, but then Wendy. That may have been a miscalculation.

It's just a lesson to me about letting my emotions get the best of me. That Baines woman, the way she keeps insisting to my face that I can't have the money. I wanted to reduce her to a flaming corpse right there in her office.

I guess that is what attracted the cripple. He knows the woman and sensed the danger she is in.

If that is so, perhaps I have a way to keep the cripple on the run and speed up getting my money. It will mean I shall have to play cat and mouse with the two of them. I may even have to eliminate them both, but it has to be done quietly.

I would enjoy frying the cripple—Doctor Leonard Wise. I haven't liked him since we met, and he is the only one who might be aware of my talent.

I shall have to plan carefully and perhaps bring a few of my other pieces into play. It will be a challenge.

But, more fun than burning up Mishan.

FOURTEEN

An hour later, after an enjoyable lunch at a nearby Mexican place with Jenny, she took me to her car and dropped me off in front of the police station.

"Thanks for the ride, Jenny," I said.

"Thanks for lunch. I'm stuffed. I think I'll just make a salad for dinner."

"Sounds great. I'll see you later."

I hobbled into the station and saw the sergeant named Tony at the desk again. McGee had been correct. Tice was nowhere to be seen.

"Hey, Professor!" Tony said as he smiled up at me. "McGee's expecting you. He's in the detective bull pen. You know the way?"

"I think so," I said. "Thank you…um, Sergeant…?"

"Williams, I'm Sergeant Williams."

"Thanks," I said and wandered past him down the short hall to once again get buzzed into the main corridor. I quickly walked to the detective's room across from processing and went in to find McGee at his desk.

"Ah, Len," he said, rising. "You're here. Can you go into Observation C and watch through the window?"

"Sure."

"If anyone asks, you're here to observe in an unofficial capacity. But if you get any impressions, I want to know about them."

He took me into the small room and shut the door that led to the squad room. I leaned against the table so I could easily look through the large one-way mirror. The lights were on in Interrogation B, and I got an unobstructed view of the room, the rectangular table, and its four chairs.

On the chairs sat Officer Galland in full uniform, and across from him, a man in a cheap suit that all but screamed public defender. Next to the lawyer was the man who'd stepped out of my vision, or off the page of the police sketchbook: Lonny Briback, aka Lonny the Match.

He was even oilier than I recalled, his hair slicked back with something from the '60s—Brilliantine or Vitalis. But the one thing I hadn't noticed was that his eyes didn't move together. One eye was either paralyzed or replaced with a glass one. This gave him an unfocused look that moved from the cross-eyed to walleyed.

"Anything you can tell me?" McGee said.

"I'm not sure," I said. "But I would estimate that the vision I saw took place several weeks ago."

"I still have Wendy's statement that he was there the day Mishan died. Though I wish to hell I had the actual witness. It would hold up better in court."

"Thus giving him motive to remove her," I said and gazed at Lonny. He couldn't keep still and shifted nervously in his chair. His hands fiddled with his shiny black hair and inserted themselves into his large ears as if they were points of fascination.

"You think he's our killer?" McGee asked.

I looked at the small man as he shifted and probed his ear with a pinkie. "I think he knows something that could help us."

McGee nodded, faced the wall, and turned a dial on a small metal box. "You can hear everything we say. If you have something to tell me, push this button." He pointed at a red button on the box. "I will hear a signal and come right out."

I nodded and kept my position on the table edge that faced the window. McGee gave me a nod and stepped through the door of the detective's bull pen, which he closed behind him. There was a pause, and then I watched as he opened the door to Interrogation Room B, a thick folder in his hand.

He sat across from Lonny, his back to me, and went through the folder carefully.

"So, Lonny, we got you for parole violation and possibly more," McGee said, not looking up.

"I didn't do nothing," Lonny said, his eyes going in two directions. "I just took a trip."

I listened to his voice amplified from the box. He had an accent, Brooklyn or the Bronx.

McGee continued. "So, you left California, ignoring the fact that you are not allowed to leave that state."

"Is this all you have, Detective?" the young lawyer said. "If you are extraditing him to California, I can't see the reason why I'm here."

I smiled. The public defender was a young man whose very presence suggested he'd had other aspirations but ended up in a job he ultimately didn't care for.

"You are here, counselor," McGee said, pulling out some papers, "because Mister Briback is a person of interest in an ongoing investigation. He also requested a lawyer, and we do things by the book in Mountainview. But I want to make it clear that he isn't going anywhere except prison." McGee went through the papers and rustled them noisily. "Now, Mister Briback, I have a reliable source that places you at a late-night meeting with one Philip Mishan at his jewelry shop, and a witness who places you in the same store the day he died."

"So?" Lonny shrugged.

I got an impression that Lonny was wondering just how much McGee knew.

"Mr. Briback, you served time for arson," McGee said, slowly standing up as his voice got louder. "And the man *burns* to death. I think *that* is relevant."

Briback shifted in his chair again, his one good eye looked around the room, perhaps for an escape.

McGee sat back down and pulled some pages out of the file. "Plus, I have information suggesting you created a weapon that shoots projectiles that start fires."

Briback leapt up from his chair as color stood out on his cheeks. "That's a load of crap…"

"Sit down, Mister Briback," his young lawyer said.

"I didn't build nothing since I got out, and if I did, I certainly wouldn't brag about it online so any fuckin' cop in the world could find it," Briback said, and sat back down, folding his arms as his voice grew sullen. "Besides, it's impossible."

"What do you mean?" McGee said.

"It can't be done. I heard the rumors and how it's supposed to work. Sodium metal can't be made into a bullet! It would disintegrate, even if you used compressed air to shoot it. It just can't be done."

His words possessed the ring of truth.

"But you just happen to know what I'm talking about?" McGee said, leaning forward to tower over the smaller Briback.

"Yeah, I heard my name was connected with this—whatever the hell it is. I went to the library, used their computer. The whole thing's a freakin' fairy tale."

"Well, Mister Briback, or should I call you Lonny the Match?" McGee said. "You'd better start explaining your visits to Mishan, or I see an indictment for conspiracy to commit murder."

"Look, Detective, I don't have all the facts of this case," the public defender fretted from his chair. "But, you are threatening my client. If you are able to charge him with a crime, you would have—"

"We pulled him in for violating his parole, and we'll keep him locked up here in New Jersey until I am sure he has no connection to Mr. Mishan's death! Right now, he was seen in the vicinity, and he has a history with incendiary devices. That makes him my prime suspect."

"It's not like that," Briback said, sweat beginning to drizzle down his face. "Look, I went to see Mishan, OK, but just to ask him some questions. Then the day he died, I was getting money off him."

"He gave you money? Why? Out of the goodness of his heart?" McGee demanded, his sarcasm plain as he leaned back in his chair. "If you got something to tell, now is the time."

Briback turned to the attorney and whispered in the young man's ear. The lawyer listened, nodded, then spoke.

"If he tells you, it would be admitting to a crime in another jurisdiction. What assurances does Mr. Briback have that you won't charge him?"

"My interest is Mishan and the town of Mountainview, New Jersey, here and now. I have no interest in pursuing crimes committed in other locales."

I smiled on my side of the glass. McGee was lying. If Briback admitted to something big enough, McGee would make sure he was charged for it as well.

The attorney gave Briback a quick nod. Briback pulled a stained white handkerchief from his pocket and wiped the sweat off his brow.

"I did a job for Mishan a few years back, a jewelry store in Ohio," Lonny said. "He paid me to burn the place down—but to do it so it wouldn't be found out. Y'know, for insurance."

"So you were blackmailing him? Cough up more money, or you'd tell the authorities?" McGee said.

"Nothin' like that," Briback said as he mopped his forehead. "I mean, I got principles, y'know. I got paid for that job, fair and square. Nothing went wrong—nobody died or nothing. But later, while I was in jail, I heard about that amusement park fire in South Jersey and that Mishan was involved."

"So?" McGee said.

"I got everything I could find about it. Had some friends send me stuff from the Internet, the newspapers. I figure if he'd hired me to burn one place, he must have hired somebody to burn that one. You get it? Same scam, different state."

"I fail to see…" McGee started.

"He hired someone, all right," Briback said as if the answer were obvious. "But I know all the best guys in the business, and not one of 'em was involved. And look, that fire was a work of art—I mean a freakin' Picasso. There was a little trace of an accelerant, but it was chemicals that you would have at an amusement park, paint 'n' stuff. The kicker was that there weren't no sign of a timer—not even a cigarette, which, y'know, is a cheap and easy fuse."

"Get to the point, Briback," McGee griped, his patience wearing thin.

"It bugged me. I mean, it had to be a set fire, because I knew Mishan. But the more I looked into it, the more I can't find any trace of arson. It bothered me. I don't know, it became, like—an obsession."

McGee leaned forward in his seat. "Let me get this straight, Briback. You broke parole and schlepped all the way here to New Jersey because of how an amusement park burned down?"

"Hey, Detective," Briback said, his eyes almost together and focused on McGee's face. "If you had a case that didn't work out, I mean you knew it was murder and couldn't prove it, wouldn't you be obsessed?"

A bleak smile came to McGee's face. He was in the middle of a case like that now.

Lonny leaned back in his chair. "I mean, I got here and went to the location of that pier, then talked to some locals and a few friends who would know. I couldn't find out nothin', and the site is a mall now."

"You're not telling me anything I don't know, Lonny," McGee growled, his police scowl returning.

"Well anyway, I tracked Mishan down. I mean, if he had something that was untraceable, I wanted it. I'm an expert with fire, and if somebody's got something this new, I want to know about it. I got my pride, y'know."

"So you showed up at his door," McGee said.

"I called him first. I mean, I didn't want he should think I'm putting the bite on him," Briback said as he looked from McGee to his lawyer.

"No, that came later," McGee muttered.

"Well, me and Mishan talk, and I tell him what a nice job the amusement pier was, and I suggest that I could stay around if he needs my help, and he laughs."

"Why?" McGee asked.

"He tells me that he don't need me anymore. Says he's got the real thing, a guy who can burn anything, anywhere, anytime. So I sez, 'How?' And he just laughs some more. Finally, he says that he has a partner and the fire just comes out of his head. That's what he tells me."

I found I was standing, but I didn't remember how I ended up that way. I stared at the glass to make sure that I'd heard him correctly.

"Come on, Briback," McGee said as he stood and began to pace the room. "You expect me to believe this load of crap?"

"It's what he said. So I decided to look into it. I found out he was involved with this company, the Nova Corporation, right?" Briback said and looked from man to man, his eyes on their independent prowl again. "Don't you get it? Nova? I mean, a supernova is a star that burns up!"

"You *still* aren't telling me anything useful, Lonny."

But he'd said exactly what *I* wanted to hear.

"That's the thing," Briback stated defensively. "This Nova Corporation is involved with a bunch of fires, in really weird ways. They bought the options on stock that a company was gonna lose money, selling short I think it's called. And BAM! A week later, one of the main warehouses burns down. Another time, a guy invests money in Nova. Then suddenly, his house burns down, the guy dies, and the money don't got to be repaid."

"I've looked into Nova Corporation," McGee said. "Most of their corporate signers don't exist."

Lonny leaned forward in his chair. "No, they *did* exist. Did you check death certificates?"

I could sense McGee felt embarrassed.

"I checked the database of—"

"But that's it. They're mostly dead. Except for this Wendy Wallace broad, and I find out she works at Mishan's store. So I check her out, and it turns out her father and stepmother were killed in a fire, too. But the police think it's an auto accident. And she gets a bundle of money, 'cause they had insurance up the wazoo, and when death occurs in a traffic accident, it's double indemnity."

I fell heavily against the table. Wendy got her money by having her own father and stepmother killed? What kind of person could do that? It seems like Jack wasn't the only monster. No wonder they were lovers; they had been perfect for each other.

And I made love to her, thought we might start a relationship…

McGee spoke up, which pulled me from my thoughts. "And all this was done by the man who shoots fire out of his head?"

"That's all crap," Briback said. "I figure Mishan said that because he's just got somebody with a technology nobody knows about. Like that projectile thing that you heard I invented. If anyone put that info on the Internet, it would have been him, using my name to put the blame on me."

"So, you found all this out how?" McGee queried.

"I got ways to check on things like that," Lonny said, his eyes both looking down at his lap.

"Be specific, Lonny. Or I swear, I'll get you indicted as a co-conspirator so fast…"

"OK, OK," Lonny said, his hands raised defensively. "I hired a PI."

"A private investigator? How did a jailbird like you—"

"Hey, I got some resources at my disposal," Lonny revealed, a Cheshire Cat grin on his face.

"I need a name," McGee said.

"Norris. Roswell Norris. He's local."

McGee sat heavily in his chair and exhaled deeply, annoyed. "I know him," he said with a look that suggested he'd just put something unpleasant in his mouth.

"He'll back up my story. I hired him to look into Nova."

McGee nodded. "I will have a talk with Mr. Norris, don't you worry about that. One last thing, you said Mishan gave you money the day he died. How much did he give to you and why?"

"We talked over the phone, and I told him what I'd found out. He asked me how much would it take to give up the information I had on Nova and leave town. He said I was stirring up trouble for him. He offered me ten grand. I figured I could pay off Norris and blow town, so I did."

"Just like that?"

Briback shrugged, one eye on McGee, and it appeared as if the other watched me behind the glass. "What I wanted was how they did it, but Mishan only ever told me the fire 'came out of his head.' I couldn't get what I wanted, so I took the money and took off." He leaned back in the chair. "Besides, with all those people getting fried, I figured I didn't want to end up on the menu."

"So you came out ahead on the deal," McGee said.

Lonny shrugged again. "Hey, look, I'm just a simple capitalist at heart. I show up, Mishan takes me in the back, and I hand him the folder. He asks if it's the only copy, stuff like that. I tell him, 'yeah,' and he starts reading it like all this stuff was new to him. So, he gives me a large envelope stuffed with the money and says, real nasty, that he hopes it's the last time he sees me. I say, 'Sure,' and I'm out of there."

"And went to…?" McGee asked.

"I'm off to Paramus. Then, the next day, I read in the paper that Mishan is dead from a fire. So, I stay put and lie low."

"And you heard about the Wallace woman?"

"No," Lonny said as if he didn't care. "She dead too?"

McGee nodded. "Where's the rest of the money?"

"I put it in a bank. What? I should walk around with it?" Lonny said.

"And do you have copies of the information?"

"No, I gave Mishan all I had. I told you, I'm a standup kinda guy."

McGee rose and shut his folder. "Sure you are, Lonny. As arsonists, blackmailers, and lowlife scum go, you're a regular prince." He nodded to Galland, who leaped to his feet. "Lock his majesty up."

"Detective McGee," the public defender stated as he rose to his feet. "My client was very forthcoming, there is no reason to be sarcastic…"

"Your client is trying to stay alive, counselor," McGee said with a glare at Lonny. "My guess is that he heard about the Wallace woman and made sure he'd get spotted and picked up. He figures behind bars, and preferably in California, he can save his bony ass."

"Hey! I was just doin' my public duty," Briback sneered as he was led out by Officer Galland.

The lawyer stood his ground. "He's not to be questioned without someone from my office here. Is that clear, Detective?"

"Very clear," McGee said, his voice flat. "But as you can see, Briback is a material witness, and worth more to me in one piece. So trust me, counselor, we'll treat him like visiting royalty."

"If anything happens to Mr. Briback, I will hold you personally responsible, Detective." The lawyer grabbed his briefcase and stalked out the door.

Watching him leave, McGee turned to the mirror and said, "Come on in, Len."

I went through the nearby door and into the room.

"Well, that went badly," McGee said. "Any comments?"

I stood for a moment and tried to gather my thoughts. How much could I—should I tell McGee?

To me, the concept of a pyrokinetic was strange, but I'd seen stranger things in the last seven years. When it all started the night Cathy died with that frightening vision in the road, I am still unsure if it was real or not. But McGee was a cop, and it would all sound implausible to him.

"I was limited in what I could get," I finally said. "The glass acts as a barrier, and I need to make eye contact."

"Eye contact? Don't you—I don't know, read the ether or something?"

"I read energy, Bill. Sometimes, I get bursts of precognition—buzzes I call them. But to get information from someone, I have to meet their eyes. It's like communication occurs from their mind to mine."

"Do you think he was being honest or not?"

"Honest?" I shrugged. "As much as he's capable of."

McGee nodded. "OK, so what impressions did you get?"

"This PI is the key. He may have information on our firebug," I said.

"If he kept a copy of his research."

"I hope so. I couldn't find much on Nova at all, and according to Briback, this guy hits the mother lode."

"I'd like to know where Norris got his research," McGee said, his mouth tight.

"I take it you are familiar with Mr. Norris."

"I'm not one of his favorite people, which is fine because he's real low on my list of scumbags pretending they are in law enforcement."

McGee shut his folder and gulped one last sip from a Styrofoam cup of cold coffee.

"Don't hold back," I said. "Say what you really think."

He exhaled loudly and leaned against the table.

"I was here about a week when Mr. Norris and I had a run in. He was working on a case, a divorce, and got some photos of a husband with his mistress. Well, the wife ends up dead, and I go to Norris, who tells me he's got nothing. I threaten a warrant. Then he tries to sell me the photos, claiming he can't afford to lose money on the deal."

"A fine, upstanding citizen," I said.

"Yeah, right! Well, I nailed the husband, and the photographs came in handy for showing motive. I even got Norris to testify, but he was uncooperative the whole time."

"Now, if you had paid him…"

McGee smiled wanly. "If I paid him, he would've told any story I wanted. Hell, he would've made shit up." He crushed the cup and threw it in a nearby trash can. "Well, I guess I've got to talk to him. You free?"

"Me? Uh—sure."

"Good, can you tag along? Maybe if he sees me with another tall guy, he'll figure we're there to beat him up, and he won't mouth off."

"I'm not sure I look terribly threatening with the cane and all."

"So, hold it like it's a weapon. Come on."

We walked out of the room, through the detective's room, and made a right in the corridor. I limped along as fast I could to keep up with McGee's gait. McGee waved at the window of the processing unit, and a buzzer went off. Then he pushed his way out the door and through the release vestibule to grab the next door while the buzzer still sounded. We stepped directly out into the MPD parking lot and got into Bill's unmarked police car.

He started up and drove onto Bloomdale Avenue, heading toward the nearby town of the same name. Soon, we'd left Mountainview, and the stores became run down and the neighborhood seedy.

Finally, somewhere on the border of the town of Orange, he turned onto a side street, then pulled into a lot and parked. Across from us, there was a car that was battered almost to a state of nonrecognition as a vehicle. Oddly, it still possessed all its glass and might have even been able to run, but I doubted it. McGee pointed to a small three-story building that rose sullenly from the one-story storefronts.

"That's his office. Third floor," he said, as he got out of the car.

I pulled myself up and out and looked at the building in the clear sunlight. Then the sidewalks appeared to move, and I felt as if the ground shifted under me.

Everything was amplified and moved very slowly. I heard what sounded like a bass drum and a whooshing of wind that I recognized as my own heartbeat and breathing. I raised my head, which felt as if it now weighed two hundred pounds and the air around me had become the consistency of molasses.

I looked up: everything was in sepia tones, shifted in black and white variations as the color had drained out of the day. I could see the building McGee pointed to, but it was different.

It was on fire.

Flames shot out of the second floor and completely engulfed the third. I heard a voice in the back of my mind.

Nothing could get out of there alive...

FIFTEEN

There was a bright light, like a camera flash, and all at once the ground was back to normal. I stood on a broken street and gazed up at the building. The flames were gone, and color had returned to my surroundings.

"Len, you coming?" McGee said. He stood and watched me, puzzled. How much time had passed? I decided not much, McGee had only walked a little ahead and turned to see me frozen to my spot.

"I—uh—saw something," I said, and closed the distance between us so I could talk in low tones.

"Saw what?" McGee asked and glanced up at the building as we approached.

I decided it was best if he knew.

"Fire," I said. "The third floor was ablaze."

He looked up at the structure again as if to scrutinize the structure for any flames. Then he returned his gaze to me. "A vision?"

"Yes," I said. "I think a premonition-or perhaps a warning."

McGee stopped in his tracks. "Could it be our firebug?"

"Hallman?" I said.

"Yeah, he might think it's a good idea to eliminate the PI."

"And perhaps the police officer on his tail as well the man who slept with his mistress. We need to be on our guard."

"What do you want to do?" McGee said.

"We'll visit Mr. Norris. But if for some reason, I say we have to leave, then and there—"

"You want to make a run for it."

"No elevators, no fire escape, just go."

"Ten-four," McGee said in police jargon. We reached the lobby of the building, which was as seedy as the facade and the neighborhood suggested. Cracked paint hung in loose flaps from the ceiling and exposed the tin, which was spotted with rust and neglect. The walls were painted a vomit yellow with marks and discoloration that covered the open areas.

I stopped. "Which room?"

McGee looked back. "302."

"You head up, I'll be right there," I said.

McGee nodded and went to a door with a filthy sign that read STAIRS. He opened it and disappeared up the dimly lit staircase. The treads, though covered in grime, were marble and hinted of a time when this broken-down building was a fashionable suite of offices.

I stepped back outside and took a quick glance at my surroundings. There was not a lot of foot traffic, even on a spring day, but a few people trudged down the broken sidewalks.

No sign of the man in black.

I took a deep breath and let my mind reach out. I wanted to be aware of him if he came close. After a moment of quiet concentration, I felt at one with my surroundings. It wasn't much, but it would have to do. If Hallman approached, I was sure I would sense it, which would give us enough time to get out before fireworks started.

I took the stairs, though it was a slow process. I lifted up with my left leg, then pulled my right up after me. In what felt like an interminable amount of time, I arrived on the third floor.

The hallway was a variation of the same puke yellow and just as foul. There were several doors with dirty opaque glass windows and plastic numbers stuck to them. I walked to 302, where I could hear McGee's powerful baritone behind the glass.

"If I have to come here with a warrant…" McGee was saying.

"You shouldn't have wasted your time coming here without one, *Detective*," another voice scolded.

I opened the door and entered the room, which caused both men to turn in my direction.

McGee leaned over the crowded desk of a man who had risen from his seat. He was short, almost cylindrical in shape, with a balding head poorly hidden by a bad comb-over. He wore a cheap brown suit with the tie open and looked as much a part of the building as the faded linoleum. On the front of the desk, piled high with folders, papers, knickknacks, and outright junk, was a small plaque reading:

ROSWELL NORRIS
PRIVATE INVESTIGATOR

The room was filled with bookcases, and each was piled high with books, papers, folders, and bric-a-brac. There were several metal cabinets, also piled with papers. The place looked like a firebug's dream—flammable objects everywhere.

Norris's eyes went questioningly to me and then back to McGee.

McGee gave a nod in my direction and blurted, "He's with me."

Norris let out a breath, which caused his flabby cheeks and chin to quiver. "What didn't you bring, the goddamn Marines?"

"I'm Doctor Leonard Wise," I said, and extended my right hand. "We believe you are in danger, Mr. Norris."

He limply shook my hand in a move that was more dismissive than friendly. "I'm in danger? The only danger here is the police trying to see confidential records. I got rights, you know."

"You barely have an investigator's license," McGee said. "Look, Norris, Lonny the Match spilled the whole thing. He had you dig up information on Nova Corporation, and I want to see it."

"And I told you I gave my only copies to Mr. Briback," Norris said, his hands up. He glanced over at me and that was all I needed, a moment of eye contact.

And one other person...

"And one other person," I said aloud, the words falling out of my mouth before I took time to analyze it. Since my episode on the sidewalk, I felt I operated in a state of higher awareness, and our brief contact made me able to instantly plug into the mind of Roswell Norris.

Norris stared and gave me a questioning look as if he wondered how I could possibly know this tidbit. If I had any hesitancy about being able to reach into his mind, I dismissed it. What he knew could get him killed, and that vision of the building in flames felt— imminent. I took advantage of his gaze to reach further, put a face with my impressions.

This images came fast and furious.

"A tall man, almost my height, dressed in black, wearing sunglasses. You signed a contract with him and gave him a folder," I said, as I followed the images playing out in my mind.

"What the hell— is this?" Norris stammered, visibly shaken.

"You gave your findings to the man from the Nova Corporation," I said. "He paid you money, but you kept a copy for yourself as insurance."

Norris shifted from my eyes and turned to McGee. "What are you trying to pull, McGee?" He backed away from us both and moved to another open space in the clutter of his cramped quarters. "What is this guy, a freakin' witch or something?"

"Mister Norris, believe it or not, we're here to protect you," I said, and gave a glance to McGee to back me up. "We have reason to believe you could end up the victim of a fire."

The color fell out of Norris's face, which instantly made his unhealthy pallor look almost deathlike. He attempted bravado, but I could tell it was forced. "What do you mean, a fire?"

"Come on, Norris," McGee said. "You did the research on Nova. Lonny said you uncovered a bunch of questionable torchings. Seems like a convenient way to get rid of someone who knows too much."

"I don't know what you're talking about," Norris said, a red flush rapidly covering his pale skin like a bad paint job. "The Nova Corporation just happens to be one of my clients."

"They hired you? When did this happen?" McGee demanded as color rose in his own cheeks.

"That's none of your business," Norris sputtered.

It didn't matter whether I could still sense his thoughts—he did not possess much of a poker face, and looked guiltier than hell.

"A few days ago, right after Mishan died," I guessed.

Norris's eyes widened and his brow furrowed. "You aren't a witch," he said, raising an arm in my direction. "You're like that guy on television—the one who talks to dead people."

"All you need to know, Norris, is that you're in danger," McGee said, stepping closer to the man in order to tower over him. "But if you level with me, I might be able to save your fat ass."

"What do you want?" Norris asked, and loosened his huge collar a little more.

Danger…

I could feel the buzz, faint but there. Along with it was the sense that we were rapidly running out of time. Even though it was McGee's call, and I was just tagging along, I spoke up. "The copy you kept of the Nova file."

He frowned again. "How can you know about that?"

"Never mind!" McGee bellowed.

"Just get it," I pleaded as I moved toward the window and looked out on the street.

He's near…

The man in black was nearby and getting close. He was on his way with one purpose, to remove a loose end. "Then we have to clear out of here."

"What do you mean?" Norris said, not budging.

I turned to McGee. I felt warm. "Bill, we're running out of time."

McGee nodded. "It's your choice, Norris. I can take off and come back with a warrant, but all that might be left of you is barbecue."

The fat man looked from McGee to me and back again. Then he moved with surprising speed for a man so large. He opened a cabinet and took out a locked box, then spun a few numbers on a dial on the front and it opened.

Out of the box, he pulled a large manila folder, which he offered to McGee. As McGee took it, the man pulled out a small revolver and slipped it into his pocket.

"What are you doing, Norris?"

"I got a carry permit," Norris said, pulling a paper from his wallet that he held out to McGee. "I protect payroll shipments, you know."

McGee glanced at the paper. "You don't lift anything heavier than a donut, Norris. But the permit is legit."

He's here…

"Mister Norris, you should take anything you really need," I said, as I began to feel more than warm, actually hot.

Danger…

The buzz was rapidly turning into a scream. I turned to Bill. "We have to go!"

"Norris, you come with us," McGee said. "I need to know where you got this information."

But Roswell Norris was busy looking around his office, as if the mess were of inestimable value, trying to think what was truly precious among the stacks of chaos.

"You really think my office is going to burn down?" he whined, his voice piteous, almost blubbering.

I looked at him, deadly serious. "Yes. And you're going to burn with it if you don't get out." I turned back to Bill. "We have to go, NOW!"

Bill, with the file held high, headed for the door. "Now or never, Norris."

Norris gave one last look at his life's work, and with nothing except the large lock box clutched in his hands, followed us out the door.

We went into the hall, which had the smell of a sauna as a dry heat pervaded the air. It stung my nose.

"Hey, the landlord finally turned on the heat," Norris said, unsure if he was making a joke or not.

We walked without delay to the staircase, and McGee touched the doorknob, then pulled his hand away.

"It's hot," he said.

I looked around the hallway. "Bill, we should warn anyone else who is here. Get them out."

Bill nodded. He covered his hand with his coat and pulled the door open. I looked in.

A flash of flames shot through the door, engulfing me. I stepped back, fire on my arms and head, burning my hair.

Then, all at once, it was gone.

"What's wrong?" Bill said, watching me wince. The door just past him lay open, and the stairway was as dark as on our way up. Cool air blew in and carried the stench of ripe garbage.

"This place will be on fire any minute!" I said as I tried to center myself. It was a vision, but so intense that it shook me.

Must go now...

"Get him out," McGee said and gave Norris the manila folder. "I'll run to the rooms here, flash my badge, that'll do it."

"This is nuts!" Norris protested. "How do you know that there will be a fire?"

I pushed Norris in the direction of the stairs. "The same way I knew about your file. Now move!"

He began to descend the stairs, his hands on the dirty walls to support himself on the way down. We reached the second-floor landing, and he paused to breathe heavily.

"I…uh…usually take the elevator," he gasped. It was even hotter on this landing.

"Keep going, get out into the street," I said, and then took the envelope from him and shoved the unwieldy bundle into the waistband of my slacks, against the small of my back, where my jacket covered it. "Stay out of sight, he's out there."

"Who?"

"Your friend from Nova, the man in black with the sunglasses."

"Jack?" Norris said, blanching a bit. "Should I hide?"

"You're the private eye. Do what you do when you follow someone!" I said and pushed the door open to the second floor. Norris nodded and continued down the stairs. With the envelope, I began to go from room to room, knocking on doors and yelling "FIRE" at the top of my lungs.

Faces began to appear at the doors, mostly men. I repeated my shout, and they quickly made their way to the stairs.

"Where is it?" one man asked as he stepped into the hall and locked his door.

"Third floor," I shouted, "can't you feel how hot it is?"

Without any further questions, the men moved quickly to the stairs. It surprised me that they didn't push or claw, but went in an orderly fashion. I saw several who went down the wrong hall.

"This way!" I said. "You need to go down the stairs."

"There's another exit— different stairs!" one of the men yelled over his shoulder to me, as he pointed down the hall to drive the message home.

I took a moment and leaned on my cane. I wanted to head outside now. I wondered if everyone was out of the building, would Hallman spare the place? It was hard to say, he got his jollies by burning things, and it was clear he liked there to be victims.

I was walking toward the first stairwell when I was struck by an unearthly silence. I felt as if pressure was building up behind my eyeballs. My flesh was warm, and I could feel sweat covering my body all at once, like a protective layer of moisture.

TOO LATE...

I stopped and stepped back, my instincts on high alert, and I knew something was about to happen.

There was an odd whooshing noise, and the door to an office up ahead—where I would have been standing if I hadn't backed up—flew off its hinges. This was followed by a red-orange burst of flames. I stepped further back as a loud percussion broke the eerie silence and the sound of the explosion filled my ears as if I were inside of it. A wave of hot air knocked me off my feet, and I fell, trying to roll as I hit the floor.

I looked up to see the entire hallway on fire, which blocked the stairs I'd descended. The exploded doorway was charred like a gaping maw, a wall of flames where the door had been.

I pulled myself to my feet with my cane as a burning liquid oozed along the floor, trails of flame in its wake.

I hurriedly limped in the direction I'd seen the other men go with the hope that exit wasn't cut off. I had only one chance because soon this hallway would be an inferno. The air grew thick with the dark smoke, which bit at my nose and stung my throat. The hallway now had a thick haze, giving everything a ghostly look.

It happens so fast, I thought to myself. And another thought came unbidden: *That wasn't his power. There was something incendiary—maybe a bomb. He planned this, planted explosives he could activate at any time.*

I began to cough and knew I would have to get close to the floor and crawl if I didn't find the door soon. The vapor had grown dense, and I moved through a fog that allowed me to see only a few feet on either side. I looked up to see an unlit lighting fixture, a triangular bulb with the word "Exit" stenciled on it in chipped and faded red paint. The door was to my left as I pushed through and slammed it behind me.

The air was cooler in the stairway, and even though it held the scent of the garbage, to me it smelled sweet. I turned to find that the lights in this vestibule were completely out. It was utterly black and windowless. For a moment, I felt panic rise up in my throat. What if instead of a hallway, I'd accidentally stepped into someone's office and was trapped here?

I calmed myself with the knowledge that offices didn't usually stink. I became aware of the moving air. The heat of the fire had created a breeze as it sucked air from the outside to feed itself. I might be temporarily unable to see, but I did have the good luck to be carrying the tool of any blind man. I gently tapped my cane in front of me, using it to feel for the stairs.

A part of me wanted to run, but I knew that a tumble down a flight of stairs would do damage to my one good leg and trap me here permanently. I heard the sound of the cane striking metal and felt the vibration of the contact. Moving carefully forward, I touched a metal newel with my left hand. I held it tightly, and my cane dipped down the first stair.

I leaned and grasped the railing, lowered my right leg down the first stair. *Success!* The marble step was under my foot. Even without my vision, I was able to move in my usual pattern going down a flight of stairs, holding tight to the banister in case a step was further away than I planned.

In moments, I was down the steps and looking at a rectangle of light, which I guessed was sunlight as it leaked in around a door.

I reached out and felt a crash bar beneath my grip, then shoved it. The light from the street poured in, dazzling my eyes. Even though it was afternoon and the sun was setting, it was still so bright, I held my hand up to shield my eyes as I stepped out into the street.

I could feel a huge pair of arms grab me and lead me gingerly away from the building.

"McGee?" I said, hoping it wasn't Jack Hallman come to finish me off.

"Yeah, it's me, Len," McGee's voice rang out, and I found I sucked at the air greedily. I went from shielding my eyes to fluttering them. They stung from my encounter with the smoke.

I coughed as I got across the street. The sound of fire engines grew nearer. McGee sat me on a bench, and his hand slapped my back—not lightly.

"You're smoldering," he said. "There are burns all over your jacket."

"I'm damn lucky I didn't get taken out," I said as I rubbed my eyes and coughed a bit more. I fought to not lose my Mexican lunch. "There was…an explosion."

"I was down the stairs when I heard it. What the hell was it?"

"A bomb or something…I don't know," I said, my voice sounding strained from all the smoke I'd inhaled. "It took an entire office with it. I think one floor below Norris's."

McGee looked up at the building, and I raised my head to follow his gaze. Although I was standing at a different location than when I had my vision, it was eerily similar. The flames came out through a set of windows on the second floor and rose up on the outside of the building to the third.

Danger...

A buzz went off in my head—a sense of warning. My head shot back to McGee. "Where's Norris?"

"I thought he was with you," McGee said, turned from me to study the crowd.

"I sent him downstairs while I warned the second floor," I said, my voice becoming more congested as I spoke, and I finished with a racking cough. I spat out a darkly colored bit of phlegm and tried to stand.

"Easy, big fellow," McGee said, giving me a helping hand.

"Says the one man bigger than I am."

"I'm all muscle. You're lithe."

"I wasn't planning a career as a dancer. Any sign of him?"

"I can't see him. Perhaps he made a break for it. We parked across from his car."

"That banged-up monstrosity was *his* car?" I said. "Great idea for a detective, anyone could spot that!"

"In this neighborhood, it fits right in. Can you walk?"

"Yeah," I said, and got my cane under me. McGee and I strode gingerly through the crowd on our way back to the parking lot. Several uniformed policemen had arrived, and they helped disperse the crowd as fire engines clamored onto the side street.

"Shouldn't you help?" I asked.

"This isn't my jurisdiction, and I'd only be in the way. I'll talk to whoever is in charge once the fire is under control and we find Norris," McGee said. "Not that I can offer much insight."

"You were—are—a witness."

"Not to very much, and I'm not sure what happened," McGee said as we turned a corner. "How did you…"

He stopped cold and stared into the distance. I was still blocked from what he could see by the corner of a building.

"What is it?" I asked as I came around the corner. In the parking lot, McGee's Chevy sat, unbothered. However, the older car I'd noticed when we arrived was on fire.

McGee took off like a shot towards the flaming heap as I glanced around and tried to sense if Hallman was nearby, ready to ambush us. But I didn't detect him. He'd accomplished his goal and left. I followed McGee, worried that he might try something foolish. The car was totally ablaze, and the gas tank could explode at any minute.

I yelled to him, "There's nothing you can do."

He got as close as the heat would let him, trying to see past the smoke to peer inside.

Going to blow…

"It's going to explode, McGee. Back off!" I screamed as loud as I could.

McGee nodded, and hurriedly headed toward his car, where I joined him.

"Christ," McGee said, visibly shaken. "He was in there. With his stupid gun drawn."

The sound of a shot made McGee flinch and duck. He gave me a "get down" hand signal, and he crouched next to the Chevy, opening the car door as a shield. I lay down behind him—I don't do crouching.

"Someone shooting at us?" I asked.

"The bullets in his gun—the heat is setting them off," McGee said. "Still might be dangerous. You stay put, I'm going to get one of the firemen." He rose up, eyes fixed on the burning car. "If we can put that out, maybe forensics can—"

As if on cue, there was another huge explosion, bigger than the one inside the building, and the car turned bright orange and red as a pillar of fire rose up, towered by smoke.

McGee fell back, on top of me, and struggled to get up. He was as large and heavy as he looked, and if the situation weren't so dire, it would have been comical as we endeavored to get to our feet like Laurel and Hardy in an old two-reeler.

"Christ!" McGee roared, as he stood up and peered at the debris of the car as it burned.

I stood a bit more gingerly. "No chance for evidence now."

"Jesus, I never liked the guy, but what a way to go!" McGee said, turning to the wall. Then, with a deep breath, he faced me. "Did he have the envelope?"

I reached into the back of my pants and extracted the thick stack of wrapped paper.

McGee nodded. "Good work, Len." He looked back at the remains of the car. It had burned so quickly that there was little left aside from the metal frame. The tires had melted flat, the rubber oozing and flaming, and there was a black stick figure in the vehicle, all that remained of Roswell Norris.

"I hope there's something in these papers that was worth dying for," McGee observed.

JACK'S DIARY: THURSDAY

Another good day, then again, every day is a good day for me. A few more loose ends, and I'll be home free. The Bahamas are becoming very tempting, and Bermuda is always nice.

I will miss my home here, with such a lovely view of my city. But a little time away will make memories short and unsolved cases get filed very deeply.

If things get too hot—now there's an expression—I'll just leave and let the lawyers retrieve the funds. However, I want to make sure the insurance company will pay out. Perhaps reducing their building to a smoldering ash would be a strong inducement?

I took care of that fool detective. There is only one way they could have gotten his name; they tracked down the firebug. I told Mishan that eliminating the blackmailing bastard was the best choice, but he didn't agree. He felt paying him off, getting the files, was the better choice.

Now it's all about containment. I paid the detective, got his copy of the folder. I made sure I could rent an office under his and then secreted several large cans of acetone there. That made things so much easier. I only had to focus on one room. The acetone did the rest.

I didn't mind arson being suspected with that building. After all, I didn't have any insurance on it. But wait until they find out who rented the office that burned!

It was such a feeling of power when I confronted that fool Norris in his car. I knew he would head right for it, could almost sense the thoughts in his head. He went to his broken-down vehicle, and there I stood behind a convenient telephone pole. It was so dramatic—I revealed myself as he started it up. Then he actually pointed his gun at me! At me! It took all my self control not to laugh at him. He was shaking so much I doubt he could've hit me even if he'd gotten off a shot.

Besides, in seconds, it was over for him, his car in flames. I would've made it take longer, perhaps let him know what was coming and toyed with him a bit, but I could sense the damn cripple nearby. I'd hoped I'd trapped him in the building, but he'd gotten out and was on the way. I had to make it quick and leave.

However, I will toy with someone. The cripple would be my first choice, yet I still sense he could be a danger to me. I dream of torturing him slowly on small, focused places on his body. Perhaps a toe, or a finger, then working to small points on his torso. Perhaps his genitals, that would be fun! And it would be a chance to practice focusing my abilities. I could make it take hours or even days.

Then again, that insurance bitch is someone meaningful to him. I wonder why. Old friend? New lover? He must not have cared much for poor Wendy if he's doing the nasty with this woman. He's so average-looking, and yet he seems to have no shortage of willing females. He probably isn't as choosy as I am.

That would be rich. Take care of my insurance nuisance and eliminate another of the cripple's lovers! I might even be able to use her to lure him to me. The coup de grace before I leave town and lay low for a while.

I like that plan. I like it a great deal.

SIXTEEN

Over an hour later, McGee and I were at the Mountainview police station, in the detective's bull pen. He left me there for a minute and came back, the soot washed off his face. He held his jacket in his left hand, wiping a damp paper towel on it where he'd tumbled in the dirt.

He'd been totally quiet on the drive back, but with a seething anger just under the surface. He'd done all the right things and spoken with the police of the City of Orange. He made a point to leave his name and number and made requests for a copy of the autopsy on Norris to be faxed to him. Now alone in the quiet room, he addressed me.

"Mrs. Hoefler is due in at six," he said, glancing at his watch. "After the job you did with Norris, I want you here."

"Sure, Bill," I said quietly.

He sat across from me heavily and looked at his watch. "You're going to have to get cleaned up, you look like crap."

"Thank you," I said as I got up.

"But before you do, Len," he said, and motioned for me to sit back down.

I lowered myself into the seat. *Whatever it is, here it comes.*

"I think you know more than you're telling me," McGee demanded.

I opened my mouth to protest, but he held up his hand.

"Now, don't start giving me a song and dance—"

"I don't dance," I interjected.

"You listen. Maybe you can read minds and get these buzzes and all that. Good for you. I'm glad you can, probably saved *both* our asses today. But I'm a cop, and I know when my partner is not being honest with me."

I was touched. "I didn't know you considered me your partner."

"On this case, I do, Len. But the point is you know something— and you're not telling me."

"It's pretty out there, Bill."

"Out there?" he rose up and began to wipe his jacket with the paper towel again. "People burning to death? Mishan, then Wendy, both with no explanation? Then, we almost get fried in a building with a goddamn bomb, and we find Norris fricasseed in his car. This whole case is completely out there, Len, and if you have a theory, I need to know it."

I sat there, stunned. Bill was a good cop and perhaps the idea I couldn't share what I believed wasn't due to his limitations, it was due to mine. I was experienced in a world of the supernatural, where the line between the known and unknown blur.

It was time to be honest.

"OK," I said, not knowing exactly where to begin. "I have a theory about all of this, and it makes sense." I stopped and decided to change tack. "Do you have a candle?"

"A candle?" he frowned. "Why?"

"It might make more sense if I demonstrate."

"Might take me a couple minutes to find one."

"Good, then I'll get cleaned up. A candle, and a lighter or matches," I said, getting up. "Where is the bathroom?"

Bill stepped into the corridor and pointed. "Second door on the left."

I tapped my way to the small tiled room. A mirror over the sink showed my face burnished by soot and my hair askew. I spent a few minutes washing and arranging my hair into a more acceptable position. I also made sure to cover the stitched wound on the back of my head as carefully as I could.

I took off my jacket and examined it. Black holes, some the size of a dime, were burned in it, some penetrating through the lining.

"Now I really have a personal reason to nail this bastard," I said aloud, my voice echoing in the empty bathroom. "He fried my tweed!"

I cleaned it up as best as I could, and looking much more presentable, I located Bill in Interrogation Room B. Bill stood there with a stubby white candle melted onto a dirty white saucer.

"Had some emergency candles from the last time the power went out. Must be years old. We have a backup generator now."

I sat at the other end of the table, facing him. "Can you please light it?" I said and shut my eyes as I cleared my mind. "And please turn off the overheads."

I heard Bill's clothes rustle as he moved. "OK, it's lit. But what is this about?"

I opened my eyes. The room was darker, though light still flowed from the bullpen through the half-open door.

The small candle was very easy to see, and I focused on it. I could see all of it, the yellow on the top becoming darker orange and fading into a dark blue which danced on the wick. I tried to *feel* it, become one with it. There was no longer a separation between myself and the flame: I was one with it.

Still focused on the candle flame, I heard my own voice as if it came from someone else. "Pyrokinesis."

I concentrated the way Doctor Kohl and I had practiced years earlier, and the flame went out.

"Damn!" Bill exclaimed.

"There's more," I said. "Watch the flame."

"Len, the candle is out."

In the room, now darker, I could make out the silhouette of the candle and Bill's hulking form behind it.

The candle flickered once, and a flame appeared back on the top.

I could hear McGee gasp, and I shut my eyes to break my concentration.

"You can turn on the lights," I said as I leaned back in my chair.

The overhead fluorescents sparked, and the room was again filled with white light, eclipsing the small candle flame.

"How did you…?" McGee said, an expression of awe on his face.

"You can blow out the candle," I said and rubbed my eyes. I was tired. I'd used a lot of mental power between my confrontation with Hallman and my reading of Norris. I had overtaxed myself with this little demonstration.

"So, what's the trick?" McGee asked.

"No trick, Bill. Pyrokinesis," I said and looked at him. "The ability to control fire with nothing but your mind."

Bill sat at the table, watching me quizzically.

"What you've just seen," I went on, "is little more than a parlor trick. I've seen people make the flame grow and shrink, even move to the left or right, through concentrated will and intention."

"Yeah, but this…" Bill said. "You snuffed it out and relit it."

"It appeared that way," I explained. "But all I did was pull the flame into my mind. For a moment or two, it wasn't burning because the energy that makes combustion occur was taken away from the candle and pulled into me."

Bill frowned. "How is that possible?"

"It might just be a mental image, Bill, but it works." I still felt tired and leaned heavily on the table. "Do you have any water?"

"Plenty, sure," Bill said, all but leaping up.

I nodded, and Bill stepped out of the room. I closed my eyes and yawned, and by the time I was done, Bill was there with a Styrofoam cup filled with clear liquid, which he placed in front of me.

"So," Bill said, a strange light in his eyes. "What if there was someone who could do your parlor trick on a larger scale?"

I smiled. My little demonstration pointed Bill's mind in the correct direction.

"Exactly," I said, as I picked up the cup. "What I just did was as far as Doctor Kohl and I took it. We used it as a concentration exercise."

"If someone took it further," he said and began to pace the floor as I drank greedily. "Someone with a gift…"

"And he practiced the one ability," I said, picking up where McGee left off. "Until he could start fires. Remember what Mishan told Briback?"

"That he had a partner who could just make fire come out of his head," McGee said with a nod. He began to pace the room again, so full of energy, he needed to let it out. "It fits. Mishan's death, then Wendy's—even Norris's." He stopped in mid-stride. "But when he did it to Wendy, why did he spare you?"

"I don't know. Maybe he thought I had a concussion from the fall."

"Jesus, Len," McGee said. He exhaled heavily and shook his head. "You're right, this is out there."

"Only a theory," I said.

"This is not something I can bring to Captain Harris or even Lieutenant Butler. And what can we do? How do we stop someone like that?"

"Let's look at it," I said as I put the cup aside. "It must take a lot of energy. And I doubt he could strike at two targets at once."

"What are you talking about? He burned the building and then fried Norris."

"No, Bill. He set off something stored in the building, and it could have been anything from cans of paint thinner to a fertilizer bomb. That takes a lot less power than what he did to Wendy or her house. So he starts that fire and waits near Norris's car. He's still got enough power to finish him off."

"What are his limits?"

"I can guess," I said, shaking my head. "There must be some physical side effects. I met the guy, he wears sunglasses. Jenny—uh, Mrs. Baines—said he claimed uveitis—that's a sensitivity to light."

"How do you know that?"

"I started out in medicine, Bill."

"Damn, next you'll tell me you were a psychiatrist."

"No," I said with a smirk. "I just studied to be one."

"And in your free time, you paint like Van Gogh and sculpt like Rodin?" Bill said. "Where do we go from here?"

I picked up the manila folder from the desk and held it out to him.

"Norris died for this. Let's hope there is something we can use to stop him."

Bill opened it and extracted Norris's file.

"That reminds me," I said. "Briback knew about Wendy's parents and knew she made money on their death. That might be in there, and it might be useful when questioning Mrs. Hoefler."

Bill glanced at his watch. "We have about twenty minutes." He handed me half of the papers and started to paw through his own stack. We each looked at our papers. I found mine weren't terribly well organized, reports of deaths, unusual fires, with cards stapled to the corner, where Norris jotted notes. Under a card marked "Wallace," I found newspaper clippings and certificates.

"Here it is!" I said.

McGee got up and stood behind me, reading over my shoulder.

"What do these notations on the card mean?" I asked, indicating a series of initials that seemed random.

"Don't know," McGee said, then stabbed at the papers with his index finger. "You're right, this is it! Let me see."

I dutifully passed the pages to McGee, who took them and studied them as he paced around the table. He let out a whistle. "Wendy and her sister both received over a million dollars for their parents' deaths. There were more than six insurance companies involved."

He let the papers fall to the table. "Damn, Norris was better than I thought. This must have been difficult to track down."

"Does it give you what you need?" I asked.

He glanced at his watch. "Hopefully enough to loosen up Mrs. Hoefler."

SEVENTEEN

At six ten, McGee brought Janice Hoefler into Interrogation Room C, the "Soft Interview" room, where I waited seated at the round table.

It was going to be tricky. I was tired and had done more mental work in this one day than in the last six weeks.

Mrs. Hoefler was flanked by her husband, who wore a shadow of a beard on his face, making him appear even more simian than before. Escorting them was the ever-present, clean-cut Officer Galland.

"We'd like to speak to Mrs. Hoefler alone, Mr. Hoefler," McGee was saying as they came in.

"Who is he?" Hoefler said, indicating me.

"Doctor Leonard Wise. Civilian consultant on this case. We just need to ask your wife some questions."

"She has to be represented by an attorney!" Hoefler said.

"And where is your attorney?" McGee asked.

"It's me!" he said as he stood up straighter, lifting his head for effect.

"Mr. Hoefler, it's an obvious conflict of interest, representing your wife in this situation. Besides, we're just checking a few facts. Neither of you is being charged with a crime," McGee said with a disarming air of ease.

I looked over at Jack Hoefler until he glanced at me and our eyes locked. I moved into his mind.

You want to call another attorney...

Aloud I said, "Do you want to call another attorney to represent you?"

From my influence the idea seemed so logical to him at that moment that he rose. "I want to call another attorney," Hoefler said, his eyes still locked on mine.

"That's fine, use the phone at the front desk," McGee said with a look of amazement at me. "This officer will escort you." He exchanged a look with Galland, who nodded as he got the message.

Hoefler broke away from me, but I felt the idea was implanted. Then he turned to his wife. "Honey, if they ask you anything, you don't have to answer until Barry gets here."

"Yes, Jack," she said. I could tell she wanted to please her husband. Hoefler gave me a puzzled glance and walked out the door followed by Galland. McGee shut the door after them, then locked it surreptitiously.

It was now just him and me with Janice Hoefler.

"How are you tonight?" he asked quietly, as he sat across from her, a smile on his face. He looked like the nicest guy in the world. "Can I get you anything, water, coffee?"

"No, I'm fine," she said, as she held her handbag tightly in her lap.

"We just have a couple of questions," McGee said, as he pulled open the file and extracted the pages I'd seen earlier.

I watched her carefully. She was frightened, as if the fact that her husband left the room, even for a moment, left her unsure how to act.

"I want to ask about your parents' death," McGee said.

"I thought this was about Wendy," Janice replied and clutched her handbag harder.

"It is. But in doing some research, I thought it seemed your parents were killed under odd circumstances."

"No, they died in a car accident," she said, the grip on her bag made her knuckles grow white.

"Yes, but there was a fire. The bodies were burned very badly," McGee said, focused on the papers. "You and your sister made a lot of money from insurance policies on the accident."

"They were old—things happen. We were just protecting ourselves," she said quietly, her eyes flitting from the table to McGee, then to her handbag and to me.

Bill went on. "I understand, Mrs. Hoefler, but it's odd that both incidents involved fire. And an organization your sister worked for has a history of fire-related insurance claims."

"I'm sure you've heard of them," I said, which drew her eyes to me. "It's called the Nova Corporation."

The effect was as if I'd slapped her. Her eyes filled with tears and she looked down. "I don't know anything about that…"

McGee dropped the file folder on the table with a thud, which made her jump.

"Come on, Mrs. Hoefler," he said, the nice guy persona gone. "Your sister worked for these people for years. She bought a big house and a fancy car. And she never told you about it or explained how she came into so much money?"

"My husband...should be coming back..." Mrs. Hoefler stammered.

"Yes, he should, but let's keep to the facts, shall we? Your parents die in a fire—a car accident, and you happen to have a lot of insurance with double indemnity for a traffic accident. It was as if you *knew* what was going to happen."

"Traffic accidents are the leading cause of death with older drivers," she said just above a whisper. It sounded like something she had been coached to say.

"There is no statute of limitations on murder, Mrs. Hoefler, and I'm looking into your parents' death. If I find there's a good reason to bring it to the District Attorney..."

"You don't understand," Janice Hoefler said, tears forming in her eyes.

McGee knelt at her chair, and his voice got low. "Look, Mrs. Hoefler, these people killed your sister, they burned her alive. I can't catch them if I don't know how your sister was mixed up in all of this."

"I shouldn't say anything until Jack gets back."

"Mrs. Hoefler?" I said, which got her to turn to me and make eye contact. I gently reached out with my mind, not to force my way, as I did with her husband, but to gently reassure her. "I'm sure there was a good reason for what happened to your parents."

Her eyes grew wide, and she reached into her bag. Pulling out a tissue, she dabbed her face with it.

McGee glanced at the door. He'd obviously gotten Galland to keep Hoefler busy, but our time was rapidly running out.

"Our—fa-fa-father," she said. "He m-m-messed with us when we were kids."

McGee's voice went quiet. "Messed with you?"

"B-b-both of us. First Wendy, then me, later on. It was horrible—he was a m-m-monster," she said, and her body began to shake all over. I gently took her free hand and held it. She looked at me.

"It's all right," I said quietly as I perceived images of dark rooms where fear and pain were commonplace.

"Wendy wanted him dead and my m-m-mother, too. She l-l-let it happen—must have known…"

"But you didn't want to hurt anyone," I said.

"No, I wanted to avoid them. Wendy got me out of that house, helped me get on my own. We had so little money. Then I met J-Jack, and he was so strong," she said, looking to the door to see if her knight returned.

"So, Wendy got a job working for Nova," I said.

"She said she met someone and said that she could take care of our f-f-father so he'd never hurt us again. And we'd have money, lots of money," she said and gazed at the door again. Her attitude changed, and she became angry. "I didn't care about the money. I just wanted that b-b-bastard to suffer!"

This caused a complete breakdown of her emotional barriers, and she began to cry in earnest into the tissue, which she rapidly tore to shreds.

There was a knock at the door, and McGee walked over and unlocked it. Jack Hoefler came into the room with Galland beside him, a looming shadow.

"Wait outside," McGee said, and Galland nodded as the door closed.

Jack Hoefler looked very rumpled at this point. He'd apparently been on the go since the morning, and this was just one more thing. He looked at his crying wife. "What did you tell them?"

"I TOLD THEM THE TRUTH!" she yelled at her husband, and his eyes grew wide.

"Janice," he hissed. "You should wait for the lawyer."

"I SHOULD! I SHOULD!" she yelled and stood. Tears smeared her mascara, which came down her face in two lines. "You always tell me what I should do, and I should do it *this* way, or *that* way. I don't have to do what you tell me."

She sat down and began to cry again while she pulled another tissue from her purse.

Color rose on Hoefler's cheeks, but his voice stayed calm. "You should know that anything she has said without an attorney will not be admissible in court."

"She has said enough," McGee went on boldly, "to indict you as a co-conspirator in the murder of your in-laws."

Hoefler's eyes grew wide. "I had nothing to do with that."

"OK, so prove it," McGee said, his arms folded.

"It was Wendy's idea," Janice Hoefler said.

"Janice," Jack Hoefler hissed. "Hush!"

"Counselor," McGee said. "If you are involved in conspiracy to commit murder, you must know that we can prosecute you under the RICO statutes."

"It was all Wendy," Hoefler spat bitterly. "Tell him, Janice."

Janice raised her head, much calmer. "We'd been going to counseling because of—intimacy problems. That's how Jack knew about—about—" She began to cry again.

"I wanted to confront the old bastard," Hoefler said. "Bring him up on charges. But Wendy, she came to me with this plan. She had us fill out these papers, insurance forms on them."

"How did you get them to sign?" Bill said, his eyes going from one to the other. "Or did you forge the signatures?"

"Wendy went to them, acted like it was a misunderstanding," Janice said, "G-got them to sign."

"Wendy was working for Nova by then," Jack said, exasperated.

"Is that where she met Jack?" I asked, the image of the black-clad man in my mind.

"Yeah, they were an item. I never met the guy, though. Wendy said he wasn't sociable," Hoefler said. "Look, I'm telling you, Wendy came to us, told me to invite her parents for dinner, and she'd take care of the rest."

"So, as the police report stated, they came to your house for dinner," McGee said.

"It was h-h-horrible," Janice said. "That m-man eating at m-my table." This began a fresh round of tears from her.

"Wendy gave Janice something," Hoefler explained. "I don't know what—Valium, I guess. So Janice was real calm and quiet during the dinner. But you should've seen Wendy. She was carrying on like it was a family reunion. She laughed and acted real friendly. Then after dinner, she pulls her cell phone out of her purse and makes a call as the parents pull out of the driveway. Says what they're driving and asks whoever is on the other end if he's in the right place and all. Then she hangs up and says, 'It's all set.'"

"She had him killed!" Janice said and raised her head again, an odd expression of mixed grief and joy on her face. "Just like that!"

"But we don't know how it was done, and we had nothing to do with any of it," Jack Hoefler said as if it were a sound defense.

"But you benefitted from the insurance payout," McGee said, as a knock came at the door. In two strides, Bill went to the door and opened it a crack. Galland stuck his head in and whispered something that made Bill nod.

"Show him back," McGee said before turning and facing the room. "Your lawyer is here, Mr. Hoefler."

"Are you arresting us?" Hoefler demanded. "Because none of this will hold up in court."

"No, but I will be letting the insurance company know, and they may press charges for fraud."

"You won't get anywhere without evidence, and there is none," Hoefler snorted.

I turned to Mrs. Hoefler as McGee and Jack Hoefler stared daggers at each other. "Will you be all right, Mrs. Hoefler?"

She had been quiet for a while and appeared to compose herself. She blew her nose and nodded.

"Yes," she said, "I'm just glad it's finally out in the open." Then she turned to face me. "Do you think what happened to Wendy—that she was being punished for what she—we—did to our parents?"

I shook my head. But once again, I was stunned that the Wendy I'd known was just an illusion. She had been very cold-blooded in using her Jack to kill her father and stepmother and make money at the same time. What kind of woman could put into action a premeditated plan to kill so callously?

"Her mistake was getting involved with Jack," I said, and met Janice's eyes. I tried to send her energy, send her love. She was a fragile soul who had been through far too much for her early twenties. The room began to fade, and only her eyes were there.

I could sense her, the real person hidden deep within her own mind, covered in layers of fear. "Can you tell us anything about Jack that might help?"

Her eyes were fixed on mine, and her voice possessed a dreamy quality. "I never met him, but she said he had a place in Mountainview."

"A place?" I said as I leaned closer. There was nothing but her eyes.

"Wendy said that the view was spectacular. You could see the entire city," she said, and I could feel her pull a bit back as confusion clouded her face. "What's happening? I feel strange."

I was not sure what was going on in the room anymore. I could hear Bill arguing with Jack Hoefler, but their voices were a million miles away. All that existed was her eyes and the beautiful soul I could sense behind them.

Shh! I said, or rather, merely thought. Our eyes were locked, and there was more between us than words could offer. *I want you to know you don't have to be afraid.*

I'm scared all the time, she thought back to me.

Let it go. You have more courage than anyone I know.

Her expression changed as the truth of this became clear to her in a moment of epiphany.

The door burst open, and a short man in a bad suit walked in carrying a briefcase, which broke our eye contact. The room grew in brightness around us, and I was aware of my surroundings again.

"This interview is over!" he announced as if he made a guest appearance on a television show.

"Yes, it is," said McGee. "And I would advise your clients to stay available."

"They are not to be seen without me present. Mrs. Hoefler is under psychiatric care!"

"Oh, shut up, Barry," Janice Hoefler said as she stood. Suddenly the weak, nervous woman was gone, replaced by someone new, and both Jack Hoefler and lawyer Barry gaped at her, openmouthed. She responded to their stares with, "You don't have to gawk, Jack."

Jack closed his mouth. "Janice," he said, a warning tone in his voice.

"And don't start with that tone, Jack," Janice insisted. "I've never liked it."

She turned to McGee. "Detective, I will be available to help, and I will testify. I don't need my lawyer. I want you to catch the man who killed my sister."

"I want that as well, ma'am," McGee said, his eyebrows raised. He gave a quick glance to me, and I shrugged.

"Very good," she said and picked up her purse. "Now, Jack, take me home."

"O-of course," he said as he exchanged a glance with Barry, who stared back.

She turned to face me. "I'm so very glad to have met you, Doctor—Wise, was it?"

"That's correct, Mrs. Hoefler."

"Janice, please," she said, a smile growing on her face. "I feel energized, better than I have in a long time," she added, walking to the door, where Jack waited for her.

"Are you OK?" Jack said, unsure who this woman was.

"Better than I have been in years, Jack. We need to make some changes…"

"We can discuss it at home," Jack said in a loud whisper.

"And believe me, we will," she replied. "Good night, Detective, Doctor." With that, she swept out of the room, Jack and Barry in close pursuit as Galland took up the rear. I leaned back in my chair, so exhausted I could've fallen asleep right then and there.

"What the hell was that?" McGee asked as he nudged my arm. "OK, Svengali, what did you do?"

"What makes you think I did anything, Bill?" I said, opening my eyes to look at my large friend.

"She comes in here Mrs. Mousey and leaves as Wonder Woman! I saw the two of you in that staring contest, and kept Hoefler busy, but what the hell did you do?"

"Nothing really, Bill. She was always that strong, she was just afraid. But deep inside, under the fear of her husband and father, there was someone who wanted to take control of her life. I just helped her let that person out."

"Len, you aren't a psychic, you're a goddamn miracle worker. What do you do next, raise the dead?"

I rubbed my eyes. "I'd be happy just to raise myself up from this chair. Bill, I'm all in, can you give me a ride home?"

"Sure, no problem. Did you get anything—you know—your special way?"

"Wendy told Janice that Jack lived in a building where he had a great view of the city. Does that mean anything to you?"

"Jack Hallman's office is on the fourth floor of a building downtown—but I don't think he can see the whole city."

"Do you have enough to make an arrest?" I asked.

"For what, innuendo? Mrs. Hoefler's testimony will help, but it's not proof that he's the firebug. We have the name Jack, and the rest is hearsay. I need more, Len, if I want to get the DA to issue a warrant to search his office. Also, if your theory is right, he can fricassee anyone who shows up. We need an airtight case, and probably a SWAT team. I'll go over these files we got from Norris and try to find grounds for an indictment."

Even as tired as I was, I said, "I want to be in on the takedown, Bill."

"The takedown? Look at you!"

"I'm serious, Bill. I believe I can neutralize his ability—though maybe only a little. If I'm there, you might have a better chance."

"I'll just have to make sure Tice isn't around," McGee said. "He's still looking at you as a suspect."

"I don't think he would accept our pyrokinesis theory."

"I'm having trouble accepting it myself, and I'm much more open-minded," McGee said while he gathered the files and slipped them under his arm. "Come on, I'll drive you home."

· · ·

Fifteen minutes later, I was unlocking the door at the Baines's house. It was only after eight, but all I wanted to do was sleep.

"Jenn?" I heard Jon say as he came out to the foyer.

"Just me, Jon. Isn't Jenny home?"

"No, she had to meet a client, seemed very annoyed about it, last minute and everything."

"Oh? Isn't that unusual?"

He shrugged. "I don't know. Back in her early days with the company, she always had to go look at busted cars and damaged houses. Now she only goes out when it's a large estate or settlement."

"But it does happen?" I asked as a feeling of uneasiness hit my gut.

"Yeah. It's rare, but she does it occasionally," Jon said as he walked with me to the kitchen. "Jeez, what happened to your jacket?"

I remembered the burns and shrugged. "I had a day."

"You look like hell. You want something to eat?"

"No, I'll just turn in," I said as waves of exhaustion replaced my fear. I headed toward my room.

"Good night, Len," he said, and returned to the living room.

I sat down on the bed, feeling like an old man, and undressed, examining the burns and holes in my jacket. It was indeed ruined. I threw it into the small trash can in the room, which it overflowed. The shirt was also a fright, and it quickly followed. I went into the bathroom and took a hot shower, washing the smell of smoke and burned hair out of my pores.

I put on my one pair of pajamas—in case I was awakened by Jenn. I didn't want to be caught again in the altogether. I slipped between the sheets and very quickly, I was dozing.

My mind, however, still operated on higher levels.

I floated in a warm darkness, but I heard voices. They seemed far away, and as I focused on the sound, a bar materialized around me. Not a noisy one, just a relaxed place. It appeared to be part of a hotel.

There was a circular bar of polished wood, and a bearded bartender stood dutifully behind it. There were tables set throughout the room with two and three chairs, backed with Day-Glo green vinyl, which seemed a glaring mistake near the good wood of the bar.

Pictures hung on the wall, reproductions—not good ones—of famous works of art. *Birth of Venus*, the *Mona Lisa*, a couple of Botticelli's, a Monet. Between the bright chairs and the faux art, the room had the atmosphere of an aging bordello.

I was in a position to watch the room clearly, but my perspective was from the corner of the room, as if I floated there, able to watch the comings and goings of people as they moved in and out the door.

What an odd dream, I thought to myself.

There was a woman seated at one of the tables who watched the door. She looked familiar, and yet strange at the same time. She wore a pantsuit with an open collar and a frilly shirt. She was wearing makeup and I couldn't quite place her. She rose and waved a hand in the air to attract someone who walked in the door.

The person who approached was Jenny Baines.

All at once, I floated near the table to watch the scene from close range.

Jenny shook hands with the woman and sat down. She called her a name, Kate or Katy. Their voices were muffled, as if they spoke from faraway. I tried to focus on what they said and caught only a few words here and there.

They ordered drinks, and a young man, tall and thin, who looked as if his waiter uniform was made for a much larger man, dutifully wrote on a pad, then went to fetch their drinks.

Everything seemed to happen so quickly, and I still couldn't place the face of the woman. Her features weren't gentle, though the powder and rouge softened the jawline. She wasn't thin, and my mind raced over the last few days to try to recall *where* I had seen her.

The drinks arrived at their table, a glass of wine for the woman, and a ginger ale for Jenny, who stirred it to remove some of the fizz. The woman held her glass firmly, almost in a mannish way. That's when it hit me.

Denise Haskell.

Wearing a wig with longer hair, all dolled up and looking quite nice in her pantsuit, she appeared far different than in the man's black suit she wore at the funeral or the white shirt and apron she'd had on in the coffee bar—but it was her.

Why was she meeting with Jenny?

As they spoke, Denise pointed at one of the fake paintings on the wall with a questioning look. Jenn turned her head, and everything seemed to stand still. From the activity going at such a clip that I could barely keep up, it now slowed to a crawl, and I could see every detail.

As Jenny turned to gaze at the picture, Denise moved her hand to Jenny's drink. In her palm was a small vial from which several drops of a blue liquid poured out and dripped into the ginger ale. The drink shifted color a tiny amount, but in the bad lighting of the bar, it was not noticeable.

Things returned to the previous speed. I wanted to grab the drink, push it away, get Jenny out of there. But I was nothing more than an invisible observer.

Jenny raised the glass to her lips and drank several times as I watched. I wanted to yell, to touch her mind, but I couldn't in my current state of nonexistence. I've undergone out-of-body experiences before, and I've yet to get the hang of how to accomplish anything in a state somewhere between reality and a dream.

They continued to talk, a pantomime of movement where I couldn't quite hear the words. Jenny's hand went to her head, and she rubbed her temples. Her mouth moved, giving an explanation as she reached for her purse to get up and leave. Denise gently touched her arm and said something, and Jenny sat heavily back on the chair. Denise looked concerned and got up for a moment to get water from the bar. The waiter came over and knelt next to Jenny in her seat.

That's when *he* walked in.

Jack, in all his long black leather coat and turtleneck glory. He wore a smile on his face as his sunglasses reflected the lights from the bar.

Jenny blinked and rose from her seat as Denise returned to the table, water in hand.

Jack seemed to possess a glow around him, like an aura, but it was orange and red— like fire.

He slipped the waiter a hundred-dollar bill, and I could clearly hear him say, "My wife isn't feeling well. I'd better take her home."

It was as if I were right next to him. I flew toward him, to smash into him, hurt him, send him reeling. But in my incorporeal state, I was quite harmless.

Jack moved to Jenny and pulled at her arm. She mumbled something like, "No, no," and her legs went out from under her. Jack kept her on her feet while Denise took her free arm. Together, they walked Jenny out of the bar.

I followed right through the wall, not having to bother with doors, and watched as they lowered Jenny into the back seat of the red minivan I'd ridden in with Denise and Char days earlier.

"Let's go, Denny," Jack said, and Denise ran to the driver's seat as Jack looked right at me. He moved into the passenger seat, and they drove off.

I wanted to follow, to do something, to warn someone, but my mind was as exhausted as my sleeping body. The scene faded out, and I fell into a deep, dreamless sleep.

EIGHTEEN

With the dawn, I jumped into full consciousness. The dream, or vision, was fresh in my mind. It was so clear, I felt as if I was still in that room.

I grabbed my cane and got up, not bothering with socks or a robe, and went out into the hall and living room. There sat Jon, fully dressed with the phone in his lap, dozing.

"Jon!" I said, giving him a shake. He leaned forward and took his face in his hands to bring himself fully awake.

"Yeah, I'm up," he said. "Len?"

"Where's Jenny?"

Jon pulled himself from the chair, which dumped the headset onto the floor. "Jenn...I don't know. She was—I mean, she didn't... I was waiting up for her."

"Do you know when you fell asleep?"

"I watched the *Tonight Show*, but I turned it off and shut my eyes for a moment. I called Jenn's cell about ten thirty—then again at eleven."

I grabbed the phone. "Why don't you make coffee? I'll call the police."

"The police? Is that necessary?" he said. His eyes were red and tired, and he rubbed them again.

"Yes, and right away." I limped into the bedroom, grabbed my phone and hit the number I needed.

"McGee."

"Jenny Baines is missing," I said and closed the door to my guest room.

"Missing? Did something happen?"

"Bill, I had a dream last night—a vision. I think I know what happened."

"What do you mean?"

"Jenny was meeting a client last night to settle some paperwork, that's what Jon told me. Well, I had a vision where Jenny was in a bar, and Denise Haskell drugged her. Then Jack Hallman showed up, and they put her in Denise's red van and drove off. And here's another fact, he called her Denny."

"Denny, like that name with all the vowels on the corporate papers. Do you know which bar?"

"No, but it was unusual. Do you know a place with a polished old-world bar, but has Day-Glo vinyl and art on the walls?"

"Art? You mean like copies of the *Mona Lisa*—things like that?"

"Yes, that's it!"

"Sounds like The Artful Dive on Route Three. It's part of the Holiday Inn."

"I got the feeling it was connected to some hotel."

"Any chance that in this vision, you got a gander at the bartender?"

"Briefly. A guy with a beard."

"Right, that's Ted. I know him, which is the only reason I know the bar. Here's what we do. Have Jon Baines pull a photo, a wedding photo will do. I'll call Ted, wake him up, and take the photo over and see if he can ID her. If so, I can get a warrant on Hallman."

"Bill, Jenny is in danger."

"Len, what do you want me to do? Go to a judge and ask for a warrant because you had a vision? I need something more, and an eyewitness will do it."

"OK, but I'm going with you. Maybe I can get a bead on where she is."

"Why would Hallman grab Jenny? Seems like a pretty dumb move."

"He's desperate. But it's more than that. He saw me and Jenny together at her insurance company. He knows we're friends."

"Are you thinking—hostage?"

"Could be."

"A hostage situation could get me a lot more help—the state—maybe even some friends from the FBI. I'll be at your place within a half-hour."

"Thanks, Bill."

I showered quickly and threw on the black suit I wore for the funeral, without a tie, and grabbed my wallet and watch, which read seven twenty-five. I hobbled to the front of the house and discovered Jon sitting at the kitchen table with a cup of coffee, the phone next to him again.

"I tried her mobile again. Then I left a message at her office…"

"That won't do any good, Jon."

"What do you mean?" he said as he stood in alarm.

"Jon," I said and took him by the arms. "I need you to get me a photo of Jenny."

"A photo?"

"Yes, Detective McGee is on the way here, and we may have a way to find her."

He moved, still in a daze, then hurriedly went to the second floor and within two minutes, had retrieved a beautiful photo of Jenny in the front yard, playing with a dog.

"I took it last year. That's the neighbor's dog."

I nodded. "Great, Jon. You should get some sleep. I'll keep you posted." I started for the front door, but Jon blocked my path.

"Len, what's going on? Do you know where she is? Is she all right? Why didn't she call?"

"Jon, I think Jenny's fine, for now. She might be in a hostage situation."

"Jenny—a hostage? For God's sake, she's an insurance adjuster!"

"And she may have ticked off a serious psychopath. But if Bill and I move quickly, she won't get hurt."

He grabbed my arm. "Len, I've got to come with you!"

"Jon, you'll slow us down. I barely got McGee to agree to let *me* go."

"Len," he said, his eyes wet. "You've got to help her. If anything happened to Jenn, I-I…"

"I promise you, I'll bring her home to you," I said, with the hope it wasn't wishful thinking.

I made for the door while the going was good, and was out in front of the house just as McGee pulled up in a black and white police car with CITY OF MOUNTAINVIEW stenciled on the side.

I went around the car and slid into the passenger seat next to McGee as I handed him the photo.

"Pretty good likeness," he said. "Then again, I only met her once."

"It'll have to do," I said.

Off we went. I wondered why Bill hadn't brought his unmarked car until he turned on the flashing lights and the sirens as we sped. The morning rush hour was in full force, and the roadways contained their usual volume. Fortunately, we were only on Route Three for one exit before we pulled off, took the first turn, and stopped in front of a modest two-story Cape Cod style house.

McGee bolted for the door. I struggled to get out of the car and tapped my way behind him, finding McGee already in conversation with the bearded man from my dream.

He nodded as McGee spoke, and when I got closer, I could hear what he was saying.

"Yeah, this was the lady. She was having a drink—just ginger ale, and she gets all dizzy. So the lady that's with her gets a glass of water, and a man comes in, says he's her husband, and the two of them help her out the door."

"Can you describe the other woman?"

"She had shoulder-length hair, but it looked like a wig. She was what I'd call sturdy. Not thin, but not fat. She looked strong. She wore a frilly shirt and a pantsuit."

Just as I saw her, I thought.

Bill was scribbling in a small notebook he'd hastily pulled out of his jacket. "And the man?"

"Tall, dark hair, good-looking, all in black," Ted said. "And he was wearing sunglasses, even though the bar is pretty dark at night."

I nodded. "That's him, Hallman."

McGee looked at me, puzzled for a moment, then shook Ted's hand. "Thanks, I'll be in touch." He went back to his car, and I followed again, still not able to keep up. I found him on the radio, finishing a conversation.

"Ten-four. I want Denise Haskell picked up and waiting for me at the station. I'll meet you at Hallman's office."

"Ten-four," crackled the radio.

"Get in the car," McGee said to me as he put the microphone on its hook. "I'm waiting for a signature on the warrant, which the assistant DA is getting right now."

"Assistant DA?"

"Yeah. New woman, Jyanette Emery."

I paused to look at Bill as a chill went up my spine. That name was somehow important, though for the life of me, at that time I couldn't imagine why.

He went on. "Galland and his partner are waiting to grab it and then will meet us at Hallman's office."

I got into the car. McGee gunned the engine, and we took off. "How did you do it so fast?"

"I did the paperwork yesterday. This pushed it forward. Galland brought it to Emery this morning. She's on her way to Judge Franks."

"But what if I was wrong?" I said, surprised that I expressed doubt about my own vision.

"But you weren't, Len," McGee chuckled.

"But if…"

"Then we wouldn't be proceeding. I've also told officers to pick up Denise Haskell for questioning. If Hallman called her 'Denny' and she is Denny Kalhaskalwicz—"

"Then she's in Nova Corporation up to her eyeballs," I said.

"She'll be at the station by the time we get there. Just relax, Len, and let me do the worrying. Hallman is in his office every day at eight. So we're heading there."

"How do you know that?"

"I've had a tail on him for days, ever since the first time you mentioned him," McGee said as he flicked on the flashing lights. "Now, if you want to talk about what is wrong with your vision, here are two things. Hallman didn't leave his house last night."

"What?!"

"And second, the description Ted and you gave doesn't match the man I met."

"What do you mean?"

"I went to Jack Hallman's office to question him, Len. He's average height. Yeah, he likes to wear black, but he's not good-looking, and his hair is thinning."

"Wait, no. The guy is at least six feet, maybe even my height. And he was very handsome and in good physical shape."

"You met him somewhere? Besides in your visions?"

"At the insurance company, with Jenny."

"It appears one of the men claiming to be Jack Hallman isn't," McGee said, glancing over at me to see the look of shock on my face. "Nice to know I can surprise you once in a while."

"It never occurred to me," I said.

"You're not a cop, Len. You take people at face value, or by whatever your weird senses tell you."

"If one of them is a fraud—which one is it?" I said.

"We'll have to ask the Jack Hallman we find."

We were back in Mountainview. McGee used a series of back streets and put us there in record time. We pulled onto Bloomdale

Avenue, with lights and sirens going, and quickly turned onto a side street where a five-story building overlooked the lower part of town and the railway station. It was a large building that extended up the block. The first floor was shops and business. The entrance we faced was for the office suites on the upper floors.

There was a second black and white police car waiting for us. McGee got out and strode purposefully toward it, and two uniformed officers stepped out. One was Galland, the other was a short African-American woman in full uniform who gave me a smile as Galland handed McGee the folded paper.

"Galland, don't you ever sleep?" McGee said.

"Wouldn't miss this, sir," Galland said and then turned to me. "This is my partner, Tylissa Booker."

I gave her a nod. "Pleasure."

"Doctor," she said. "Heard you got a witness to spill the beans?"

I shrugged. Word certainly traveled fast in a small police department.

"Booker, you stay out here and keep things under control." McGee stated.

"Yes sir," she said with a nod.

"Galland, you're with us."

I followed McGee and Galland in the building and onto the elevator. As we rode up, I turned to McGee.

"If this is the Jack Hallman I told you about," I murmured to McGee. "Do we have enough firepower to stop him?"

"If not, we'll need you more than ever, Len."

Galland glanced at both of us with a confused look but rode on in silence. We got off on the fourth floor. Then McGee marched down the hall and banged on a door.

"Open up, Hallman, it's the police. I have a warrant to search the premises."

Grumbling came from the other side of the door, and it was opened to reveal a man of average height with a craggy face, thinning hair, and bland features, wearing a black turtleneck and suit jacket.

"What is it this time, Detective?" the man said. "I have half a mind to sue you for harassment."

"Wrong, you just have half a mind, period," McGee said, turning to me. "Len, is this your man in black?"

"Not even close."

"OK. Jack, you have any ID?"

"You know who I am, Detective," he complained.

"Just show it," McGee barked.

With another grumble, he reached into his jacket, withdrew his wallet, and showed his driver's license. The picture was of poor quality, but it was obviously the man standing before us.

"So, now that we know who you are, let us in, Hallman," McGee said as Galland handed him the warrant in one practiced move.

McGee pushed the door open and stepped into the lawyer's office. It was a nice suite, organized to the point where I couldn't imagine a bit of dust daring to be there. Several wooden bookcases were built into the walls and were lined with books. The floor was a dull linoleum covered by cheap, but handsome, Oriental carpet. His desk was an older style roll-top, but modern enough to hold a laptop computer. The machine was up and running with a a rather cute semi-clad woman dancing along its face as a screen-saver. There were tall wooden file cabinets, all with small cards on the front that identified their contents.

"Let me see that warrant before you go touching anything, McGee," Hallman said as he grabbed the warrant to read it.

"So, who is walking around claiming to be you, Jack?" McGee asked nonchalantly as he watched the stripping figure on the laptop screen.

As he read, Hallman replied, "How the hell would I know?" He spied something on the paper and stopped to read it again. "What is this? I'm a suspect in the kidnapping of Jennifer Baines? Who the hell is she?"

"Hallman, I'm going to ask you a couple of questions. If I don't like the answers, this officer," he indicated Galland, "and I will take apart this office splinter by splinter until I get them."

"Sure, sure," he said as he handed back the warrant. "I always try to be helpful to the police."

"You represent the Nova Corporation, right?"

"I have had some limited business dealings with them, but any communication with them is privileged."

"You hear about the fire last night?" McGee said. "Killed an old acquaintance of both of us, Roswell Norris."

"I heard about it, tough break for Norris," Hallman griped, uninterested.

"He was also in the employ of the Nova Corporation," McGee said. "I should also advise you that the office under his, where the fire originated, was rented by you, according to leasing records."

"What?" Hallman said, his mouth falling open. "That's impossible! I made sure—" He stopped abruptly as he realized he'd stuck his foot in it.

McGee smiled. "How would you know that was impossible unless you rented the office under the name of Doctor Leonard Wise?"

"What?" I said, stunned.

"A little tidbit I was saving, Doc," McGee stated. "Funny how the paperwork said Leonard Wise, but the realtor gave me a description that fits you, Jack."

"I look like a lotta guys, McGee. You said yourself there is someone walking around claiming to be me," he sneered.

McGee walked through the office, looking around, then he gave a know-it-all smile to Hallman. "I think your usefulness to the Nova Corporation is about to come to an end. Considering how Roswell ended up, I think you know what happens to people who are no longer useful."

Hallman grew pale.

"I'll give you a list of people who wore out their welcome, see if it clicks in your memory: Philip Mishan, Wendy Wallace, and now Roswell Norris."

Hallman's color faded even more.

"So, if you know something about the Nova Corporation or the abduction of Jennifer Baines, you'd better tell me, because you have a better chance of staying alive if you work with me."

I spoke up. "We're looking for a man my height, dresses in black, and wears sunglasses due to a sensitivity to light."

He avoided my eyes, which made me unable to reach into his mind. I was angry at this point. I wanted to turn him to face me, make him meet my eyes, force him to experience the images of Wendy bursting into flames, of Philip Mishan falling and burning, of Roswell Norris's charred corpse.

"I don't have anything to say," Hallman said, but his bluster was gone.

"We need a name, Hallman, and a place. We think he's holding the lady there," McGee said.

"I don't know anything," Hallman said. "All I was doing for Nova was regular corporate stuff."

"Including picking up large insurance checks for all those fires, right, Jack?" McGee said.

"If you have a problem with Nova, you should talk to *them*."

"You're their agent," McGee said. "How do I get in touch with them, and who the hell *is* in charge?"

"John Gingold," Hallman replied.

I felt a chill go up my spine. I could perceive the rightness of it. Why didn't I see it sooner? His name glowing on the paper, the attraction I had for it the first time I'd seen it.

"John Gingold," I muttered in annoyance. "Also known as Jack."

Hallman turned to me. "I don't know his nicknames—or aliases, if he has any. He's a big investor from the Bahamas."

"He's taken a hostage," I said, and Hallman finally met my eyes. "She was the insurance adjuster on Mishan's store."

"I don't know anything about that," he said, just as I pushed into his mind and made contact. I saw images of Gingold in this very office. He sat with his imperial style as if he were a king holding court.

"I met Gingold," I said, and I didn't allow him to break eye contact. "He claimed to be you."

"Yes," he said, confused why he couldn't look away. I could sense that he was moving into a light trance.

He's too sensitive. If I do anymore, he'll fall asleep or slip into a hypnotic state, I thought.

McGee helped without knowing it. He grabbed Hallman by the arm, which startled him into full awareness.

"I need a place, Hallman," McGee insisted. "I need to know where he is and where he could be holding her."

"What?" Hallman said, turning red. He glanced at me as if to say, "What just happened?"

"Look, I've got your description as the signer of the lease on the office that exploded. Today, forensic evidence will prove it was arson. I got enough right now to arrest you."

"Look, McGee. I only have two addresses for the corporation. A post office box in the Bahamas and one in Upper Mountainview."

"And what are the odds that you rented the box in Upper Mountainview?" McGee said.

"I opened it, sure! It's what lawyers do. It wasn't illegal," he argued with an exaggerated shrug.

"So, how do you get in touch with him?" McGee barked, his patience wearing thin.

"He calls me when he wants me," Hallman said. "That's the way he does things. Look, Detective, I just act as an agent of the corporation."

"Did you fill out his certificate of incorporation?" McGee said. "Do you know that everyone on that paper beside Gingold is dead?"

"And you have to know about the insurance claims," I added.

"I told you, it's all privileged conversation, and everything I did was legal," Hallman said.

"You really are one stupid-ass guy," McGee said. "He's going to get away and leave you to take the heat, if you'll pardon the expression. Look, Hallman, your only hope of staying out of jail is to give me every scrap of paper you've got on this clown."

A very dangerous clown, I thought.

"Detective," Hallman said, "you've got the goddamn warrant. Find it yourself!"

"Galland!" McGee bellowed, as he grabbed Hallman's arm roughly and shoved him toward Officer Galland. "Kindly escort Mr. Hallman downstairs and have Officer Booker take him to the station."

"I want my lawyer," Hallman said.

"Don't annoy me, Hallman, or I'll have Galland cuff you," McGee said as he passed the small man over to Galland. "But I'll tell you one thing, Hallman. This lady ends up dead, and I guarantee you're going down as a co-conspirator for murder one."

"I told you, Detective, I don't know anything," Hallman said as he was pulled by Galland out the door.

"Work on your memory, Hallman," McGee shouted after him. "And think about what I said about people ending up dead. You might just want my protection." Then, as an afterthought, he called after Galland as they reached the elevator. "And Galland, get your ass back up here. I'll need you to work on his computer."

"You want Galland to check his computer?" I asked. "It's probably encrypted."

McGee smiled. "Galland was a serious hacker a few years back. Fortunately, he's on *our* side, and the warrant allows us to go through his computer. Whatever it is, Galland can get past it."

McGee went to one of the wood—oak file cabinets and pulled out a drawer. "Shall we go for the obvious?" he said, extracting several thick files, and starting to go through the papers. I joined him, and McGee gave me a portion.

"There are a lot of insurance policies," I said.

"And lots of correspondence with insurance companies," McGee added as he held up a stack of papers with a large metal clip at the top.

"And all of the policies are for fire; no theft, no flood, just fire," I said as I went through my stack. "I doubt there will be any papers mentioning a secret lair."

"Yeah, if you find one marked 'Hidden Lair,' let me know," McGee said. "In the meantime, write down the properties insured by the policies. That's a start."

McGee and I started taking notes as Galland returned with a small device in his hand.

"What's that, Officer?" I asked.

He held up a flash drive. "My own special brand of software. I load it in, and it makes accessing hidden files a lot easier," Galland said. He sat at the laptop and inserted the device in the USB port.

"Your own special brand?" I asked.

"He writes the code himself," McGee said without looking up from his stack of papers.

"He writes…" I said, then turned to Galland. "Wow!"

McGee and Galland chuckled together as Galland sat at the desk, doing a few things that looked like magic to me. He flew past the risqué screen saver and quickly through the password lockout. He then began to load the program he'd inserted.

"What do you need, sir?" Galland asked.

"See if you can find any references to properties held by Nova Corporation," McGee said, his eyes fixed on his work.

"Try to look for a building with a view," I said.

"A view?" McGee repeated, his eyes meeting mine.

"Yes, remember Janice Hoefler? She said Wendy's boyfriend owned a place with a spectacular view of the city."

"But which city?" McGee said, picking up his handwritten list. "I mean, if it's a view of New York, he could be in Jersey City or Hoboken." McGee quickly scanned the list. "There's a warehouse listed in Hoboken."

"I got the impression it was here in Mountainview," I said.

"We are a city of small buildings, Len. This building we're in is one of the tallest."

I was close to something, an impression lurked just outside my reach, but it was too ephemeral to grasp. Something I'd seen, but couldn't connect.

"You lose your steam, Len?" McGee asked.

I jumped a bit. "Oh sorry, I was close to something."

McGee lowered his voice. "Looked like you were close to drooling. If you're going to conjure a vision or something, why don't you go take a seat in the corner."

I nodded and put down the pile of papers. As Galland's fingers went ticky-tack at the keyboard and McGee took notes and opened folders, I sat in a chair at the far end of the room and closed my eyes.

I'm scared, I thought. *Scared that I'm going to let Jenny down just like I let Cathy down—and Wendy.*

And they ended up dead, the voice in my head responded. I pushed the thought away. Fear would bring nothing, except to close me down. I wouldn't be able to help her then.

I focused on my breath and hummed, using a variation on an ancient Hindu form of meditation called *Jappa*. I was trying to change the vibration that my mind operated at, attempting to shift to the place where the information could come. I let go of my fear and allowed peace to descend on me.

Flashes of light, all created in my own mind, sparked and shot like lightning. I could sense something, and it was close, agonizingly close.

My skin grew cold when I felt *something* on my hand. It seemed to slither, leaving a trail of damp mucous as it moved. In my deep meditation, I slowly opened my eyes to see a black worm crawling up my hand. It was large, and it moved by compressing its body and pushing onward, expanding and contracting in its shambling, invertebrate way. As I looked at it, it lifted its body and opened a maw filled with tiny teeth.

"AH!" I yelled, and jumped to my feet, my meditation broken.

"What?" McGee said, turning to me.

"You all right, Doctor?" Galland asked as he rose from the computer.

The thing was gone. I stood there breathing hard as my heart attempted to thump its way out of my chest. My body, riding the rush of a sudden burst of adrenaline, was shaking.

"I'm f-fine," I said and swallowed to keep my last meal where it belonged. I touched my skin, but there was no trail, no slimy residue. It was entirely a vision. But what did it mean?

"Any luck?" McGee asked.

I glanced at my hand one more time, not sure that if I looked again, it would be back. "No, just crazy stuff. Maybe a message. I'm receiving, but not translating." I sat next to McGee, still shivering, and picked up some papers.

"Can't you control it?" McGee asked. "Your information about last night—"

"My conscious mind wasn't trying to interpret," I interrupted. "Right now, I'm worried about Jenny—and it's getting in my way. And impressions come as they come. It's up to me to figure it out."

"So, what did you see?"

"A worm that bites," I said, as I returned to the files and gave a shudder.

McGee lifted an eyebrow. "How nice."

NINETEEN

We stayed at Hallman's about an hour, compiling a list of properties owned by Nova from the insurance policies. Many of the
places had burned down, claims had been paid, and the extent of
Nova's financial gains from each transaction was becoming obvious.

Finally, Galland had printed a list of properties he'd found on
the laptop. McGee then called for backup to finish going through
the office. We left Galland to continue his excursion through
Hallman's files as McGee and I returned to the police station where
Jack Hallman waited.

It was a short drive, but McGee was on the radio to the station
to check on the officer who had been sent to pick up Denise Haskell
for questioning.

"The officer reports she's not at her listed address," the female
voice on the radio responded.

"Tell them to try the coffeehouse," I said.

McGee nodded and told the dispatcher to have the officer go to
the Halfway House.

The dispatcher asked one more question before signing off. "Detective McGee, is Doctor Leonard Wise riding with you?"

"Yes, why?" McGee said into the microphone.

"The LT told me to make sure he comes to the station with you. Do you copy?"

"Ten-four," McGee said, returning the microphone to its clip.

"What was that about?" I pondered.

"I have no idea," McGee replied.

He parked on Bloomdale Avenue, in the same spot as the other day, and as I got out of the car, I was again filled with an extraordinary sense that what I wanted was close, but I still didn't have it.

We walked into the side door of the MPD station, which brought us in past the locker room and the bunk rooms, where officers could catch a few hours of sleep when working multiple shifts. McGee led the way to the main corridor where we found Sergeant Tice, apparently waiting for us. Next to him was a man I didn't know. He wore an MPD uniform, and I could plainly see the gold bars on his lapels.

And next to him was another officer, who wore a brown and tan uniform from another district.

"Here they are now," Tice announced and looked at the lieutenant.

The lieutenant studied me from head to toe, turned to the officer next to him, and said, "All right, cuff him."

"What?" McGee said, which stopped his headlong march. "Lieutenant Butler, what is this about?"

The officer in tan stepped forward to block my path. "Doctor Leonard Wise, you are under arrest for arson and second degree murder."

The man came behind me and, in one quick move, took my cane from my hand, pulled my hands behind my back, and slipped a pair of cuffs on my wrists. I shifted my weight to stay upright.

"LT, we should talk about this," McGee said, his face growing red.

"You gave me free access to your files, right, McGee?" Tice sneered. "When were you going to let someone know that this is the man who rented the suite where the fire started in that building in Orange?"

"Look, McGee," Butler said. "I don't like this either, but this officer is from the Orange police and they have an arrest warrant."

Tice added, "And we're happy to deliver him."

I stood silent and looked pleadingly at McGee.

"It was a setup, LT. Look, Jack Hallman rented that office using Doctor Wise's name," McGee said.

"You have proof of that? Maybe a signed confession?" Tice taunted.

"What's your proof, Detective?" Lieutenant Butler asked.

"I got a description—verbal—from the man in the rental office," McGee said. "And I questioned Hallman. I know when a suspect is trapped in a lie, sir."

"Then your doctor friend won't be held long," Tice said.

Lieutenant Butler shook his head. "I have to go with Sergeant Tice on this one, Bill, sorry. If it's all a frame-up, you should be able to get him out in a few hours."

The officer from Orange gave me a tug toward the door.

I stumbled as I fought to stay upright.

"He's got a crippled leg!" McGee called out as he came over and helped me stand. "Can't he just walk with you?"

The officer looked at McGee, and it seemed the possibilities ran through his head. He was young, and I got the impression he was either inexperienced or not the brightest bulb in the chandelier.

"I can't do that, sir," he finally responded.

"Can you cuff his hands in front? At least then he can use his cane!" McGee said as his color rose again.

"That sounds reasonable," Lieutenant Butler pointed out, sensing the young man's lack of expertise. "Unless you want to carry him to your vehicle?"

Again, the officer took his time considering this proposition. He finally relented, and using the key, he opened the cuffs and moved my hands in front of me.

"LT, we are in a hostage situation, and Doctor Wise had information that could make all the difference."

"What's the matter, McGee?" Tice blurted. "Can't handle your own case?"

"We have to do this by the book, Bill," Butler said, giving a nod to the officer, who tugged my arm again.

I looked into McGee's eyes and said quietly. "Find her, Bill. You have to find her."

"I will," he said adamantly.

As the young officer escorted me, I heard McGee say, "I've got the lawyer who claimed to be Doctor Wise in interrogation."

We went through the door, past the elevated desk in the main lobby and out onto the street. I used my cane as best I could to keep up, my mind racing. How long would it take to get out of this situation? Could I end up at the Orange police station for hours? All day? What would that creature do to Jenny?

Images of Wendy's body bursting into flames replayed in slow motion in my memory.

The officer crossed Bloomdale Avenue with me in tow, heading to the small municipal lot where his cruiser, emblazoned with CITY OF ORANGE was parked. I allowed myself to be led, and hung my head like a puppy. Gingold and Hallman had planned this, with Tice happy to act on it and pull the lieutenant in for additional support.

As we approached the police car, I turned and gave the police station one final look. My eye was drawn to the odd building next door, its red brick in dark contrast to the yellow pillars of the municipal building.

But my gaze went up to the top, to the large dark windows that faced the city in all directions. My perspective shifted to the tile work on the front bearing the name LEACH.

I froze, unable to suck in breath, the sound of my heart pounding in my ears. Although the weather wasn't hot, I was suddenly drenched with cold sweat. I now understood the meaning of my vision at Hallman's office. I had seen a creature resembling a leech to trigger my mind back to the name Leach that I had seen on this building the other day.

I gazed toward downtown. Mountainview is built on a hill, the police station near the top, the train station at the bottom, with Bloomdale Avenue on an incline. From the top floor of the Leach Building, the view of the city must be spectacular. I could now tell that the windows, which reflected the sunlight so brightly, were *tinted*—as if to protect someone with a sensitivity to light.

I was jolted back to reality by an unpleasant yank from the officer, who unlocked the door to his cruiser.

"Wait," I said. "There's something important I have to tell Detective McGee!"

"You'll get one phone call at the station," he said as he opened the back door.

In a flash, I knew where Gingold had taken Jenny. He owned this building, like the others. But what could I do? One thing was clear, if I went into the back seat of that police car, I was locked in with no way out until Orange. And then would they let me call McGee and tell him that Gingold was right next door? And could McGee take him down? Would it be too late for Jenny?

All this galloped through my brain at breakneck speed as the officer waited for me to move. "Look, mister, either get in the car, or I'll put you in. I'd rather not hurt you."

I met his eyes.

Using all of my mental strength, I let go of any inhibitions or reservations and dove into his mind with every fiber of my being.

He looked at me questioningly for a moment but didn't look away. I reached farther and deeper as I tried to find the core of his being, much more than I'd done with Janice Hoefler.

All at once, I knew a great deal about this man, Mike Mackenzie. Everyone called him Mack. He was a good man, and he worked hard to be a good cop. He'd been a poor student, and it was more difficult for him to remember all the rules and information. He made up the difference by working twice as hard as other officers. He went with less sleep, reviewed police materials and procedures on a regular basis, and made sure to follow orders *exactly* as he was told.

I had entered his mind so strongly, I had pulled him into a trance state. This morning, Hallman slipped easily into a similar state without prompting. But either through my fear for Jenny or my desperation at the situation, I'd reached the same deep place in Mackenzie's mind.

But now, I had no qualms about taking advantage of it.

"You received a call," I said aloud.

I did? His mind answered, his lips unmoving.

"You were told to let me go," I said, my eyes totally focused on his.

I was told to let you go, he thought back to me.

Unlock the cuffs, I passed to him without a word.

He moved slowly to take the keys from his belt.

"Keep your eyes on mine," I said aloud.

I was afraid if we broke eye contact, I might not be able to maintain our connection and bring him to this place again. He lifted the keys, and held them up, selecting the handcuff key, his stare meeting mine.

I don't remember getting a call, flashed through his mind, a moment of doubt.

Yes, you do. You went to the car and there was a call on your cell phone.

He slipped the key into the lock and made a brief turn, releasing the ratchet and expanding one metal bracelet. He repeated the action on my left hand. The cuffs came off, and I rubbed my wrists, irritated from the tight metal.

"Sorry for the misunderstanding," he said aloud, his eyes glassy.

"Quite all right, officer," I said, still in contact, but I was getting weary. This took a lot of energy, and I had to end it quickly. *You have to go.*

"I have to go," he said as if it were his original thought.

I nodded, blinked, and broke the eye contact. I quickly crossed Bloomdale Avenue, and only glanced back to see him standing there puzzled for a moment. He then got into the car and drove off.

I exhaled deeply with relief as the car disappeared down Bloomdale Avenue.

I stood and faced the Leach Building. It would've helped if I'd actually had a plan. All I wanted to do was get free from the officer, but now—I couldn't go back into the police station and get McGee. Tice and the lieutenant wouldn't let me get ten feet before they'd throw me in cuffs and call the Orange police again.

But to barge into the Leach Building alone with no backup— that was also not a smart idea.

The activities of the morning had tired me out. I'd used a lot of mental energy on Hallman and now Mackenzie. Was I strong enough for a face-to-face with Jack Gingold?

I pulled out my cell phone and moved to the text screen. I hate to text, as my fingers are too large for any touch screen, and I end up writing incomprehensible messages, especially when the autocorrect kicks in.

But I went ahead anyway.

Bill-

It's Len. Gingold is on the top floor of the Leach building, next door to the MPD station. That was what the worm that bites was all about. Get some backup as soon as you get this message and go there. The top floor.

I sent the text.

I looked up at the building and knew I had to go in. Probably a very bad plan. If McGee crashed in there with a thousand SWAT guys, I could end up shot. However, I didn't know how long it would take for Bill to read the message as he was interrogating Hallman.

Go...

I sensed the buzz. I needed to make my move—now.

I glanced at my watch. Just a little after nine. Hopefully, Gingold was a late sleeper, and I could get the drop on him, as they used to say in old gangster movies.

I decided on a frontal assault, going in the front door. I approached the facade and noted that there were two businesses on the ground floor. One was an insurance company, the other a moving and storage company.

I nodded. This made sense: a storage company.

If any of the buildings Nova owned had anything valuable in them, he could store it here and then claim an additional loss when it burned down. It also gave him a front, a legitimate business that wouldn't arouse suspicions or have any connection to Nova.

I stepped to the door and entered the moving company's office. There was a short, heavyset man with an unlit cigar stuck in his mouth like it was a part of his lips. He sat, unshaven, behind a desk with an open newspaper in his hands.

He glanced up at me, but the paper didn't fall. "You need something moved?"

"No," I said, and smiled as I tried like hell to make my voice nonchalant. "I have an appointment with Jack." He didn't respond, just sat and stared at me. "Uh, John—Gingold?"

He nodded, and I relaxed. Though I couldn't imagine this man would pull out a large gun and blow me away, I was unsure of how elaborate Gingold's security might be.

"You got to go to the back of the building," he said, moving the cigar to the other side of his mouth with his tongue. "You ring the bell, and he buzzes you in, then you take the elevator."

"Thank you," I said with a nod and then walked to the door. I peeked back to see if he went for a phone or a hidden button. But he just returned to his paper without a break to his routine.

So far, no alarms.

There was an alley next to the building, and I took it to avoid the police station and the chance I might be seen. The alley wove right and left, maze-like, between the extensions that had been added to the buildings over the years. I walked out to a view of the police parking lot, filled with cruisers and fire department vehicles.

I drew closer to the back of the Leach Building. There were large metal rollup doors and an enormous moving van with the name of the company emblazoned on it. I passed by the locked doors covered with flaking red paint and discovered a doorway. It looked much newer than the rest of the building, like something from a private residence. However, it was heavy metal, with a tiny window reinforced with wire in its center.

There was a door buzzer on the jamb near the knob with a small cardboard insert that read Gingold. A small box with a speaker was next to it.

I stood there for a moment and studied the door. If I buzzed and Jack asked who it was, what would I say?

So much for the element of surprise.

I went back to the metal rollup doors, which were used to load large items in and out of the warehouse, but they were securely fastened.

I returned to the door and examined the lock more carefully. There was a small gap between the lock and the door jamb. It was a wide enough space to slip a credit card in and if I had a small screwdriver, I might be able to force it open. I pulled on the door, and it quivered a bit, so there was some play in it to force something under the catch.

Looking around to make sure there was no one watching, I touched the button on the head of my cane, and with the sound of metal, the sword slid from its wooden sheath.

I held the blade for a moment as it flashed in the sunlight. It was not a wide blade, as it was fitted to the cane, but the end came to a fine point.

Perfect.

I scanned the street again and slipped the sharp tip of the blade into the space between the latch and the door. My experience as a burglar was limited, and though I did spend years doing magic, I never mastered escapes. I struggled as I manipulated the lock and thought how my magician brother Thomas could have done this in seconds instead of minutes.

Sweat began to drip down my face and sting my eyes. The idea occurred to me that scaling the building like a superhero might be an easier solution, but just then, the blade caught the small metal cylinder and slipped it back. The door came open in my hands.

I almost fell backward, but held onto the doorknob, so it didn't close on me, and I didn't end up on my butt. Then, picking up the wood of my cane, I returned the blade to its hiding place, quietly stepped inside, and gently shut the door.

I tried to see if there were any cameras trained at the door or hidden in the corners of the room, but I saw nothing.

He knows you're coming... flashed into my mind. The sweat was gone, but I felt cold.

JACK'S DIARY: FRIDAY

I love it when a plan comes together. Then again, why wouldn't it? I have always had an enormous amount of luck, and it's still working.

Drugging the bitch was certainly no trouble—she was oblivious to it—and when I stepped into the bar and helped her out, she was too gone to fight back. The advantages of better living through chemistry. A little Rohypnol goes a long way.

I brought her back here and put her in my bed—in the vault. I didn't touch her, not that way. I've never forced myself on a woman. God know I don't have to. They find me quite attractive enough.

But she passed out completely, which was a pity. I thought in the privacy of my abode, I could—well—play with her. With my power, I wanted to start with a few little burns and see the look of fear in her eyes. That's the fun part, the exciting part. Like Mishan, Wendy, and even old Roswell Norris. The look in their eyes when I strike. I think it makes me stronger.

But she lay comatose, so I took off her shoes (I am a gentleman) and placed her on the bed, covering her with the satin sheets. I opened the sofa bed in the other room, and after carefully locking her in the bedroom (didn't want her wandering around during the night, did I?), I went to bed myself.

This morning, I woke earlier than my usual time. I forgot to cover the windows, and the light was pouring in through the tinted glass. Even that was too much, so I put on my glasses. I walked to the large vault door and opened it with the combination, but dear Miz Insurance Bitch was still out.

I watched her for a few minutes. She is an attractive enough woman, though nothing extraordinary. But I imagined how she'd look with her face twisted in agony as she begged and pleaded for mercy, tears streaming down her cheeks. Now that would be an entirely new level of attractiveness. Perhaps tying her to the bed would be an idea?

I started my morning coffee and sat to write this. It's a bore that she's still sleeping, but not unexpected. It's one of the side effects of Rohypnol, makes the user sleep for up to ten hours. That will be fine, I'll give her a chance to wake up. The day is young, and I have nowhere to go and no one to see, so she can have all my attention. Yes, all *my attention.*

Will the cripple come? Is he good enough to find me? Ah, such questions, but I have a sense he's on his way. I'll feel him when he gets close.

In the meantime, I wonder if they know that dear Denise is missing? I doubt that they will find her.

Ever.

TWENTY

The elevator lay straight ahead of me as I crept into the building. It appeared quite large, as if used for moving furniture. It was fronted with two silver sliding doors polished to the point of being mirrored.

"If there's an elevator, there have to be stairs," I whispered to myself as I approached the end of the hall. He might know I was on my way, but I didn't want to just ride up and be trapped inside the large metal coffin, with nowhere to run—not that I was much of a runner.

I noticed a large door to my right, reinforced with metal straps like in a warehouse. I quietly turned the handle and pulled it open. A dark hallway stood beyond, windowless in the center of the building. The floors were of thick pine with warps that appeared in several boards, creating gaps. There was another door across from me that probably led to the storage area.

A set of rusted metal steps waited to my left. The banisters and rails, also metal, were painted a sickly green, a shade I would call crypt green. I started to climb the steps as quietly as I could, pulling my right leg up behind me. The tapping of my cane, though faint, seemed to reverberate around the open space up to the top floor. This structure had the odd angles of a bell tower, and I fought vertigo as I ascended.

I could detect him above me, his energy glimmering like a golden nugget at the bottom of a cloudy stream, so I kept going.

White, white, nothing but white, I thought. *A white wall and white carpet in a white room with no doors and no windows, just pure, plain whiteness.*

I didn't want him to sense me, or if he did, I wanted to keep my true thoughts away from him. I didn't know his limits, and I certainly wasn't sure of my ability to face him. But I didn't want him to know that.

What would I do once I arrived at the top floor, which loomed above me ever further? What if the door up there was locked? Even worse, what if it wasn't?

All at once, I got an image of Gingold like a James Bond villain, holding a martini and explaining his plan to destroy the world. I shook my head and ignored it. What did I expect, to see him standing there with a white cat?

I wanted a drink, the first time since the night of Wendy's death. That night, my drinking had made me next to useless. Now I wanted it to calm my nerves.

But that's the problem with being an alcoholic: there's always a reason to drink. If I feel good, it's to celebrate; bad, it's to cheer me up; scared, it's to give me courage; excited, it's to calm me. It doesn't matter, there is always a reason when it's what you want.

I felt cold as the sweat dried on my skin, but that was good. Cold, like the cold at Scudder House. I could still recall walking in there and feeling the air change, becoming frigid. It was almost like it welcomed me, as if I was expected.

. . .

Scudder House was a fantastic creation in its day, built for Elias J. Scudder, the last of the great railroad tycoons. It sat on a many-acred estate that overlooked San Francisco Bay casting a huge, dark shadow with its turreted towers and magnificent Victorian woodwork.

The day the family moved in, they threw a party for the entire railroad company and guests, everyone from conductors and motormen to the vice president of the United States. It was a summer's day in 1894, with a spectacular buffet set outside on ice in the heat. Guests dressed to the nines drank the finest champagne and ate caviar.

There were tours of the house in its magnificence, showing off the crystal chandeliers and gold plated bathroom fixtures. It possessed all of the most modern fixtures, indoor plumbing, gas jets for lamps, huge fireplaces for warmth and show, and a coal burning furnace.

But even that first night, it became evident there was something inexplicably *wrong* about that house.

Fireworks were set off from a ship in the bay, and all the guests were watching, oohing and aahing over the sparks as they flared in the sky. Elias's youngest daughter, only five, merrily watched the display. She wore a frilly dress, and she'd played with the ribbons hanging from it all day. As she watched, she backed up and proceeded to step into a sinkhole that the land surveyor said could not have existed on that property.

Her cries were muffled by the dirt and sounds of the explosions. And as she lay there, the dirt closed up again and quickly suffocated her.

The discovery of the body was a horrible shock and made news from coast to coast. Elias Scudder took his wife and five remaining children, closed up Scudder House, and moved back east.

Years later as the Roaring 20's came to an end, an older and much poorer, though not broke by any means, Elias Scudder returned to the abode that bore his name. But he and his wife lived as recluses and seldom ventured out. The few servants they hired insisted on staying away from the house at night, only coming in during the day to do what needed to be done.

Then the series of deaths began.

On the day of the stock market crash, Elias Scudder jumped out of the front tower with a rope around his neck. His neck was broken in an instant, and the servants had to take the hanging corpse down.

His wife stayed in the house, but died within ten years. She grew more paranoid and less coherent with each passing season. The doctors ruled that Mrs. Scudder died of natural causes. But that didn't explain why her eyes were open and wide, as huge as silver dollars, and the fact that her hair had turned stark white all at once.

A daughter moved in, a rather stern woman named Francis. She was the odd one of the family. It was rumored she was a lesbian and had several liaisons with other well-to-do women in the house.

Her death was also unique.

She was only in her fifties, but she died by leaping from the same tower her father had used and eviscerating herself by plunging onto one of the house's decorative and quite sharp fence posts. She landed in such a way that it penetrated her through her sex and into her heart. The house made headlines yet again.

A brother then took up residence since there was a trust fund to maintain the house. He was, by all regards, the most normal of the Scudder family and did not commit suicide.

Instead, one night, his bed collapsed in a freak accident, and he was trapped by the mattress and pillow, which compressed against his face and head. He suffocated before anyone arrived to help.

His death was said to be caused by what was now referred to as "the Curse of Scudder House".

The last resident, a cousin named Nat Hewing, moved into the house. He wanted to find a large, unaccounted for sum of money and valuables that were supposed to be hidden there. He sold off the furniture, the fixtures, and tried to disassemble the house brick by brick. For exactly two months.

When they found his body, it was burned beyond recognition. He may have been trying to burn the house down and instead set himself on fire. He was dead from the fire, and yet the house was not damaged in any way. Even the floor under his body was unmarked.

. . .

Fire rising up on his body, like Mishan, like Wendy.

I stopped dead. The steps seemed endless, and I was only up the first flight.

I considered why I was thinking about Scudder House. Could there be a correlation between it and this situation with Gingold?

Cold, the house was cold…

. . .

I walked into that house, which was still huge and grand even after years of emptiness and neglect. The estate's land had been sold off over the years, except for the acres directly around the house. But as I rode in the car with Doctor Kohl up its cracked driveway, I couldn't help feeling that the darkened windows with the tattered drapes watched me, expecting my visit.

I went into that house and did my best to keep my mind blank to all that was around me, although I felt the energy—the *urgency*—as it tried to reach out to me.

Doctor Kohl and I set up the equipment while there was daylight. We intended to work for a while and then vacate the house before dark.

I kept my mind focused on the tasks at hand, or on a wall—a white wall. Nothing in, nothing out, a solid barrier of my mind. But behind that wall, I could sense the buzzing of something, like the loud hum of a powerful machine. Is that when I began to call my hunches buzzes? I think so, because it was like a buzzing at the base of my skull, like a nest of bees had taken up residence there.

Then and there, I knew why Doctor Kohl spent months to teach me blocking techniques and made me practice the exercises over and over. He'd been correct, because I was wary of the unbidden perceptions that tried to force themselves on me. The years that followed the accident were filled with nights where I knew things I didn't want to know and saw things I didn't want to see.

When Doctor Kohl fired up our portable generator outside, and our equipment began to operate through the extension cords that snaked their way into the house, it was nearly sunset.

"All right, Leonard," he said, touching the button on a digital recorder. "Ve can begin."

By that time, I was wired to an electroencephalogram, the pads on my forehead reading my brain wave activity.

"I've only tried to be a medium a few times," I said to him. I looked up at the high ceilings, the darkness of the woodwork, and the frayed remains of curtains hanging over the windows like a shroud. The room possessed a heaviness, a weight that seemed to press down on my shoulders and on the back of my mind.

"Don't move, you vill schnap the vires!" Doctor Kohl said, a flash of humor in his eyes.

I breathed deeply and let the protective wall come down.

I remember nothing after that.

My first recollection is lying on the back seat of Doctor Kohl's car as we raced away down the nighttime streets.

"What?" I said as if I came out of a dream. My head ached and my muscles were tight, like I'd escaped a straitjacket or done ten rounds with a famed fighter.

"Leonard, are you avake?"

"Water," I said, my mouth so dry I couldn't feel my tongue.

"There is bottled vater on the floor."

I touched the floor of the vehicle until I feel the plastic container. I sat up, pulled off the cap, and began to gulp down the cool liquid.

"Do you know who you are?"

"That's an odd question," I said, my tongue feeling too large for my mouth.

"It is you! Tank Gott!" Doctor Kohl said, appearing greatly relieved. "Do you know vat happened?"

"The last thing I remember…we were beginning…" I stammered and lifted my hand, which now weighed two tons, to my head.

"Yah, that vas three hours ago. Come, I take you back to the hotel, away from that *damn* house."

I leaned back and felt more tired and thirsty than I'd ever felt in my life. But even so, it was an odd experience to hear Doctor Kohl refer to any site of what he called "an experiment" as *damned.* His philosophy was that there are only phenomena, which are neither good or bad.

Except at Scudder House.

The next day in the hotel, there were six of us. Fritz had brought in Doctor Janis, a professor from the University of San Francisco. He was an expert on Scudder House and had arranged our excursion. With him were a female assistant and two young male students. They all assembled to hear the recording Doctor Kohl had made while we were in the house.

I was fully recovered after a good night's sleep and able to listen to those digital recordings, but it was an odd experience. It was my voice, but I had no recollection of saying the words. On the recording, I kept changing my voice and timbre, as I appeared to jump from one persona to another, each with a different personality.

As the team reviewed what was said, reading the transcripts, we became aware that there were several mentions of hidden objects left by the former inhabitants.

"If ve could go through the house," Doctor Kohl said, "If ve could find them, it vould be proof of consciousness surviving after death."

So, as a five-man, one-woman team, we returned to Scudder House.

When I walked into that house again, the buzzing in my brain started again, but this time sounding like not just bees, but angry ones ready to strike.

"Whatever we do, we need to do it quickly," I told Doctor Kohl.

He checked his notes and led our group. The others seemed unaffected, but my head ached as I fought to keep everything out.

We worked our way up to a bedroom on the second floor and wandered along the floor, noting any gaps in the floorboards. I'd spoken on the tape in a high, girlish voice about a lost cameo, even recounted which room and possible location. After just fifteen minutes of crawling on our hands and knees, one of the students gave a yell. He reached between the boards with a handy pair of tweezers and extracted the shiny object, then handed it to Doctor Janis.

"Lucy Scudder!" Doctor Janis said as he took it in his gloved hands and turned it over to note the inscription. "This is quite a find!" he added as he inserted it into a plastic bag.

"Let us see vat else ve can find," Doctor Kohl said, as he glanced at his notes and then led us to the bedroom next door.

"You spoke of the molding in the corner being a hidey-hole," Fritz said to me.

I nodded. "I heard the recording, but I don't know where it is." Yet I found I moved to the window, where there was a diagonal piece of trim at one end of the sill that pointed into the room.

Fritz's eyebrows went up. "Is that it?"

"I don't...I'm not sure," I said, staring at the wood. I reached out and touched what looked like a nail that wasn't hammered in all the way, and an entire section slid loose, coming out on a hinge.

One of the young men moved quickly in and extracted latex gloves from his pants. He put them on and carefully reached inside.

I got the briefest flash of a trap, something in there that would take off a finger or two, and reached out my own hand to grab his shoulder, and pull him away.

But he had found something and was pulling out a brown and silver object… all his fingers intact. I exhaled deeply as the others crowded around to look at his find.

"A revolver," Doctor Janis said, as he examined it. "Nineteenth century, no doubt about it."

"Remember that poem he said that mentioned another hiding place?" Doctor Kohl said, giving a quick glance out the window. It was about three in the afternoon, and we all wanted to be gone before dark.

"Can you play that one part again, Fritz?" Doctor Janis requested.

Doctor Kohl nodded, pulled out the small digital recorder, and pressed the play button. My voice spoke, once again making my skin crawl to hear this person who wasn't me.

> "In the lowest floor of all
> You'll find a space, and not a hall
> Tenth row down, sixth one in
> It is the place I hide my sin
> Fifteen, thirty-eight, turned with stealth
> Then twenty-one if you'd see my wealth"

"What does that mean?" the young woman, Cheryl, asked.

"Perhaps we could find out," I said, and my legs pulled me toward the door. It was an odd, disjointed feeling because I didn't want to see, I didn't want to find out what this poem meant, but my legs moved as if with a mind of their own.

No, I thought, *a mind other than my own.*

The group followed me as I led them to the basement. Doctor Kohl turned on the light, and I hobbled down the ancient wooden stairs.

It was cold, the coldest part of the house. But the cold wasn't just the air; it was like a living thing that chilled the blood and made the more sensible part of me want to run—and not look back.

The electric lights helped but couldn't cut the gloom. The walls were a stone foundation, huge blocks of cut granite. Even here, there were curved arches of brick and decorative concrete and brick designs in the walls and floor as you went from room to room.

But the feeling of heaviness and sadness increased in this dark place shut away from the sunlight. My nerves yelled, "Get out, get out!"

"Can you play that one poem again, Fritz?" Doctor Janis said.

Doctor Kohl nodded and pushed the button. The poem repeated itself, the eerie voice coming through the tinny speaker.

"It's no clearer down here than it was upstairs," Cheryl said.

"The numbers sound like a combination," one of the young men said. "Like for a locker."

"There's no locker down here or anything else with a lock," Cheryl said.

"There are the legends of the hidden fortune that Nat Hewing was looking for."

"Which he died for," I said. I wondered why I was being led to find these things. In the past, those who tried hadn't found anything and may have died in the attempt.

Propelled forward again, as if in answer to what I'd been thinking, I walked through an archway. There stood a brick wall at the far end of the room, which made me stop. All the other walls were granite, and this was the only brick wall that wasn't a room divider or archway. There was nothing hanging on that wall, and nothing was stored or placed along it. I approached and ran my hand along the red rectangular masonry.

"Tenth row down," I said as if I was in a dream. My hands tapped bricks, counting them. "And sixth one in."

I pushed on the brick and heard a *click*.

It moved.

Suddenly, a part of the wall swung loose like a door. The entire group gasped, and I moved effortlessly to pull it aside to reveal a large, rectangular metal door. It appeared to be an old-fashioned bank vault.

"Oh my God!" Doctor Janis exclaimed eagerly. "This is what Nat Hewing was looking for!"

I walked to the vault door and started to turn the numbered wheel. It was cold—so cold—in my hand, like dry ice, and I pulled away as if I'd been burned.

"Are you all right, Leonard?" Doctor Kohl asked.

I nodded and reached out again, turning the dial right to fifteen, then left to thirty-eight, and finally right to twenty-one. When I pulled at the handle, it made a rusted click, and the door creaked open.

At that moment, I remembered a talk-show host who had received minimal amounts of fame for doing a live broadcast of the opening of Al Capone's safe—it had been empty. I thought the same thing would happen here, which would be fine. All I wanted was to get out of that cellar and leave that house.

Doctor Janis pulled out a flashlight and shone it into the darkness behind the door. His light flickered back with a dazzling flash of gold.

As we all stood in stunned silence, we could see it was filled with shelves that held gold bullion in large heavy blocks of the glittering metal, bars of silver that were brown with tarnish, and stacks of currency from a different age.

Doctor Janis looked in and held everyone back. "Don't touch anything. We must take pictures, document this." He rapidly gave orders for his team, one to get a still camera, another a camcorder from the car. As they scurried off, he turned to Doctor Kohl and me.

"This is an amazing find," he said, breathing heavily with excitement. "We always believed the vault was just a legend. I mean, if Elias Scudder had all this capital, why commit suicide the day after the stock market crash?"

That had nothing to do with it, flashed in my mind. And I knew it was true.

It was this house that had killed him.

Doctor Janis went in with an entire team over the next week and photographed, categorized, and put everything into a display he called *The Lost Treasure of The Last Robber Baron.* In his estimation, the discovery was equal to that of the discovery of King Tut's tomb. With research, he found that the false wall had been so well built that even an architect or a master mason couldn't have found it.

But I did. I'd tapped into the energy of a long-deceased man and was able to find evidence in the here and now. Janis credited me and Doctor Kohl with the discovery, and the news reports began to refer to me as the Super Psychic.

Another reason I decided to leave California.

Despite the publicity and the acclaim, I was unsatisfied. Although I possessed no recollection of the actual medium experience, I knew one fact that continued to bother me.

I didn't finish the job.

"I didn't make a difference," I confessed to Doctor Kohl a few weeks after the experience, when reporters kept calling for interviews that I declined. "Whatever was there is still there. The consciousness that I touched is still trapped in that place."

Fritz nodded, his white hair shaking in the loose shape I called an Einstein because it made my teacher resemble that famed scientist.

"Yah, Leonard," he said. "But you are learning. You made a difference in how the vorld accepts vat you do. That vill have to be enough—for now."

There was something in that house—something that led those people to their doom, drove them mad. It was still there, and I should have done something. But I wasn't strong enough to take it on in its environment.

Or was I just too scared to try?

TWENTY-ONE

On the top landing, I realized that once again, I was scared. But if I didn't push on, Jenny would suffer. It wasn't just me or some trapped consciousness, but a friend who resembled the woman I'd once loved.

Cold—Scudder House was cold—and this man's ability is fire. A cousin tried to burn down Scudder House—but the *cold wouldn't let him.*

I focused my mind, trying to recall the chill I received at Scudder as I walked in the door of that famed house. The cold that seeped into my bones even on a warm day. I must have that cold on me, in me, right now.

I reached the door and bent to look at it. There was a small gap in the locking mechanism, just like the front door downstairs. If it was locked, I might be able to pry it open. At least then I would have a weapon in my hand. I held my cane tighter.

But when I turned the knob, it opened with a click.

Cold, I thought. *I'm nothing but ice. A white wall made of ice.*

I pushed the door open and stepped inside. I was in a wide hallway with faded light streaming in from an open door to the next room. It wasn't much brighter than the dark stairwell, so my eyes didn't need to adjust. There was a washing machine and a dryer on one side of the room and white shelving covered with Formica on the other. The shelving held cleaning liquids, canned foods, and supplies of every kind.

I stealthily crept forward.

He was near. I could all but smell him.

"Come in, *Doctor* Wise," came a voice from beyond the end of the hall.

I moved into a kitchen. It was a very modern design with a large island that contained a range and refrigerator, ovens, and micro-wave, all state-of-the-art.

The jig is up. I might as well go in.

I walked through the kitchen and stopped at a wall that separated it from the rest of the apartment. I peeked around it and caught a glimpse of the spectacular living room. It was decorated tastefully, with large leather sofas and a desk in the corner, a computer on top. There were large clay pots, artfully painted, sitting on top of several short columns that were placed around the room.

There were also multiple sculptures with metal blades that stuck up in the air. I think they were supposed to represent a fern or some kind of plant. They rose like bayonets, adding to the sterile, threatening nature of the chamber.

From my vantage point, I couldn't see the entire room, but I could glimpse windows on two walls. They were tinted so the room wasn't nearly as bright as it should be. The view of the town of Mountainview below was indeed spectacular.

"Give it up, Gingold. The police are on their way," I said, my back against the wall.

"Do come in, *Doctor*," he repeated in his mocking tone. "If you're going to arrest me, at least you should face me."

I took a deep breath and thought, *Cold, nothing but cold* before stepping into the room.

He stood leaning against the wall, as usual, wearing nothing but black. A black turtleneck, black jacket, pants, and soft-soled shoes. His hand drummed the door of a large, closed vault.

Like the one at Scudder House, but larger... burst through my brain. I looked at the metal door a second time, trying to note each detail.

"Where is Jenny Baines? What have you done with her?" I asked, watching his face, his sunglasses reflecting like the eyes of an insect.

"Right here," he said as he tapped the metal door. Then he turned and walked over to his desk and turned the flat screen monitor to face him. "And I don't believe that your friends the police are coming. I would have seen them enter the vestibule downstairs."

I cringed. Cameras had been there, but hidden. He'd seen me a mile away and watched me the entire time.

"If you've hurt Jenny..." I said, just as I realized how hollow my threat sounded.

"You'll what? Thrash me within an inch of my life?" Gingold said, the smirk evident. "You'll make me rue the day I was born? Please, Doctor, let's not fall into clichés, shall we?" He stepped away from the desk and gazed at the town below him. "Besides, your bitchy friend—or is she your lover? She hasn't awakened from her little trip to dreamland, and it's no fun to play with someone who is asleep."

I exhaled, suddenly aware I'd been holding my breath. I'd arrived in time.

"Now, please," Gingold went on, his smile pleasant. "Don't start to tell me that this is between the two of us, and to let her go because 'it'll be easier on you in court.' Just don't waste my time." The smile was gone, and his mouth became a hard line. "I'm in charge here, and you have invaded my home. I am perfectly justified in killing you."

"You can't get away clean. I've made the police wise to you," I said, as I attempted to stall, to keep him talking.

The smile returned. "And they'll arrest me for what? Wishing for buildings to burn down? Sending bad thoughts to people I don't like?"

"Arson is one thing, but murder? They'll hunt you down. And Mishan wasn't the first person you killed. There were Wendy's parents…"

"My, my, you've been busy. Yes, I did take care of them, a little fire in their car on the way home. That one was tricky. I had to make sure their tank was full."

I nodded. "So you could ignite the gasoline."

He sat behind his desk and opened a drawer. "It's a lot easier to set off something with a low flash point."

"But Mishan was different. Was he the first one you performed the spontaneous combustion routine on?"

"No, actually, the first was a wino in a building I was planning to burn." His eyes closed for a moment as if to savor the memory. "I was wandering about, trying to find the perfect place to start the fire, deep enough in but close enough to the door so I could escape. And I walked right into this old fellow. He asked me for money." A smile appeared on his face. "I told him I had something for him and handed him five dollars. He looked up to me with such gratitude." He began to chuckle. "It was quite a sight. You should have heard his screams—he sounded like a little girl once he started to burn."

I couldn't see his eyes behind the glasses, but his hand rummaged in the drawer. "I needed to rest for two days after that, but I made sure to keep practicing. Mostly on the homeless. After all, who could they complain to?"

"What did Mishan do?" I asked as I carefully moved toward the vault. If I could get in and get Jenny out, there was still a chance.

"Mishan didn't follow orders. I told him I wanted to waste the nosey firebug…"

"Lonny the Match?"

"Hmm. It appears you *are* familiar with the cast of characters," he said, almost with good humor. "But I'm not surprised. The Super Psychic of Scudder House the papers in California called you."

My eyes must have widened in shock, which pleased Gingold.

"I can do research as well," he said with a smug smile. "But enough of that! Yes, I wanted him to kill Lonny, but Mishan insisted on paying him off, getting the files he'd found with that detective. I agreed if he'd give them to me without reading them."

"His only fault was reading the files?"

"That would have been enough. And Doctor—the vault is securely locked, so don't bother."

I backed away from the door.

"Mishan's fault was that he tried to use the files to blackmail me," Gingold said, shaking his head sadly. "Can you believe it? The utter gall."

"And Wendy? I thought you loved her."

He shrugged. "As much as a god can love any woman," he said. It appeared that his hand had located the object of his search in the drawer. "We shared some very nice times. You should have seen her with Denise."

"Denise Haskell?"

"Oh, yes, they were quite lovely to watch once they got into the thick of it. And they did, right in that room where Mrs. Baines is now locked." He sighed. "We did have some fun times."

"But you killed her. Because of me?"

His face turned stony. "After I'd shared my generosity, she insisted it all had to stop." The relaxed smile returned. "I believe some of my particular desires were a bit too esoteric for dear Wendy."

Or a bit too painful... flashed through my mind.

"But she was still dear to me. A precious, pretty thing. Mishan chose jewelry, but I truly have the eye for pretty things." He reached into the desk drawer and extracted a handgun—small, silver, and sleek.

"Like this pretty thing. So lovely and yet so deadly," he said as he inserted a clip of bullets in the bottom of the handle. He pulled back the slide catch, which loaded the chamber. Then he raised it toward me. "My dear Wendy, and you came along and soiled her—there was nothing left to do."

"You've been sloppy, Gingold. You've left too high a body count. If you'd stopped at Mishan..."

"You might be correct, Doctor," he said as he moved from the desk in one fluid motion. "But I have to play it as it's dealt." He glanced down at the monitor. "And look, no police. I might have a few minutes to play before I leave for Bermuda."

"What about the money? Your man Hallman is under arrest. The police have his Nova Corporation files."

"I have other lawyers and other corporations, with other insurance policies," he shrugged.

Only fire policies... ran through my mind.

"Perhaps it is time to cut my losses," he said. "Then again, if I go to collect through another attorney, perhaps the insurance company will be more willing to work with me. That is if your Mrs. Baines isn't there to stand in my way."

"You want to kill her? Why, when you might never get the money? They're on to you, and the insurance company will never pay," I exclaimed, surprised by the forceful tone of my voice.

"The bitch was rude to me!" Gingold shouted. He lowered his voice and went on, "Bad form, Doctor, falling in love with a married woman."

I could feel heat on my face and was sure I turned beet red. "She's a friend," I stated, in a tone that was unconvincing even to my own ear.

The smile flickered again. "It's a shame about you. You have abilities. I can feel them, even now. But nothing like mine. I am a god of fire!" He walked around the desk, the pistol aimed at my chest. "I don't have to take the little annoyances of day-to-day living like the sheep out there on the street."

My gaze went to the silver weapon in his hand, which appeared to gleam evilly. "So why does a god of fire need a gun?"

The smile returned. "I'm not stupid. You're different. I don't know what you can and can't do. Consider it insurance. You do know how much I like insurance."

"I know, Jack. But you're wrong. You *are* stupid. You've let your ego and your temper tantrums run the show. That's why you botched the whole thing. You could've killed Mishan and gotten away with it. But you couldn't let Wendy or even Roswell Norris continue living for nothing more than the simple fact that they annoyed you."

His mouth became a hard line. "I'm afraid you are no longer amusing, Doctor." He approached and waved the gun. "Step away from the door, and believe me, I have no compunction about putting a bullet in you."

"What's one more body?" I said, watching the light reflect off his sunglasses. They were for more than just protecting his eyes. With them on, I couldn't make a connection with his mind. I thought of what to do to touch his mind like I'd done with the officer. It might be the one way to save my life as well as Jenny's.

I shifted away as he walked to the door of the vault. He stood at an angle where he could watch me as he dialed the combination.

I thought about jumping him, but if I did and succeeded, could I get Jenny out? What if there was a limited amount of air inside? I had to wait until the door was open before I could risk a move.

The image ran through my head again of James Bond and the villain spilling his whole plan. And I realized this wasn't my fantasy; it was his. He wanted to extol his genius, no doubt while wearing a tuxedo.

I stood my ground, leaning heavily on my cane, as he finished with the dial and pulled opened the latch. There was a resounding *click,* and the door creaked on ancient hinges.

"After you, Doctor," he said, waving me forward with the gun.

He stood behind the open door and moved the pistol into his left hand as he opened the vault. Though he could still shoot me, I doubted his left hand was as practiced with the weapon as his right.

I leaned heavily on my cane with my right hand, as if I needed it far more than I truly did. I approached slowly, focusing my thoughts on my meditation mantra. If he could reach into my mind, I didn't want to tip my hand.

I stepped toward the door, and as I came close, I slipped on my cane and fell against the door, which pushed him back. The gun raised but didn't fire, and in one quick move, I transferred the cane to my left hand, grabbed the tip with the right, and pivoted, so the heavy, brass snake head swung up. The stick revolved in a perfect arc, and the heavy metal smashed against his hand, which knocked the pistol from his grip.

He yelled out in pain as the weapon tumbled and slid on the polished oak floors across the room and came to rest near one of the large, smoked-glass windows.

Gingold backed up to put distance between my cane and himself. He cradled his left hand, which now bore a large red mark.

"You bastard!" he spat. "That hurt!"

"It hurt a lot less than burning to death!" I said. I approached him, swinging my cane by the tip wildly to keep him from going for the gun. "Or is pain only real when it happens to you?"

He looked at his hand, and I could almost see tears behind his glasses.

"Not much of a god now, are you?" I taunted.

His mouth set in a firm line. "You should fall down and pray. Pray that I'll make your death easy."

He raised his undamaged hand and pulled off his sunglasses with one quick yank.

I almost expected his eyes to be glowing red, no pupils, no irises, just a red light, as I'd seen him in my vision days earlier. But the eyes that peered at me were light blue—so light, they were almost white.

I tried to reach out, touch his mind, and take control.

Don't look, danger...

I didn't quite understand this, but I'd learned not to question that voice in my head. I averted my eyes and stepped behind the open vault door.

"Look at me, you bastard!" he bellowed, angry that I wasn't going to play along. I could feel the air in the room growing warmer, as if sunlight poured in and heated every corner.

That was it! I finally knew the one part of the process Gingold needed to kill his victims.

Eye contact!

It needed to be established just like when I touched other people's minds. It made sense. Mishan had turned to look at him through the window when his clothes started smoking, Wendy stared right at him from the porch, and Norris must have met his eyes as well when Gingold approached his car.

The other times he'd ignited objects, he'd used things that could burn easily. In Norris's building, he'd used an accelerant in the office one floor below. When he killed Wendy's parents, he'd set off the gasoline in their car. Even Wendy's house must have had hidden accelerants, a plan for the day he might need to be rid of her. The trick with the candles didn't really require much ability. I could already do one candle.

But what had the coroner said? That Wendy's body was burned from the *inside.* That meant he'd reached *into* them to burn them to death. I had to avoid his eyes at all costs.

Cold, I thought, *nothing but cold.*

I was trying to reach out to the very air and change the atmosphere of the room, like at Scudder House. I could not only remember the cold in that place, I could sense a deep cold within myself that I'd carried with me since, and I focused on that feeling and pushed it out all around me.

I peeked around the door. Gingold did not look happy. He stared in my direction, but I wove in and out behind the door so he couldn't get a fix on me or reach into my mind with his fire. I held my cane at the ready to belt him again if he approached.

Instead, he decided that winning was more important than valor, and he made break for the gun that lay near the window. I was right after him, and I fell forward, hooking my cane between his feet. He stumbled, went flying, and fell at least two feet short of his intended goal with a resounding *whack.*

He turned to face me, his pale blue eyes flashing with rage. I held my hand out to block my eyes but far enough away so that I could see what the rest of his body was doing.

The room around me grew hot again. I could actually feel the very air, hot and dry, as I breathed it in, like in a desert at high noon.

I had to keep him off balance, break his concentration. Even without eye contact, he had the ability to produce heat or fire. In this enclosed space, that might be more than I could handle.

Cold, nothing but cold...

I pulled myself up from the floor and swung my cane at him to chase him away from the gun.

He scuttled along the floor away from me.

So far, he hadn't been able to make me burst into flames, and I did hold a weapon. I needed to eliminate the gun as one of his choices.

I spun around, and with a move that reminded me of how I once played hockey as a kid, I used my cane like a hockey stick and whacked the gun in one tight move.

It slid along the floor, rattling as it passed through the open vault door.

Goal!

I turned back to Gingold.

He was bleeding from his mouth, a small trickle caused by his fall. His left hand wore a red mark, but he was able to use it. Holding my hand up to shield my eyes from his, I backed away toward the vault door.

I thought it was a good plan: get into the vault, get the girl, get the gun. Then I realized that if I was in the vault, Gingold could lock me in and set the building on fire. Even if the vault was lined with metal, it would get so hot, Jenny and I would be cooked like Christmas turkeys.

I inadvertently backed against one of the standing columns with a pot on top and glanced back to make sure I hadn't bumped into an assailant or that I'd knocked the pot over.

In the moment that I looked at it, a burst of fire shot out the top of the pot. It was an odd fire, dazzlingly bright like a photographer's strobe, and at the same time, the air filled with sparks as if it was a flash-pot used in a rock-and-roll stage show.

I dove forward to the floor and almost eviscerated myself on one of those sculpted ferns with the leaves like knives. I rolled as I kept my legs straight. I'd wondered about the large pots stationed throughout the room—the *faux-art* look of them. I now knew their function. Booby traps containing chemicals that he could set off with little effort.

I jumped clumsily to my feet, feeling the adrenaline rush through my body as a combination of anger and fear that could easily become panic went through me.

I saw only a huge pink ball everywhere I looked, my retinas dazzled by the explosion that went off so close to me. I waved my cane blindly and tried to strike anything I could.

Don't panic…

The buzz wasn't much help. But I had to focus my mind if I was to succeed. My vision rapidly cleared, but now the room had started to fill with smoke, which made my eyes water. The pot merrily burned away.

I peered through the haze and didn't see Gingold. Did he make a break for the vault and the gun? Did I dare risk a move to lock him in there with Jenny? Could I approach the blazing pot and look into that darkened chamber?

Cold, nothing but cold…

I felt the connection inside me to the cold in Scudder House and reached out my mind to the blazing pot, trying to push what was in me out toward it. The flames within it quickly lowered, and I could no longer feel the heat against the skin of my face. Then the fire flickered once and went out.

Nothing but cold…

I hopped to the door and wrenched it open, looking in. It was too dim to see inside. For a moment, I was sure I was a dead man, about to be shot by Gingold as I stood in the doorway, silhouetted by the light.

"How did you do that?" a voice behind me demanded. I whirled around to see Gingold standing near the sofa. He must have ducked behind it when he set off the pyrotechnics, knowing just how bright they would flare. Instead of a face, all I could see was the diminishing pink dot.

At least he didn't get the gun. But how many explosives were hidden in this aerie? I needed to keep him off-balance.

"You think you're the only one who can do things?" I said. "You're no god of fire, just a spoiled brat with a few cheap tricks."

Another pot on the other side of the door made a huge *whoosh* and fire exploded out the top of it. The room grew much hotter. There was another *whoosh* and another, and I could see two more of the large earthenware displays as they spewed flames and crackled gleefully.

I coughed as the room filled with smoke rapidly, and none of the windows looked as if they could open.

"You can die from smoke inhalation as easily as I can," I bellowed, bending my good leg and lowering myself closer to the floor, my bad leg sticking straight out behind me.

"You can't stop me!" he said, coughing. "You're the one with tricks! Your abilities are nothing compared to mine."

I began to think he was right. The apartment walls would catch unless he'd had the whole place fireproofed.

I saw a shadow move through the smoke and swung the head of the cane where I thought he was, but I hit an end table with a thud. It upended and spilled its meager contents.

I coughed and knew there was no way out unless I could stop the fire. I concentrated again on the cold, allowing it to fill me.

Then I stood up and focused on one of the blazing pots. The flame immediately diminished, flashed once, and snuffed out.

I leaned back against what I hope was a piece of furniture. It was hard to tell in the haze. I hoped I wasn't about to lean against one of the fern-bayonets. I felt exhausted, but there were two more of the pots. I didn't know if I had the strength to shut them down. Maybe this was his plan, to wear me out, push me to my limits. I couldn't even see him in the thickening smoke.

I turned and grabbed the spilled end table and moved to the pillar, upending the small round table and placing it on top of the pot, over the flame. It crackled and made noises as it started to catch, but it cut off the oxygen supply. A couple of snuffling sounds and the fire went out.

I looked at the final pot and pushed the cold out with as much force as I could. The flames danced for a moment, went down, but started to blaze up again. Then it fell away, and the pot was dark.

I grabbed the table, the legs were now warm to the touch. I carried it and put it on top of the pot I'd just extinguished, just to be sure.

The room was still filled with smoke, but it didn't look as if the walls had caught fire or that anything else was aflame. I coughed and wiped tears from my eyes as I tried to look around the room to find him. I moved toward where I thought the vault door and Jenny waited.

"Get back!" Gingold said, emerging from the metal doorway with Jenny. He had his arm around Jenny's neck and the small silver gun pointed to her temple. Jenny's eyes were glassy, and she looked as if she'd just been awakened. She blinked, her eyes brimming with tears, no doubt from the smoke.

I backed away, my cane in my hand. When I fell against a wall, I felt the cold glass of a window right next to me.

"Let her go, Gingold, the police are on the way."

"They won't find anything except your charred remains," he stormed, almost insanely. I think the smoke had frightened him as well. He liked to watch his destruction from a safe distance, like with Wendy and Mishan. He liked the sense of power it gave to him. Now, there was danger to himself, which he didn't enjoy.

I raised my hand to block my eyes from him and tried to center myself. If I could cool down the entire room, that might scare him more and turn the tide.

He held the gun tightly against Jenny and yelled, "Put your hand down! I want you to meet my eyes."

"I don't like long looks on the first date," I said, leaning over as a fit of coughing took me.

"Funny!" he snapped, unamused. "You're good, the best I've run into. I want to find out who is more powerful. Meet my eyes, or I'll blow the bitch away."

"You'll kill us both anyway," I said and slid my cane into my right hand, still holding up my left. I was out of time, I needed a solution.

"I want to beat you first," he said as he pushed the gun so hard against Jenny's temple that her head lolled at an ugly angle.

"All right," I said and dropped my hands to my sides. I raised my head and stared into his eyes.

I could see his pupils expand a little as I tried to reach in. But it was so hot.

COLD…

There wasn't cold—there was fire everywhere—all around me, on me, burning me.

NO! IT'S ICE...

I wasn't on fire and I fought to reach in and touch his mind.

Sweat began to pour off me, and I could feel the air becoming too hot to breathe.

"See!" he said, not breaking eye contact. "You're nothing compared to me." He brought the hand with the gun away from Jenny and raised it toward me.

I swung and whipped the cane up, smashing the window behind me with all of my strength. The glass spattered out, and the window collapsed as sunlight blazed into the room.

"AHHHHH!" he yelled, raising his hand with the gun to cover his eyes. Jenny, her stare gone, lifted her elbow and brought it against his ribcage with such force, the air went out of his lungs with an "Oomph!" He released his grip and she twisted out of his clumsy grip.

I hit the catch on the shaft of my cane and slid the sword free. "I'll see you in hell," Gingold yelled as he lunged blindly at me, giving a cry full of his hate and fury.

When he leaped at me, I thrust my arm out, and the blade plunged into his chest as I sent it home.

Blood began to pour out of his shirt, and his enraged battle yell faded into a pathetic gurgle. The gun fell from his hand as he staggered back, taking my blade with him.

He stumbled for a moment, then lost his footing and fell onto one of the fern sculptures with the full force of his weight. The other blades penetrated into him as he cried out.

The large earthenware pots burst into flames again, all of them this time. I grabbed Jenny, pulling her into the kitchen and towards the exit as the room quickly filled with a dense fog of smoke. We pushed through the door, and were out on the stairs.

She coughed, and I gasped for air.

I slammed the door closed behind us.

"We…have to…get out," I said as I dragged her toward the stairs.

"Those pots…the flames…what was that?"

"Death throes of the god of fire," I said as we descended, holding onto the railing and each other as we went.

TWENTY-TWO

We finally got outside and walked through the alley to the front of the building. The entire top floor was engulfed in flames, and dark smoke poured from the one window I'd smashed.

In the firehouse next door, a lot of activity had started. Men opened the large garage doors and pulled on their coats and helmets. One man ran out to the street with a rolled hose and quickly attached it to a nearby fire hydrant.

"We should get to the police," I wheezed, my lungs aching from the smoke.

"Let me help you," Jenny said, and I leaned on her as we walked, the staff of my cane in my hand.

We walked around the building onto Bloomdale Avenue and burst through the door to the Mountainview police station. Then both of us fell into nearby chairs.

Sergeant Williams was behind the elevated main desk, and he cried out in surprise as we entered.

"You!" he bellowed. "They told me you were under arrest!"

"There was a mistake," I sputtered, and I rose up on the stem of my cane, now a few inches shorter due to the snake head being part of the sword in Gingold's gullet. "Get McGee," I said and fell into another fit of coughing.

He picked up the phone on his desk and made a quick call, several in fact, as I returned to the seat and fought to catch my breath.

Sergeant Tice arrived first. He came down the short hallway yelling, "You're supposed to be in custody."

I held up the wooden rod in my hand threateningly and said, "Get McGee, or I'll give you a damn good reason to arrest me for assault."

"Calm down!" Tice said and backed away. He knew I was serious, and although he didn't fear me, some distance between us didn't hurt.

At that moment, McGee strode down the hall into the lobby, took one look at me, then Jenny, and then Tice, who just shrugged.

"That bastard threatened me with his goddamn stick," was all Tice said.

"You two look like hell, but I'm glad to see you, Mrs. Baines," McGee said.

"What about his threat?" Tice said.

"You're the one with the gun, Tice. You two, come with me. Len, can you walk with your cane like that?"

I rose and nodded. He led us past the short divider around the tall desk, through the electronic door with his ID and took us directly into a large conference room one door down. Using a wall phone, he immediately made a call to emergency services. Then he got us water and coffee. Jenny was still sleepy from the aftereffects of the drug.

A few minutes later, a pair of EMTs came in and checked us out. Smoke inhalation is the most common killer in a fire, and sometimes it can be sneaky, the effects coming on hours later. The two young men looked down our throats and gave us each a shot of corticosteroids. One brought a small oxygen tank and had Jenny put on a clear plastic mask and breathe as I spoke to McGee.

I quickly told him of my confrontation with John Gingold in the building right next door and even mentioned the sword from my cane.

McGee was shocked with each revelation, and even more by the fact that I'd carried a pretty dangerous weapon since the day he'd met me.

"What would you have done if I'd mentioned it?" I asked quietly as I watched the EMT with Jenny.

"I would have confiscated it, for your own protection," McGee said.

"Then it's a damn good thing he didn't, Detective!" Jenny said, having overheard us.

At this, McGee smiled and nodded. "Mr. Baines is probably worried sick about both of you. But for your own safety, I want you both in the hospital for observation until you're given a clean bill of health. Then I'll take your official statements."

"Detective, what is going on?" Lieutenant Butler asked as he walked into the room with Sergeant Tice.

"LT," Tice said. "This man is still wanted for questioning by the Orange Police. He appears to have done something to the arresting officer."

"Done something?" McGee said. "What, Tice? Pulled a rabbit out of a hat? Made magical passes in the air?"

"I don't know, but he *was* wanted for questioning," Tice persisted.

"McGee," Lieutenant Butler demanded, "the last I knew, this man was taken for questioning by the Orange police. Now he's here with the woman you said was a hostage?"

"Jack Hallman has already confessed to renting the office in the doctor's name. And these two need to get to the hospital for observation."

"Lieutenant," Tice whined. "He threatened me! Aren't you going to take that seriously?"

McGee's jaw set. "They confronted the man who held Mrs. Baines against her will. I'm still sorting it all out, LT, but these two should be in a hospital. Tice, if you don't get out of the way, I'm going to threaten you myself."

Tice's face turned a shade of red that quickly darkened to purple. "You can't—"

"On my authority," Butler ordered, pointing at me and Jenny, "get them to an ambulance, but I expect to see a report on my desk by the end of today."

"Yes sir, thank you, sir," McGee said.

"And Tice," the lieutenant added as he headed for the door, "lighten up."

Jenny and I held back our desire to laugh right in Tice's face and followed the EMTs and McGee out of the MPD through a side door, where an emergency vehicle waited.

Bloomdale Avenue was now a flurry of activity. There were fire engines out on the street with ladders extended as men with hoses finished spraying out the last of the fire. What I could see of the top floor was blackened and slick from the water.

"He was right next door," McGee said, shaking his head.

An EMT opened the back of their vehicle. Jenny got in, and I followed. I was forced to lean on her a bit to get my leg in. She kissed my cheek.

"What's that for?" I asked.

"Saving my life," she said.

We arrived at the hospital in minutes, and Jon was there to meet us, having been called by McGee. He wore an old jogging suit and picked Jenny up in his arms as she squealed in delight. Then he put her down and hugged me.

"Easy," I said, suddenly aware of all the sore muscles from my encounter.

I was checked-in, checked out, an I/V stuck in my arm, and I lay in a bed as the concoction of drugs took effect.

I fell into a long, dreamless sleep.

EPILOGUE

Released the next morning, Jon picked us up and took us home, where he proceeded to fuss over Jenny. I took my ruined clothes from the previous day and put them in a trash bag, then showered and got dressed in what little I had left.

"Feel better?" Jon asked as I entered the kitchen. Jon held both of Jenny's hands, like newlyweds, and they kept exchanging glances with a look of gratitude.

"I do," I said and turned to Jenny. "You?"

"Much better," Jenny said.

I looked at her, and all at once, I was puzzled.

"What?" she said, noticing my stare. "Did I grow another head or something?"

"No," I said. "You just look different."

"I'll say," Jon said, giving her rear end a quick squeeze.

"Jon!" Jenny said, shocked, and then laughed. "What do you mean, I look different?"

"Oh, it's nothing. Must have just been the light," I said as I walked over to get coffee. But she did look different, profoundly different, and yet it wasn't in any one specific way. As I poured myself a cup, I knew what it was.

She didn't look like Cathy.

There wasn't any particular change in her features, hair, or body type following her adventure with Gingold. But to me, she no longer had that pull of my lost love. I could see her as she truly was, my best friend's wife. I could care about her, love her, yet felt no *desire* for her.

I exhaled deeply. I'd saved her life. I'd done something right, something good, and it somehow made up for Cathy, whom I'd lost. I could be free to really love a new person, not someone who would be a substitute.

Jon made breakfast, putting out eggs and toast, and the three of us ate and laughed.

"So, Len, what are your plans, now?" Jon asked.

I shrugged. "Guess I'll be heading back to California. I still can work with Doctor Kohl."

"Well, I have another idea," Jon said. "I was talking to the dean and, well, it was actually Trisha's idea…"

"Your assistant?" I said.

"Yeah, and let me tell you, she knows everyone. She has a lot of clout with the administration and—"

The doorbell chimed.

"Damn! Hold that thought," Jon said and headed to the door.

One minute later, McGee walked into the room with an object wrapped in newspaper in his hands.

"Sorry to invade," he said.

"Want some coffee?" Jenny said, getting McGee a cup.

"Sure," McGee answered. "I assume you're both all right? Gingold didn't do anything to you, Mrs. Baines?"

"No, Detective," Jon said with a smirk. "I checked—very thoroughly."

McGee smiled and blushed a bit, which surprised the hell out of me.

"Any sign of Denise Haskell?" I asked.

"We found her in the downstairs of the warehouse."

"Dead?" I asked, feeling the festive mood sinking.

"No, actually, she was alive. Gingold clunked her on the head and stuck her in a shipping crate. Would've been dead if she'd stayed there or the fire had gotten any worse. But the fire department put it out before it could spread to the rest of the building. We broke into the place and found her, got her to the hospital. I just came from talking to her."

"Was she any help?" I said.

"Filled in a lot of the blanks. Turns out she was one of the Nova Corporation partners under her full name. She was in on the insurance scam, but didn't know that Gingold was killing people. She thought the fires were all set. It also turns out that she was involved in a three-way relationship with Wendy and Gingold."

"Gingold mentioned something about it," I said.

"Well, it gets better. It turns out that all Gingold could do was watch. Major league hang-ups. He'd watch them and get himself off."

I smiled. "Gods don't have sex the regular way."

"What?" Jenny asked.

"Nothing," I said. "Go on, Bill."

"The problem for Denise was that she fell in love with Wendy. Wendy thought it had been good for a few laughs, but she didn't want Denise to become a permanent fixture. So she dropped both Denise and Gingold—decided that it should be just business."

"Which made Denise and Jack fast friends. Both of them were jilted," I said.

"Exactly. So, when Mishan buys the farm, Denise moves in to start helping Jack, taking Mishan's place. But when Wendy bites the dust, Denise gets scared. She just wanted to get the money and go. But she was already in too deep, and when Jack called her to grab Mrs. Baines, she figured it was time for her to leave town."

"You can call me Jenny, Detective."

"OK, so they get Jenny, and at this point, her story matches what you told me one hundred percent, Len."

"What story is this?" Jon asked.

"I'll explain when I take you out to dinner," I said.

"No way, I'm buying the celebration dinner," Jon insisted.

"Gentlemen, please let me finish and then you can fight over the check all you want," McGee said. "So, she decides once they drop Jenny off, she's gone."

"But Gingold surprised her and stuck her in a box," I said.

"With her red minivan in the building's garage."

"One more fire and he would've been home free, every possible witness gone," I said, as I shook my head.

"That's what we figured he'd planned," McGee said as he stirred his coffee. "Galland was able to pull juicy stuff from Hallman's computer, and guess what? The guy isn't so dumb. He started singing like a bird, deciding that he would much rather cooperate with the police."

"Trying to get a deal for when his part of the conspiracy goes before a grand jury?" I said.

"Yup!" McGee replied. "Looks like we're going to have this case wrapped up in one neat bundle. And I have you to thank, Len." He stood, picking up the newspaper-wrapped bundle. "Oh, and I have a present for you."

He handed me the bundle, and I tore the papers away. Within its folds, discolored from soot on one end and by what looked like burned blood on the other, was my cobra headed sword.

"I found that at the crime scene, but I think it got lost on its way to the station. I think you can still use it if you clean it up," McGee said, shrugging. "Of course, I don't know anything about it."

"Thanks, Bill. This was a real life saver," I said.

"Amen," Jenny added.

"What did you tell the lieutenant about the COD?" I asked.

"Cause of death was that he impaled himself on one of his fancy sculptures," McGee explained. "My reports suggest that he inhaled too much smoke and fell. Doctor Latrell has found the blades of— whatever the hell hit his vital organs. Of course, the scene has a lot of fire damage."

"So my involvement can be kept to a minimum?" I questioned.

"If that's what you want," McGee answered. "You'll still have to explain your presence in the aerie and the actions you took. But I think your sword should be our secret."

"I would prefer it that way."

"So, where to now, Len?" McGee asked as he took a swig of coffee. "I mean, I know you're planning to go back to California and all, but I personally would love to have you here. We work well together."

"I really don't have any other prospects," I stated.

"Hold on, Len!" Jon said as he rose and stepped to the center of the kitchen. "That's what I was trying to tell you! You do have other prospects."

"What do you mean?" I said.

"Trisha Heywood, my assistant, you talked to her the other day about where you studied with Doctor Kohl. You told her his program was the only one like it in the country, remember?"

"Yes, so what?" I said.

"She did a little checking and found out you were right. There is a veritable gold mine in the study of parapsychology and the science of the mind."

"Jon, sweetie, get to the point," Jenny requested with a smile.

"The point is that Dean Walters loved the idea after Trisha and I told him about it. He wants to start a parapsychology department at Garden State University. And I have been authorized to offer you the position of associate professor and head of this new department."

"Me?" I said, my mouth hanging open.

"Of course you, who better? Look, you've got the summer to plan the courses, and we still have time to offer them in the fall! We'll start small, but within one or two years, we can build it into something huge."

"Congratulations, professor!" McGee said, slapping me on the back.

"What do you say, Len?" Jon asked, his arm around Jenny, who was beaming.

"I-I accept," I stammered. "But I can't stay here—in your house."

"Ah, yes, did I mention the perks?" Jon pointed out. "It seems there is an apartment on campus that is currently empty. When I told Dean Walters of the concept, I also sold him on the idea that you MUST have that apartment or it was no deal. You can move in next week."

I looked from face to face, as all of them stared excitedly at me.

"I guess…it's all settled then!"

Everyone around the table gave a quick round of applause, and I took a small bow.

"First time your psychic abilities didn't warn you, huh, Len?" Bill said.

"I'm completely surprised," I replied.

"I'm glad you're staying," Bill said, shaking my hand. "With you around, I'll make lieutenant in no time."

. . .

Jon, Jenny, and I went out to dinner that night. We dressed up, went to a nice restaurant, where they had wine, and I had seltzer. I even let Jon pick up the check.

I felt good that night and didn't even crave a drink. I had a purpose and had been pulled into what I knew I was supposed to do. Create a new department and, at the same time, work with the police to help solve cases. Whatever my abilities were or are, I could use them to help people—really help.

That night was an epiphany of sorts for me. I was finally able to let go of some of the things that had driven me from New Jersey. I also could see how everything that happened to bring me back was for a reason.

Everything happened on purpose.

There was, indeed, a fire in my mind. It's different from the one Gingold possessed—or that took possession of him. He only craved more—to be fed more bodies and money and broken lives. Mine is a cooler fire, one tempered with compassion, intelligence, and I hope even love. It does not consume me.

But it burns bright, indeed.

THE END

FREE PREVIEW

SEDUCTION IN THE MIND

DOCTOR WISE
BOOK 2

COMING SEPTEMBER 2017

ARJAY LEWIS

PROLOGUE

Harold Stoller stood in the library of his upscale home in Upper Mountainview, New Jersey, and tried to pour himself a drink. It was difficult because his hands shook so much.

The ice clinked as it tumbled from the ice bucket into the cut crystal glass, and sloshed the fifty-year-old scotch in as best he could. Some of the amber liquid spilled onto the top of the small table where the tray, decanter, and ice bucket were kept.

Using both hands to raise the glass to his lips, he sipped the liquid into his mouth. It burned as it went down his throat, but he could feel it relax him.

The room was mostly filled with exquisite wood paneling and shelf after shelf of fine books: collector's items, first editions, and rare finds he had amassed over the years.

There was one mirror on the wall, with an ornate and hand-made frame, which was meticulously gilded with gold leaf.

The man who looked back from the reflection frightened him. Gaunt, with bags under his eyes. But worse, his eyes looked haunted.

He'd been a heavy man before. In fact, carried too much weight, which is what made his doctor insist he lose some of his girth.

Before *her*.

At first, the weight loss pleased him, and he felt better. But as the months wore on, he grew tired, more restless, and began to fear going to bed.

Because of the dreams.

The wonderful— horrible dreams.

She would come to him in the night and they would do unspeakable acts, things he'd never even thought of doing with any other woman.

If she was a woman. Or was she a monster?

His mobile phone vibrated in his pocket, and it made him jump. It was from his therapist, the one person who actually helped him. He glanced at the message on the screen:

Do you need me?

He wanted to text her back, tell her something, but then he heard the music.

A woman's voice, a cappella and full-throated. It was rhythmic, an eerie tune, filled with all the excitement of sex and with an ululation that sounded like her climax.

He froze for a moment, put the drink down, and pinched himself. He was awake, and he could hear her!

He stared at his mirror image, the fear so clear in his eyes.

He ran to the library door, and turned the lock which sealed it. Though it appeared to be a plain wooden door, it was reinforced with unseen steel bars, which strengthened it far beyond what one would expect.

He went from window to window and made sure each one of them was closed and locked. As the room was so high off the ground, they were not reinforced but they fit snugly into their sills. But still, he heard her song and though faint it grew louder, as if she approached.

He went to the pair of glass double doors that led onto the balcony to assure himself they also were secured.

The song grew more powerful, he could feel the music, as if it caressed his very flesh.

He looked up, and stood frozen in place. Outside the glass doors on the balcony she stood in all her glory. A slight glow illuminated her amazing body. She wore an odd garment, that appeared to be only a cloth wrapped about her. But the cloth was almost transparent, and showed off her pert breasts, the curve of her thighs, and the hidden valley of her sex.

He made a sound, a cross between a moan and cry of fear. It was her, just as she came to him in his sleep. But now he was awake and observed her in the flesh. Or was she merely a projection of his mind?

"I've gone mad," he said as he licked his lips.

He could see her mouth move as the song began a new chorus. Her throat vibrated and her chest heaved as she drew in air. She gestured for him to come outside, to join her.

He opened the doors and the song grew to full volume. He tentatively stepped onto the dark balcony, unsure of what would happen.

"Ella?" he said.

She nodded in affirmative, her smile grew broader and her arms opened to welcome him.

He shook his head, and told himself, "She can't actually be here, it's impossible."

Her body was incredible to gaze at, her smile was so inviting and the song on her lips intoxicated him.

He approached, but she remained in one place. He noted that she appeared to hover a few inches above the balcony— or was that an illusion of the unlit terrace under the cloudy sky that no stars could peek through?

Still unsure, he put out his hand, as he carefully approached her. The song grew more sweet, the ululation in her throat coaxed him closer.

His hand touched her shoulder. He gasped.

"*She is here, she's actually real!*" his mind screamed.

He gently moved his hand to her breast, and she threw her head back with a sigh of pleasure.

"My—my God," he said, as all the memories of their intense sensual encounters flooded his mind.

With a smile she shifted out of his grasp.

"Ella, you're real!" Harold shouted, his tiredness forgotten. He was fully aroused, and wanted to make love to her in this solid form, unlike the wisps of dreams that had plagued his nights.

He moved towards her, to take her in his arms, but she evaded his grasp easily.

"Don't toy with me, Ella, my darling, my love," he said. He knew he would beg, he would plead, just to be one with her flesh, her so very solid flesh.

He reached towards her again, and with a bell-like laugh she slid aside.

He was so excited. He *had* to have her, to feel those incredible legs wrapped around him, to hear her whisper words of love in his ear as she did in the dreams.

He lunged at her, as she laughed.

He went through her shape as if she was nothing but mist, and continued over the edge of the balcony.

The scream escaped his lungs as he fell the three stories to the ground and landed on his back on the solid stone patio.

The pain was immense. He felt he may have broken his back or his ribs. There was an intense pain in his chest, and he could taste blood as it oozed out of his mouth.

He watched her as she glided down, as lightly as a butterfly, and looked down at him with pity. She bent and gave him a kiss so gentle it felt like a breeze.

As the light faded in his eyes, black bat wings grew from her back, and with the cry of a bird of prey, she took to the sky.

It was the last thing Harold ever saw.

ONE

I leaned on my cane. "And so, I hope the assignment is clear and that there are no questions."

I stood in front of my class: the young people were a good group, a nice mix of the student body of Garden State University. They ranged in age from eighteen or nineteen to some in their late thirties.

This class, Parapsychology 101, was my final seminar of the week and I was dog-tired. I'd spent every night with the police working to help solve a kidnap and ransom case.

Though it was touch and go for a while, Detective-Sergeant McGee and I— along with the Mountainview Police Department and an exemplary new officer named Tom Harrigan— not only succeeded in a rescue of the eight-year-old son of a renown businessman, we were able to recover all of the ransom money, and discover that the entire plan was the brainchild of a no-account cousin of the housekeeper, who abetted the crime. She broke down and confessed to the whole scheme.

I looked forward to the weekend to rest and recharge, my final task was to get this assignment out to my students.

I hobbled over to the blackboard, shifted my weight to my good leg and pointed with my cane at the words inscribed in bold letters:

DANIEL D. HOME

"You are to write and give full biography of Mr. Home," I said. "Some called him the greatest medium of his time. However, no less than Harry Houdini called him a charlatan and a fraud. Give me both sides of the argument, and then clearly articulate your personal conclusions. I do not care which side you come down on, but I want it clear, reasoned, and well explained."

I lowered my cane and faced the class. "Also, I should warn you I wrote a paper on this gentlemen, and if you try to copy a paper from the internet, it will probably be mine."

This caused a titter of laughter through the room.

"If I find you are turning in *my* paper, I must warn you, I will fail you. I know all of my own arguments, and I find them tedious."

This caused another round of broken laughter.

"Due in a week, please make it at least ten pages, double-space and footnote all your sources. Thank you, ladies and gentlemen!"

The class rose as one person, and ambled their way for the door. It amused me that each one of them immediately took out their smart phones and became lost in the tiny screens.

I shook my head. "Glad I can put mine down every now and then," I muttered to myself, just as the pert Aubrey Andrews approached.

I sighed. "Yes, Miss Andrews?"

The cheerful blonde wore jeans, ripped in the most fashionable places— mostly the knees, shoes that lifted her enough to make me concerned she might fall forward, and a frilly top that plunged to show off her ample bosom, which due to the angle of her shoes appeared to lunge forward at me.

She was not a bad student— bright if she applied herself. However, she'd taken it on herself to spend time to try and engage me in conversation.

"I thought your insights into the history of the Spiritualist movement were very informative, Doctor," she said.

I almost expected her to pull out pompoms and yell, "RAH."

"Thank you, Miss Andrews. I think it is important to point out the flaws as well as the myths of these people. I believe there were many good-hearted members of the movement, but far too many of them were con artists."

"I still haven't found the entire syllabus for the semester on-line, yet, Doctor."

I sighed heavily. "That is because I haven't completed it. I promise it will be up by next week. I had other— projects."

She drew close, pressed into my personal space. "The kidnapping?"

I met her eyes, surprised.

"It's been in all the papers. I figured you were lending a hand," she added.

"Miss Andrews," I said, impressed that she had quickly reasoned out the situation. "I am not at liberty to discuss anything that might involve the Mountainview Police Department."

"Of course not, Doctor," she said, with a gleam in her eyes. "I just was so impressed they solved it so quickly."

"We can all be thankful for the fine work of our local law enforcement," I said. "Now I'm really tired—"

"Doctor, I noticed that you posted on the university website for a Teaching Assistant."

I raised my eyebrows. "Are you interested in being a TA?"

"Well, not for just anyone," she said, and glanced down shyly.

I pondered it for a moment. "I was looking for at least a junior or senior—"

"I'm a sophomore, but the field really interests me."

"How so?" I said skeptically.

"Your entire approach," she said, as she got excited. "The idea of parapsychology and energy reading as the next wave in forensic investigation. It's really cutting edge."

I nodded. "It's not a commonly accepted concept, I should warn you."

"But think of the long term good it can do," she gushed. "I mean, a trained psychic investigator working side by side with the police— like you do—"

I held up a hand. "My work with the police is—

"I know, I know, on a volunteer basis, and you can't discuss it, and blah—blah—blah."

I smiled. Her mode of self-expression varied from a thirty-year-old adult to an eight-year-old child all in the same sentence.

"Nevertheless, Miss Andrews, I am looking for a junior or senior, not a sophomore. And to be perfectly blunt, you are very bright and it is early in the semester, but so far your work is not at a level I would expect from my TA or someone really interested in pursuing the field."

This made her pause, to fully absorb what I said.

"I see, but I only really understood what you are doing in the last week or so," she said. "If I can bring my work up, and maybe do some extra-credit, will you at least *consider* me for the position?"

I looked her in the eyes, and slipped into her mind, just a peek, really, just to see if she meant it.

She was quite sincere.

I pulled myself free and looked away. No reason to go in any deeper.

"I'll consider it along with the qualifications of any other candidates," I said, as I picked up my laptop computer and shoved it into my bag. "Now, I really need to go."

She grabbed my hand in her excitement. "Thank you, Doctor, you won't regret this!"

She traipsed her way up the stairs to the door, happiness in every step. I was amazed that anyone could move so effortlessly in shoes as ungainly as hers.

I shook my head. To be honest, there wasn't a barrage of people who sought to be the TA for the newest Associate Professor, in a department that is probably the only one like it on this coast. To find the most qualified person might not be possible. At least Miss Andrews' enthusiasm might make it work out.

I grabbed my cane and headed for the stairs, which I would have to take more slowly than the skipping coed had. The car accident that necessitated my walking stick, and caused the loss of my right knee, forced me to live with my right leg fused rigid at all times. It was lucky I didn't lose it. I tapped my way slowly up the stairs, one at a time and out of the room.

I was soon outside in the clear fall weather. There was a slight chill in the air, but it made the autumn smells of rotted leaves and first fires waft about me. I went on my way to my office, a small room in the administration building.

It was a lovely day to stroll the manicured grounds of GSU. Though not Ivy League, it was still a highly respected school, which offered a remarkable choice in courses and degrees to people from around the country and the world.

When my dearest friend, Jon Baines, invited me here for a lecture last spring, it was planned as a one-time event. Little did I know that I would be offered a full-time position, and get to meet Detective-Sergeant Bill McGee, who had sought out my assistance to solve a baffling murder.

The success of that case, and the fact that I had absolutely no desire for publicity or even recognition, led McGee to use me as a resource again and again. The only downside was that he really only brought me in to cases that were difficult. But so far luck, coincidence, synchronicity, or a combination of them all had, combined with my unique skill set, helped me find answers and Bill McGee to solve cases. He and I had rapidly become a good team, and it looked very possible that he could be considered for Lieutenant down the line.

Bill had a pretty open-mind about what I do, whether it was the knowledge of what people thought, or my visions of recent or future events. However, many of the other officers were wary of me. They were convinced I was a charlatan, a witch-doctor, or just plain crazy. However, as long as Bill closed cases, the brass didn't complain. Bill took the credit and I stayed in the background.

Just the way I liked it.

I arrived at College Hall, the administration building, which had once been an estate. It stood three stories high, capped with a large domed roof.

Because of renovation several years ago, they had rebuilt the main entrance that faced the quad with glass all the way to the top. It was nice, with the lights on at night, you could see inside to the two huge curved marble staircases as they rose up from the ornate floor. The negative was that the post-modern addition did not really match the stoic interior of the classical construction.

As I approached, I could see a smoky reflection of myself in the glass front wall.

Once inside, I limped my way towards my small office which I am always grateful is on the first floor.

As I walked down the hall with fine wood paneling on both sides, and the glorious marble floor, I passed the Associate Dean's office and heard my name called out.

"Len, Len," came a woman's voice from the half-opened door. In a moment, it opened and Trisha Heywood, Jon Baines' personal assistant, stepped into the hall.

"Trisha," I said. She looked distraught, and I was compelled to ask, "Is everything all right?"

"Yes, I mean, no, I mean, Doctor—" she said. This was unlike her. Trisha was the woman who ran this university with machine-like precision, even though she was only officially the Associate Dean's assistant. But we all counted on her. To see her flustered meant whatever happened could not be good.

I gently touched her arm. "What is it?"

She exhaled deeply. "There are some people here— to see you. I hope you don't mind, they are friends of mine— and it's a very delicate situation."

"Anything you need, I'll do my best," I said. After all, she was the one who suggested GSU create a Parapsychology Department as well as hire me.

"Thank you, Doctor."

I raised my eyebrows.

She smiled. "Thank you, Len."

"That's better," I said. "My office is kind of small, can I talk to them in a meeting room?"

"I have them waiting in Conference Room A," she said. "There's coffee."

I smiled again. She knew I always took a cup after Friday class, usually with her.

"Thanks, that's fine," I said. "What is this about?"

"I'd rather they tell you, if you don't mind," Trisha said as she walked with me towards the conference room.

I gave a nod and opened the door. Two people sat in overstuffed leather chairs at the far end of the room, away from the large center table. The older gentleman rose, a bit bent from the years that had worn him down. Even so, he possessed an air of elegance. He wore a suit, which although expensive, the cut and style suggested a different age.

"Doctor Wise?" he said and took my hand to shake it. "I'm Charles Stoller."

He indicated his wife who sat neatly coiffed with salt and pepper hair. She wore what looked to be a Chanel suit, with a lovely pearl necklace and matching earrings.

"My wife, Abigail."

She remained seated so I approached her and took her hand.

"Mrs. Stoller," I said, and she gave a slight nod of her head. I walked over to a regular straight-back chair, and pulled it over so I could face both of them. I sat down as Charles returned to his padded chair. "Trisha said you needed to talk to me. How can I help?"

Mr. Stoller looked at his wife, who cleared her throat delicately.

"Doctor," Abigail began, "we have a matter that needs to be looked into— delicately—"

"Due to our standing in the community," Charles added.

I looked at each of them. "I can assure you, I any situations I am involved in is handled with the utmost discretion."

"That is what Trisha— um— Ms. Heywood said," Abigail said. "I also understand you have assisted the police in matters—"

"I have. You'll understand that I'm not a liberty to discuss any details."

"That's good!" Charles said.

"Ours is a private family matter," Abigail said.

"Of course," I replied.

"It's about our second son, Harold," Charles said.

"Is he in some kind of trouble?" I asked.

"I should say so," Abigail said, her chin up. "He's dead."

My mouth dropped open in shock that such a genteel woman said this so casually.

"Recently?"

"As a matter of fact," Charles said. "Just last week. The funeral was yesterday."

Abigail sighed. "I cannot tell you the grief that this has caused us, Doctor."

She took a lace handkerchief out of her small purse, and daubed her nose delicately.

"How can I be of assistance?"

"It's the damn police," Charles griped. "They ruled his death a suicide."

"I'm not familiar with the situation," I said.

"Our son fell off the third floor balcony of his home," Abigail stated.

"Or was pushed," Charles added.

Abigail went on. "The detective who investigated said that it was suicide, as the door to the library— that's the room with access to the balcony— was locked from the inside. And the position of the body on the stone patio below suggested that he dove off the balcony."

"Who was the detective?"

"Some sergeant named Tice," Charles said.

"He was very dismissive of our concerns," Abigail said.

I nodded. I was very familiar with Tice. He was dismissive of everyone, and was one of my biggest detractors at MPD.

"You see," Charles went on, "it's the fact that Harry went to a lot of therapists over the last few years."

"He was quite broken up when his most recent marriage fell apart, about two years ago," Abigail pointed out. "But he had made a lot of progress, started getting into shape—"

"He got too damn thin, if you want my opinion," Charles said with a look to his wife.

"He told me he'd been having bad dreams lately," Abigail said. "So the police decided it was suicide."

"And you are not sure you agree," I said.

"No, Doctor," Abigail said. "I am convinced my son was murdered."

TO BE CONTINUED IN...

SEDUCTION IN THE MIND

ABOUT THE AUTHOR

Arjay Lewis (aka R.J. Lewis) is an award-winning magician, entertainer and author. He has experienced every level of show business from street-performing to Broadway.

Arjay's published stories have appeared in *H.P. Lovecraft Magazine Of Horror, Weird Tales* and *Sherlock Holmes Magazine.* He also has been published in the Anthology *The Ultimate Halloween.* His Novel *THE MUSE,* is a finalist in the 2016 Paranormal Novel Competition for Chanticleer Book Reviews.

He has collaborated on several films including: *DOWN IN FLAMES, The True Story Of Tony 'Volcano' Valenci-* which has won seven Film Festival awards. His screenplay for *DUMMY* (co-written with Pamela Wess) is the winning screenplay for the 2017 Garden State Film Festival. It also won 4th place in the 2016 Writer's Digest Screenplay Competition and was a Finalist in the 2016 Filmfest Screenplay Competition.

Arjay is married to his wife, Debra, and has one daughter Rayna. He is currently performing with Princess Cruises as the 'Magic Maker' in the hit show, MAGIC TO DO.

www.arjaylewis.com

71346529R00201

Made in the USA
Columbia, SC
26 May 2017